8 24

THE LIDO

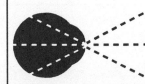

This Large Print Book carries the
Seal of Approval of N.A.V.H.

THE LIDO

LIBBY PAGE

THORNDIKE PRESS
A part of Gale, a Cengage Company

Farmington Hills, Mich • San Francisco • New York • Waterville, Maine
Meriden, Conn • Mason, Ohio • Chicago

LIBRARY OF CONGRESS CIP DATA ON FILE.
CATALOGUING IN PUBLICATION FOR THIS BOOK
IS AVAILABLE FROM THE LIBRARY OF CONGRESS.

ISBN-13: 978-1-4328-5423-2 (hardcover)

Published in 2018 by arrangement with Simon & Schuster, Inc.

Printed in Mexico
1 2 3 4 5 6 7 22 21 20 19 18

For Alex Page,
my swimming sister

CHAPTER 1

Step out of Brixton underground station and it is a carnival of steel drums, the white noise of traffic, and that man on the corner shouting, "God loves you," even to the unlovable.

"Tickets for the Brixton Academy tonight," yells a ticket tout at the station entrance. "Buying and selling, tickets for the Brixton Academy!" Commuters shake their heads at promoters and preachers who try to thrust leaflets into their clenched hands. You push through the crowds and walk past the Rastafarian selling incense and records outside Starbucks. Across the road is Morleys, the independent department store that has stood on the street for years. "Love Brixton" glows in neon lights in the nearby window of TK Maxx.

Today spring flowers bloom in buckets at the flower stand: daffodils, tulips, and fat peonies. The florist is an old man in a dark green apron with soil under his nails and a gold chain around his neck. Whatever the weather, he sells "Sorry"s and "I love you"s at a reasonable price. Wrap it in brown paper and tie it up with ribbon.

Next to the station is Electric Avenue: it heaves with people and market stalls selling everything from vegetables to phone chargers. The air smells of sweet melons and the tang of fish. The fish lie on beds of ice, turning it from white to pink throughout the day and reminding you that you should never eat pink snow either.

Market traders fling prices across the street at each other, discounts thrown like Frisbees. Catch it quick and throw it back.

"Three for a tenner, threeforatenner."

"Don't miss out, three for a fiver, THREEFORAFIVER."

"Three for a fiver? I've got five for a fiver!"

On the other side of the street Kate walks quickly home from her job as a journalist at the *Brixton Chronicle*. She doesn't have time to examine vegetables. Or maybe she just wouldn't know what to look for. It may be spring, but Kate is living under a cloud. It follows her wherever she goes, and however hard she tries she can't seem to outrun it. She weaves through the crowds, desperate to make it back to her house and to close

8

the door behind her and climb into bed. When she is not at work, her bed is where she spends most of her time. On the street, she attempts to block out the sounds around her, trying not to let them fill her up and overwhelm her. She keeps her head down and focuses on the pavement.

"Excuse me," she says, stepping past a plump elderly woman without looking up.

"Sorry," says Rosemary, letting Kate pass. She watches the back of the young woman hurrying away — the woman is petite with a midlength light brown ponytail flicking behind her with the speed of her walk. Rosemary smiles, remembering what it was like to be in a rush. At eighty-six, she rarely goes anywhere fast. Instead she carries her shopping and walks slowly away from the market and toward her flat on the edge of Brockwell Park. She is dressed plainly but neatly in trousers, comfortable shoes, and a spring mackintosh, her thin, wavy gray hair pulled back from her face and secured with a clip. Over time her body has changed to the point that she barely recognizes it anymore, but her eyes are still the same — bright blue and smiling even when her mouth isn't.

Today is Rosemary's shopping day. She has made the rounds at all her favorite shops and stalls, said hello to Ellis the fruit and veg man, and collected her weekly brown bag of food. She has popped into the secondhand bookshop run by Frank and his partner, Jermaine. The three of them chatted for a while, Rosemary sharing the window seat with their golden retriever, Sprout, and looking along the shelves for something new or something she might have missed last week. She likes stopping there and breathing in the musty old smell of hundreds of books.

After the bookshop, Rosemary steps inside Brixton Village and is hit by the smell of cooking spices and the noise of people talking and eating at tables in the passageways — the same noises and smells she has become accustomed to through her weekly visits. The market is airy and some restaurants provide blankets that people drape over their shoulders or laps as they eat. Strings of lights hang from the high ceiling, making it feel like a Christmas market even in the spring.

To Rosemary and her friend Hope, whom she meets here for a weekly catch-up and slice of cake, it's still Granville Arcade, the only place where Hope could find the Caribbean foods she so missed when she first moved to Brixton when she was twelve. It is now filled with independent restaurants, shops, and stallholders. The change still unsettles them but they like the coffee shop where the young barista knows their orders and starts making them as soon as he sees them approaching through the window. And the cake is delicious. Hope speaks proudly about her granddaughter, Aiesha, and her daughter, Jamila — busy as usual with work. When Jamila passed her final medical exams, Rosemary had sent her flowers with a card that read, "Dear Doctor . . ."

Hope and Rosemary reminisce about when they worked in the library.

"Do you remember the first time Robert plucked up the courage to ask you out?" says Rosemary with a laugh. Hope's husband, Robert, had been a bus driver before retiring a few years ago, and when they were both young he would visit the library every few days after his shift, looking around eagerly for Hope's hourglass figure.

"It took him long enough," Hope says, laughing. "I'll always remember how you used to disappear up a ladder and stack books when he was there so he'd be forced to speak to me."

The two women chuckle together, both of them relishing this part of their week. But now Rosemary's feet hurt and she is ready to be home.

"Same time next week?" says Rosemary as they part, hugging her friend and realizing that at sixty-eight, Hope, too, is now an old woman. She squeezes her a little tighter — to Rosemary she will always be the cheerful young girl who started at the library when she was eighteen and who Rosemary took under her wing.

"Same time next week," says Hope, giving a final wave as she turns off down the street to collect Aiesha from school (the favorite part of her day).

Now, Rosemary passes the queues for the bus stops and crosses the junction where the old cinema stands on the corner, the names of this week's films spelled out in white letters on the black board. Opposite is a large square where elderly men sit in chairs and smoke while teenagers skateboard around them.

As she gets farther away from the station, shops turn into terraced houses and blocks of flats. Eventually she reaches the Hootananny, the rickety old pub famous for its live music. A strong, sweet smell floats from the benches outside where people sit and drink pints and smoke. Here she turns left and follows the road that wraps around the edge of the park toward the mid-rise building where she lives.

The lift, often broken, is working and she is relieved.

Rosemary has lived in the flat on the third floor for most of her life. She moved there with her husband, George, in 1950 when the building was newly built and they were newly married. The front door leads straight into the living room, where the most noticeable thing is the bookshelf that runs the full length of the right-hand wall.

The kitchen next to it fits a table, two chairs, and a television that rests on the washing machine. When Rosemary has unpacked her shopping, she crosses the living room, opens the doors, and steps onto the balcony. Her navy swimsuit hangs from the washing line like a flag. There are plants out here: just a few potted lavender, nothing too extravagant — it wouldn't suit her. Rosemary can see Brockwell Park stretching ahead of her, taking her far from the noise and the crowds at Electric Avenue.

Spring is in bloom and the park wears a new green coat. There are the tennis courts, a garden, and a small hill with an old house that used to be a manor and is now used for events and a concession selling ice cream and snacks to sticky-fingered children. Two sets of train tracks loop around the park:

the real one and a miniature one that is only for the summer and very small children. The sun is just starting to set and Rosemary can see people, enjoying the lengthening days. Runners make their way up the hill and down again. And on the edge of the park closest to her balcony a low redbrick building wraps its arms around a perfect blue rectangle of water. The pool is striped with ropes that split the lanes and she can see bright towels on the decking. Swimmers float in the water like petals. It is a place she knows well. It is the lido, her lido.

CHAPTER 2

Every morning on her walk to work Kate Matthews passes strangers as they wait for the buses or dash out of houses and into parked cars. But there are familiar faces too. She sees them every day, their changing outfits and hairstyles like the changing weather marking the passing of time.

On the main street she passes a very tall blond man with a high forehead who wears a black leather jacket, whatever the weather. If she passes him when she is at one end of the main street, she knows she has time to stop and get a coffee before work; if she passes him at the other, she breaks into a half walk, half run, for she knows she's running late.

There is the college girl (or so Kate imagines her) with dark hair and an animated face who nods her head to her music and sometimes sings along. Often she is accompanied by a man in Doc Martens. When

15

he is with her she hangs her headphones around her neck and talks to him, her arm linked through his. Today she is alone.

As they pass each other Kate nearly nods, but then she remembers she doesn't know this woman. She doesn't know her name or where she heads every morning in the opposite direction to Kate. They have never met, but she is just as much a part of Kate's Brixton as the bricks that build it.

The sky suddenly clouds and it starts to rain. Kate curses herself — she left her umbrella at home. The shower quickly soaks her and she arrives at the *Chronicle* office dripping. As she arrives she passes Jay, the photographer, on the stairs. He smiles at her, his mouth traced by a strawberry blond beard, his curly hair a wild halo around his head. He is tall and broad but soft around the edges, taking up most of the space in the stairwell. They haven't worked together much, but they always say hello in the morning and nod or wave if they pass each other in Brixton. He always seems to be smiling and even on her worst days it makes her smile, too, even if she can't quite get her mouth to show it.

"Morning!" he says, as they squeeze past each other on the stairs. His voice is thick with a strong South London accent.

"Morning. Are you off?"

"Yes, I've got an assignment to do" — he gestures at the camera bag on his shoulder — "for a review. A new restaurant is opening on the site of an old pub. My dad said he remembers drinking there when he was my age."

"Okay, well, see you later," replies Kate, "And don't forget your . . ."

Before she can finish he gestures at an umbrella hooked on the back of his rucksack.

She nods and heads up into the office.

"Been swimming, have you?" asks her editor as she sheds her wet coat and hangs it on the back of her chair.

Phil Harris is a man whose body hasn't been treated with much kindness. His cheeks are a permanent shade of purple, the color of the claret that he glugs every night at the local pub with his wife or, as the rumor goes, sometimes with Not His Wife. You can see steak and chips sitting around his middle like a rubber life ring that will eventually drag him to his death. He is not rich (he never managed to make it up the national newspaper ladder), but his wealth is in the eating and drinking.

She shakes her head. "No, just got caught in the rain. I can't really swim."

17

This is a lie. She can swim. If she fell into a pool by accident, she could make her way to the side. She understands the basic principles of where your arms and legs should go to keep you afloat. She just hasn't been swimming since she was a teenager. They had lessons at school but as soon as she could make the decision to stop, she did. It happened around puberty when the girls' bodies felt to them like uncomfortable clothes they'd love to wriggle out of. She remembers the transformation: the giggling rabble became a subdued group by the water's edge, arms wrapped around themselves to cover the shame of their perfect, hideous bodies.

"That might be a problem," says Phil. "We've got a job for you at the lido. Of course, it's not essential that you swim — but it might help you get into the story more, you know, understand what all the fuss is about . . ."

Kate tastes chlorine and the fear of getting seminaked in front of her school classmates. Without explaining, Phil throws a folded leaflet across the pile of books separating their desks. It lands on her keyboard. On the front is a black-and-white photograph of an open-air swimming pool. There is a high diving board and a man is captured midflight, his arms outstretched like the wings of a swallow. Inside is a color photo of what Kate assumes is the lido today: bright blue water and children with their arms on the side, legs kicking vigorously.

"Save our lido" is handwritten in large letters on the leaflet. She reads the text inside: "Our lido, open since 1937, is under threat. The council have announced troubled finances and a private bid to buy the building from a property company, 'Paradise Living.' They want to turn our beloved lido into a private members' gym. Will we stand for it? If you think you can help the campaign, speak to staff at Brockwell Lido."

"The Swimmers of Brockwell Lido" is signed in neat writing at the bottom. Kate thinks the whole thing looks as though it has been made with a pair of scissors and a photocopier. It is an accurate assumption.

"You want me to write about this?" asks Kate.

Kate currently reports for the *Brixton Chronicle* about missing pets, scheduled road construction, or planning notices. The bits that go near the back, but not right at the back where the sport is. The bits that people don't read. They are not stories she would show the tutors who taught her

19

journalism master's classes. Her mum still collects them in a scrapbook, though, which makes it even worse.

"When you're famous you'll be glad I kept these," she would say, and Kate would sink further into the embarrassment that she wears like a coat.

"Yes," says Phil, "I think there's something good in this. You know Paradise Living have already built four buildings in Brixton? They're selling the flats for millions. They think having a private members' gym at Brockwell Lido will help them sell the flats for even more money."

He turns to Kate.

"So, you said you wanted a story," he says. "This is your story."

When Kate was younger, stories were her friends when she found people challenging. She searched them out, hiding among them in the library and tucking herself into their pages. She folded herself into the shape of Hermione Granger or George from *The Famous Five* or Catherine Moreland from *Northanger Abbey* and tried to be them for a day. When she started secondary school her friends were the characters she met in the pages of her books. They sat with her in the library as she snuck mouthfuls of sandwich behind books so the librarian wouldn't

20

see. (The librarian always saw, but pretended not to.)

Now she tells other people's stories. Even if it's just interviewing someone about their lost cat, once she gets past her own nerves Kate finds listening to others' stories fascinating. Often, people are surprised by the questions she asks them. "What is your earliest memory of Smudge?" "How do you think your life would have been different if you hadn't bought Milo?" "If Bailey could talk, but could only say one sentence, what do you think he would say?"

Usually her interviews get edited to just the most basic information ("Smudge, a 3-year-old tabby, has been missing from the Oliver household since the 3rd September. Reward offered"), but she keeps the stories in her head, turning them over like the pages of a beloved old book.

The story of the lido is her opportunity to prove herself. She is going to try hard not to mess it up.

CHAPTER 3

A swimming pool looks lost without its swimmers. It is early and the lifeguard is rolling back the cover, sleepy and silent as he tugs at the plastic. From her spot on her balcony Rosemary can see the mist rising from the surface as though the water is a living, breathing thing. The sky might be blue but the air is still as cold as a shrug. She wraps her hands around her bowl of porridge and watches the lifeguard tucking down into his fleece. He returns inside as soon as the job is done and the water is uncovered.

The pool is silent until the pair of mallards arrives, skittering along the surface as they land. Rosemary likes to watch the pair enjoying the emptiness of the pool each morning as sunshine dapples the water like confetti. Eventually more swimmers arrive. They are quiet, partly from sleep and partly in respect to the stillness and the mallards.

They know the ducks well and swim around them until the pair decides it is time to leave and runs away along the water and flies over the lido walls.

The lifeguard surveys the pool from his chair like a tennis umpire on his throne. Watching the swimmers go up and down is his morning meditation, and Rosemary's too. She finishes her porridge, heads inside, and takes her swimming bag from its spot by the door.

Rosemary arrives at the lido at seven o'clock every morning. Once she is ready, she pushes open the changing room door and steps into the cold. She would dash if she could. Instead she walks to the edge, her feet arriving about three minutes after her mind. Her body is not as strong as her will: growing old has forced her into patience.

As she makes her way to the ladder she watches the other swimmers: a pool full of arms breaking the surface. Only the breaststrokers have faces that you can recognize.

Lowering herself down the ladder Rosemary feels like a tree in the wind. Her branches creak. She lets go and is taken by the water, letting its coldness surround her and getting used to the temperature before kicking smoothly off the side. She begins her steady swim into the mist. She can't see the deep end but knows that if she keeps kicking she will eventually reach it. Rosemary is eighty-six but in the water she is ageless.

Rosemary has lived in Brixton all her life. Even during the war she was one of the few children who stayed behind. Apart from times when the water was being siphoned by the fire brigade to put out local fires, the lido remained open, and she swam whenever she could. At first she felt guilty for being in the water while her father and her friends' fathers were fighting. There were close calls, too, like when the bombs fell at night on the park just beyond the lido and on Dulwich Road that ran alongside it. She remembers visiting the park the day after the hit and seeing families stumbling bleary-eyed among the rubble trying to salvage any possessions, and hearing the cries of a woman who'd lost her sister to the blast, some neighbors comforting her, others turning their heads the other way and allowing privacy for her grief.

But despite it all, the lido was there. And as the months passed it became impossible to remain somber all the time — it was like sitting for too long in her Sunday best. Eventually she just had to fidget and untuck her blouse and scuff her shoes and be a teenager again. During those years the lido was quiet; Brixton's children were mainly evacuated outside the city to the safety of the countryside, and with the men away and women working, lifeguards were hard to come by. Rosemary often had the cool blue water to herself.

Over the wall of the lido she hears a bus pulling away from a bus stop. There is train noise, too, a pause at Herne Hill before chugging round the corner to Loughborough Junction. Rosemary's life has been built inside the walls of these names. There are all the hills: Tulse Hill, Brixton Hill, Streatham Hill, Herne Hill. Then the "villages": Dulwich, West Noorwood, Tooting. The names taste as familiar as toothpaste in her mouth. She knows the bus numbers by their shape and the road names by their sounds — App-ach, Stradella, Dal-keith, Holling-bourne, Tal-ma.

She used to know all the shop fronts, too, but they are becoming harder to remember. Sometimes she thinks someone is playing tricks on her. Every time somewhere she knew gets replaced with something she doesn't she has to scratch the old place off the map inside her head and replace it with the new estate agents or coffee shop. It is hard to keep track, but she tries. If she doesn't know these places, she would be lost in a new city that is no longer hers. She wishes that there were some kind of recognition for all this information she has amassed in her life. If she emptied her mind of all the stored numbers and names and streets, then perhaps she could learn something useful, like a new language or how to knit. Knitting could certainly be useful in the winter.

Rosemary swims a steady breaststroke, dipping her head in and out of the water and letting her ears fill with pool. She can see her fingers ahead of her wrinkling in the water, although she can't tell how much is the water and how much is just her age. Her wrinkles always surprise her. Young girls don't have wrinkles. She is a young girl swimming in the morning under the watchful gaze of the big old clock and the lifeguard who twiddles his whistle in his hand. She is swimming before heading to her job in the library — she will have to get changed quickly if she is to make it on time. Her hair will drip behind her as she makes her way up and down the shelves of books.

"Have you swum the Channel yet, Rosy?" George will say when she gets home in the evening.

"Still working on it."

Now, though, the library is closed and George isn't here. Rosemary stops in the shallow end and leans against the wall before walking slowly to the ladder. She imagines this lido as a private, residents-only gym, and although she is used to the cold water, a shiver runs through her. When she climbs out she is painfully aware of the existence of her knees. She never noticed that she had knees when she was young; like her free bus card, it is a part of her life now that she resents. She still always pays for her bus ticket, on principle.

CHAPTER 4

Kate's walk home from work takes her through the housing estates that wrap around the main street. Every now and then as she walks past flats and down residential streets she glances up from the ground and into the windows of flats, imagining the stories inside the buildings.

A family have dinner in their front room, the glow from the television flashing on their faces. Two floors above, a young girl practices on a secondhand violin, the surprising sound of Bach drifting from the high-rise.

One floor below the violinist, a couple passes a joint between them on the balcony. They are fully dressed but their bare feet are almost touching. The sweet smell is the first thing that the woman in the flat next door notices when she arrives home from work. She opens the balcony door, throws her coat on the sofa, and lies down on top

28

of it, hands crossed over her stomach, breathing deeply.

In a ground-floor flat, an elderly couple finish eating dinner, holding hands beneath the table. Both look out the window at a fox making its way across the communal garden.

As Kate walks she imagines that somewhere in the city, someone like her sits in their room alone and eats peanut butter from the jar. She wonders if any of these strangers she passes would understand that some days she doesn't want to get up at all and that she has forgotten what it feels like to be happy.

Of course, she won't admit to anyone that she is lonely. You're not supposed to be lonely in your twenties. Your twenties are for making friends for life and having inappropriate boyfriends and reckless holidays where you drink shots off each other's stomachs, having the Best Time. On Facebook it's as though all the life has been served up to other people having the time of their lives and there are no scraps left for her. Or at least that's how it feels. She doesn't tell anyone that often she feels like a matted teddy bear you might see forgotten under a bench on the underground. She just wants someone to pick her up and take her home.

Kate rents a house with four other people — two students and two who do something but she's not quite sure what. They come in at different times and shut their bedroom doors, occasionally passing on the way to the (one) bathroom. They are people that she has heard grunting in the heat of sex (thin walls) and whose hairs she has untangled from the shower plug, but she doesn't know where they all came from before arriving here in this house, or what their favorite films are. She doesn't really know them at all.

And they certainly don't know her. But what is there to know really? Siblings: yes, one older sister, Erin. Parents: a mother, a stepfather, and a father who lives in Antigua with his girlfriend and who only phones on special occasions (birthdays, Christmas, and graduations).

"Happy birthday, K."

"Thanks, Dad. Still sunny there?"

"You bet. Still rainy there?"

"You bet."

"I miss you."

"Okay. Bye, Dad."

"Bye, Kate."

Kate and Erin grew up in the Bristol suburbs with their mum and stepdad, Brian. Their mum worked at a creative agency; she dressed in a riot of colors and liked to tell jokes. Brian was always much quieter. He was an academic specializing in a specific time frame in medieval history that Kate could never quite remember. He wore heavy wool sweaters and round glasses that he was very amused to hear had become popular among her school friends. Brian had moved in when Kate was seven and she was too young to question anything: her life then was something that happened to her. Erin, six years older, had been more wary, like a cat giving a visitor a wide berth and dashing under the sofa at any sudden movement. But over time the four of them had settled into the comfortable ease of family. They had their established roles and played them well: Kate's mother taking them to new galleries and asking them questions about what they thought of the pictures, how they made them feel; Brian reading aloud from the newspaper, offering to help with homework, and occasionally slipping Erin some money so she could go out with her friends. Kate and Erin had their roles, too: Kate the shy younger sister with her head in a book, Erin more aloof, bossing Kate about and handing her affection occasionally like biscuits given to a well-behaved dog. On Kate's first day at secondary school her older sister showed her how to adjust her uniform just the right way so she wouldn't display "nerd" or "mischief" in the length of her skirt or the number of stripes on her tie.

Kate stayed in Bristol for university because it was cheaper to live at home, but also because she didn't feel ready to leave. After her degree she left for London to do a master's in journalism and then found a job at a local paper in Brixton.

Kate assumed she would meet lots of people when she moved to London. But she has been here for over two years and it still hasn't happened. All she has are housemates who leave dishes to pile up like a game of Jenga in the kitchen and think black mold is the perfect decoration for a bathroom.

Her friends in Bristol never wanted to come to London — too expensive and they didn't see the point. They were right about it being expensive, but Kate couldn't afford to keep visiting Bristol. About a year ago she'd stopped. Not one of her friends seemed to notice. She hasn't spoken to them since.

Kate's loneliness sometimes feels like indigestion; at other times it is a dull ache at the back of her eyes. When she must take the tube, she tentatively flicks through the London magazine *Time Out,* imagining the things that she could be doing — perhaps going speed dating in Shoreditch, or dancing at a silent disco on the top of a building in the city, or learning how to crochet an ironic pair of underpants at a cocktail bar that is also a retro events venue. But then her anxieties put her back in her place and she remembers that speed dating is just repeating your name and occupation to thirty strangers, that silent discos are less fun on your own, and that ironic underpants are less ironic when it's only you laughing at them.

So instead after work each evening she heads straight home, unless the fridge is completely empty; then she'll make a quick stop at the local supermarket, picking her favorite prepackaged meal and whatever wine is on sale. She comes home, waits three minutes for her food to heat up in the microwave, and then shuts her bedroom door.

Her bedroom is not big, but it is large enough for a double bed and a small desk. She doesn't have bookshelves, so piles of books are balanced precariously against one of the walls. On her desk there is a laptop and a scrawny potted plant that her mum bought her when she moved in. "Bee happy in your new home," reads the tag still attached to the flowerpot, on a card shaped like a bee.

Once inside she opens the wine and sits on her bed watching documentaries with names like *The Boy Who Wants to Cut Off His Arm*. And she cries, because weirdly she knows exactly what it feels like to want to crawl out of your own body, or failing that, to chop it off and float away. Or maybe that's just the wine. Each night she drinks one glass too many, because it makes her head feel foggy, which is better than being conscious of fear sitting on her shoulder and the cloud above her head.

She stays up late, staring into the glow of her laptop screen, hoping to find some comfort there, to feel a connection to people whose faces are also lit up by their computers. When she grows too tired of searching, she closes the laptop and puts it next to her bed. Sometimes she keeps on crying, her pillow growing wet around her face. She tries to stay quiet so her roommates don't hear, but sometimes she finds herself gasping for air as though she is drowning. When she cries loudly like that, she wonders whether part of her does want someone to hear: to knock on her door and scoop her up and tell her it will be okay. But no one ever does. Once she is empty of tears she lies in the dark with her eyes wide open, feeling completely numb. Eventually she falls asleep.

CHAPTER 5

The swimming club children are fearless.
Rosemary watches them wriggling like
tadpoles up and down the lanes. They are
young enough to be completely unselfcon-
scious as they stand on the edge waiting to
dive in. Jostling each other, they pull their
brightly colored swimming caps tighter over
their heads.

As she watches from the café she spots
the natural athletes: the ones with bodies
that are too long for them and torsos that
taper to look the shape of ice cream cones.
Some of the children are smaller and have
little tummies that make hills of their
swimsuits, but their bravery still surprises
her when they jump into the water. When
the instructor blows his whistle, they dive
one after the other like knocked-over bottles,
ever trusting in the water and in the fact
their bodies will know what to do once
submerged. Rosemary wishes she had that

confidence in her body — she can't always rely on it doing what she tells it to.

"Are you Rosemary?"

Rosemary turns away from the pool and looks up at the small young woman standing next to her. She is holding a notebook and pile of papers. Her clothes, in various shades of gray and black, look like they have fallen on her, and her hair is tied back in a messy ponytail.

"I hope you don't mind me joining you?" asks the young woman. "I was told at reception that you would be a good person to speak to about the lido?"

"I am Rosemary, yes. What do you want to know about the lido?"

"I'm Kate Matthews; I work for the local paper. We're interested in writing about the potential closure of the pool. Did you make this?"

She holds up the "Save our lido" leaflet.

Rosemary blushes. She feels embarrassed about the handwriting and the photocopying — she can see now that it looks amateurish.

"I did. But I'm not sure if I can help you."

There is a scraping of metal on stone as Kate pulls out a chair and sits down. She follows Rosemary's gaze into the pool.

"They're so cute," says Kate. "And good

too." Together they turn to watch the children following the instructor shouting to "pull" or "kick harder." Despite being so small they are quick as fish.

"I wanted to help." Rosemary watches the pool for a moment, the water white and frothing with busy feet and arms that are eager to please. The class is coming to the end of one set of lengths and the fastest children are already pulling themselves out and hopping up and down on the side. The last swimmers continue to the end, kicking even harder than their faster classmates.

"I couldn't just sit here and do nothing. But I hear that Paradise Living is offering a lot of money, and that the council just can't afford to say no."

Rosemary pauses, looking across at the water. The sun catches the surface and shines on the children as they swim eagerly up and down.

"Paradise Living." Rosemary laughs. "They clearly don't know anything about paradise."

"I've heard about them," says Kate. "Our paper has written about them before — some swish new high-rises they've built."

Kate pauses.

"I'd like to interview you, Rosemary," she says.

"What do you want to interview me for?" replies Rosemary.

"It's for the paper. I think it would be nice to have a profile of you alongside the news story. It would make a great addition to the news piece to have a human story, too — to hear from someone who's been coming here for years about what the lido means to them. I was told by the manager that you are the lido's most loyal swimmer."

Rosemary smiles, thinking about Geoff, the lido manager whom she has come to know well. She then looks at Kate, wondering whether to trust her. She is naturally wary of reporters, although she has never actually spoken to one before. This young woman doesn't look like how Rosemary imagined a journalist to look. She looks like a child.

"How long have you been coming to the lido?" Kate asks gently.

"Oh, forever."

Rosemary can't remember a time when the lido wasn't in her life — it is as much a part of her daily routine as the cup of tea she drinks on her balcony.

"Do you swim?" Rosemary asks Kate.

"Oh no, I don't really, I mean I . . ." Kate's voice trails off and she shrinks farther into her chair. At the deep end a man does a perfect swan dive into the water. Rosemary watches Kate anxiously watching the man. Her scruffy ponytail looks in need of a wash, and there are dark circles under her eyes. She sits low in her chair, her shoulders slightly sloped forward as though they are trying to protect the rest of her body from something. Rosemary's previous wariness breaks like the surface of the water beneath the diver's splash.

"I'll do the interview if you go for a swim," Rosemary says.

Kate looks startled, her brown eyes darting uncertainly. For a moment she is silent, but eventually she nods.

"Okay," she says slowly. "When would work for you for the interview then?"

"No," replies Rosemary. "Swim first — then we'll sort a date. Here's my email address. Write to me once you've been for a swim." Then she adds, "And don't worry. It's like riding a bike. You don't forget how to do it."

As Rosemary heads back to her flat after saying goodbye to Kate she wonders why she forced the poor woman into the agreement. But there was something about Kate that made Rosemary think she was in great need of a swim.

Chapter 6

At the lido a pregnant woman gets changed. Her body amazes her. She is a beach ball, a taut balloon, a planet, a world. She pulls the tankini over her bump. Only it isn't a bump anymore — it is a mountain. She can feel him kicking in the core of her earth.

"That's right, my love," she says quietly. "We're going for a swim, sweetheart."

No one in the changing room seems to mind her talking to herself. Madness seems to be accepted when you are pregnant, she has found, just like mood swings, toilet breaks, and eating two (okay, three) hamburgers a week.

Her bikini bottom sits low on her hips and a moon of flesh pokes out from her tankini. It fit her last week. She balances her towel on her mountain as she puts her clothes into her bag and shuts her locker, taking the towel again and hanging it over her shoulder.

A teenage girl holds the door open for her. The pregnant woman will miss the kindness that seems to radiate around her pregnancy. She smiles and steps out onto the deck and the sun on the lido smiles back at her. Her feet slap softly on the wet concrete. Her ankles are swollen and her toenails are bare: she can't reach over her stomach to paint them anymore. She feels people watch her walking the length of the pool and she watches them watching her.

She has never had as many conversations with strangers as she has had while pregnant. Pregnancy is like the weather: everyone wants to talk about it. She has been advised to lie on her left side to cure her swollen ankles, she has been shown countless photographs of grandchildren, and strangers have suggested numerous birthing plans to her. In reality she likes the attention. It helps that it is something that is hers and not her husband's. Not that she would admit it to anyone, but she is terrified that her baby will love its father more than her.

Lowering herself down the ladder is a struggle, but as soon as she is in, the weight that has grown for eight months is gone — the water carries them both. It is a pleasant kind of cold. A cold that soothes a body that is so often hot now with the heaviness of her child.

As she swims she thinks about mundane things, like *she must remember to buy cat food and did the recycling bin get collected today and don't forget to call my mother-in-law and thank her for lunch.* Her strokes are slow but strong, the two of them moving through the water like a steadily coasting ship. The sky is spotted with clouds the color of elephant skin and there is a breeze arguing with the trees. As she swims through the shadow of their branches she thinks about their small elbow of garden and whether it will fit a swing. Perhaps he will need to learn to walk beforehand. Or which comes first? Perhaps they could get a baby swing.

She kicks and she feels him kick.

A woman seated on the edge pulling a swimming cap over her child's head smiles at the pregnant woman. *This is what exceptionally beautiful people must feel like,* she thinks as she swims.

The pregnant woman's husband is cooking dinner tonight; in fact, he has been cooking most nights recently. She wonders what she will be eating — she hopes not stir-fry; her body suddenly squirms at the thought of noodles, not that she particularly dislikes them.

When she first told him she was pregnant, they both cried happy tears. That night he wouldn't stop kissing her stomach. His lips pressed tenderly on her belly button and then between her thighs.

A few weeks later they both cried terrified tears. She can't even remember what one thing triggered it, but she suddenly felt like a child handed a secret that was much too big for her. At first she felt excited, then she was crushed by it. Her husband must have felt the same because they both cried and trembled and suddenly wished themselves alone with each other again. They only had two oars and just enough strength and experience to keep them both rowing in a straight line. A third person would surely send them off course.

It was he who finally calmed her. He bought the books and made them sit and read them together. She had been avoiding them, worried that the references to breast pumps and how soft babies' skulls are would overwhelm her. But they sat together and studied like teenagers for exams and it became okay.

In the shallow end she rests for a moment, her back against the side and her hands on the damp fabric stretched across her stomach. She used to hate it when pregnant women stroked their bellies in public like that — it seemed too intimate. But now she can't help it.

She cannot wait for her baby to be born. Her body aches from carrying and her heart aches from wanting. But as she swims she wishes it could be like this forever — just the two of them, both as close as they will ever be to another person. The water holds them and they hold each other.

CHAPTER 7

Kate didn't expect that buying a swimsuit would be such a challenge. She stands under the fluorescent glare of the changing room light and examines her body in the mirror. She has always been petite but over the past year she has put on a little weight from living off microwave meals and peanut butter. Looking in the mirror she sees someone she hardly recognizes. Hips: too wide. Thighs: too round and mapped with cellulite. Breasts: still too small.

Kate is not a Naked Person. She gets into the shower quickly and dresses again in the bathroom. Even getting into her pajamas is done in a rush. As a child her house wasn't one where her parents walked from bedroom to bathroom across the hall in the nude. She was not from a family of Topless Sunbathers or Let-It-All-Hang-Outers. Prudishness flows in her veins.

Her clothes sit in a pile in the corner of

the changing room. The jeans hold the shape of her legs. She desperately wants to reach for them but there is one more swim-suit to try on (the fourth). She needs to make a decision.

When Rosemary said she would be inter-viewed if Kate had a swim, Kate nearly said no. But this was her first proper story and a chance to prove herself to Phil and to start writing the articles that might be truly worthy of her mum's pride.

And Rosemary's words have stuck with her: *It's like riding a bike. You don't forget how to do it.* Because there was a time when Kate had enjoyed swimming. When she was little, before she caught the infection of self-consciousness, she used to go with Erin to the local pool where dolphins and seals were painted on the bottom and a fountain sprayed squealing children. Erin would swim through Kate's legs underwater and lift her onto her shoulders. She remembers the carefree happiness she felt in the water with her sister. Perhaps if she gets back in the water, she can swim back to that feel-ing.

Kate confronts her stomach in the mirror. It is soft and a line of dark hair makes a dash from her belly button down into the waistband of her pants. Hair. That had been

47

a terrifying part of growing up. Why did all that hair have to sprout from such unlikely places? Since she was fourteen she has tried shaving and waxing and using hair removal creams that smell of Play-Doh. Nothing quite cuts or pulls or washes away that initial teenage discomfort at discovering all that hair though.

She reaches for the swimsuit currently slumped at her ankles and shimmies it over her hips and up over her breasts. The smell of Lycra clings to her throat and makes her feel like she is drowning before she has even made it to the pool. It is hot in the shop, so hot that she starts to feel a familiar prickle under her arms and a spinning in her head.

It is the Panic. *Not now,* she thinks, *not here.* But the Panic is already in the changing room with her, making the space unbearably small. It is all around her, filling up the tiny cubicle, pressing down on her from the outside, and bursting out of her from the inside. It forces her down to the floor until she is kneeling in the swimsuit, her breathing overtaking her in gulps and gasps. There is not enough air. Her lungs will not breathe like she wants them to. She needs water, but a fumble in her handbag tells her that she left her bottle at home. Her lungs heave as she tries desperately to stay afloat. The Panic puts two hands on her temples and squeezes hard.

Don't cry, don't cry, she thinks, as the tears descend her cheeks.

One. *It's too hot.* Two. *Please stop.* Three. *I can't.* Four. *Deep breath.* Five. Six. Seven. Eight. Nine. After a few minutes she has managed to reclaim control of her breathing. She sits on the changing room floor. The mirror has a crack running through the middle. *Just like me,* she thinks. She stays crouched on the floor, exhausted.

Kate had her first panic attack in the beauty section of a department store. It was just after she arrived in London and started her journalism master's program. While Kate was growing up, anxiety had always lurked in the background, waiting. She never liked crowds; when other children invited her to parties at theme parks or cinemas, she would pretend to her mum that she had a stomachache and couldn't go when really she was just knotted with the fear of being among so many people. She preferred sitting quietly with a book. Her mum sometimes found her curled up asleep in the bottom of her wardrobe with a book open on her lap. It's where she went to read, feeling safe and cocooned in the small space with her mother's clothes and the smell of her perfume protecting her.

Kate felt more comfortable in her books than she did in real life. She liked to reread her favorite stories: knowing what was going to happen made her feel calm, as though she was directing the story herself. And if she didn't like the direction a new book was taking, she could simply close the pages, take a break, and return when she felt ready or move on to a different story. But real life wasn't like that.

When she moved to London she felt like her life was a car driving away and she was being dragged behind, bumping and scraping along the pavement. Everything was new, and big and strange; she felt small and alone.

On the first day of her master's program, the lecturer went around the class and asked them all to say something about themselves. Kate told them about Bristol, about her family, and that she now lived in Brixton.

"And like a true Bristol woman I love cider."

Then the other students spoke in turn.

"I'm Josh, and I was the editor in chief of my university newspaper. My investigative series on racism on campus was nominated for a national award."

"Henrietta here. My comment pieces have been regularly published in the *Independent* and the *Guardian.*"

"My name is Lucas and I have a first in English Literature from the University of Cambridge, where I was also head of my students' union and received the highest grade in my year group."

And it went on from there. With each new speaker Kate felt smaller. Doubt flooded her body: What was she doing here? She admired them really but she didn't have the language to talk about herself like that and it made her cringe.

After the lecture she headed to Oxford Street, the first place she thought of to go shopping to buy a present for her mum's birthday. It was rush hour and she had never seen so many bodies squashed together on the tube. She was taken by the crowd as though she was a piece of driftwood on the sea, pushed along the platform, right to the edge, then forced inside the doors and up against the body of a stranger.

Once she was out at street level, it was no better. People in suits heading home slalomed through crowds of shopping tourists. Kate pushed through to the crossing then made her way slowly down the street. Every few paces she was stopped behind a pram or a group of shoppers. She felt her heart rate rising as people bumped into her or jostled her with their shopping bags. It was the end of September but unusually hot, and she felt herself sweating under a coat that she couldn't take off because of the crowds pressing around her.

She couldn't remember deciding to head into the department store. Suddenly she was standing in the fragrance pit with eager sales assistants squirting at her from bottles, aggressive smiles painted perfectly on their faces.

"Can I help you?" a woman in a white uniform like a dental assistant's said as Kate swayed past her. Kate's mouth was full of the taste of too many perfumes. The smells were sickly and sweet, like sticky candies that have been left for too long in a coat pocket.

The people around her seemed like a swarm of insects. She was spinning and saw herself reflected a thousand times in the thousand mirrors — on the side of the escalator, on the pillars, on the makeup stands, in the compacts that the sales assistants held up while customers tried on a new shade of lipstick. Even the floor was reflective and showed her terrified face in its shiny black surface.

Everything was hot and heavy, and she had a pain behind her eyes that felt like someone had just ripped open the curtains and sunlight that was too bright to bear was pouring into her head. And then she realized she couldn't move. She was crouching next to the Estée Lauder stand, terrified. She was crying and her makeup was dripping down her face and staining black circles on her white top.

Kate never thought she was someone who would sit down on the floor in the middle of a department store and cry for no reason that she could possibly express. If she could have escaped her body and looked at herself from a distance, she would have wondered who that crazy woman was and what the hell was wrong with her.

Back in the sports shop Kate dresses again and wipes her face. She smooths her hair, opens the changing room door, and walks to the counter.

"I've decided, thank you," she says, "I'll take this one."

You wouldn't tell from looking at Kate that she is a young woman who is visited by the Panic. Only she knows that.

CHAPTER 8

The lido empties of people when it rains. Rosemary watches it, sheltered from the spring shower by the balcony above. There are only two swimmers in the water. She can't understand why; swimming in the rain is one of her favorite pleasures. It's a secret thrill like the extra spoonful of brown sugar in her morning porridge or the feeling of slipping feet into socks that have been warming on the radiator.

When it rains the line between sky and water is blurred. "Above" and "below" fade from black and white to a murky gray where everything is water. The few other swimmers look at one another smugly, like proud new parents who know that their baby is cuter than all the other babies. They know that they have something extra special, and that only they can see quite how special it is.

It was raining a few weeks ago when she

first heard that the lido might be closing. She had gone for her usual swim and Geoff had stopped her to tell her. He was a middle-aged man with a face Rosemary thought of as kind. He insisted on wearing a shirt and tie to work, but trainers were his one concession to his surroundings. They were bright red and smiled out beneath the hem of his smart gray trousers.

"Mrs. Peterson, before you go I have something I need to tell you," he said when he saw her passing the reception desk. That's when he told her that the lido had been struggling to make ends meet for a long time, and that a property development company — Paradise Living — had made the bid to the council a week ago. He said they wanted to turn it into a residents-only gym — another thing to help them sell the flats they were building across Brixton.

"And I didn't know if I should tell you this," he said, "but I've heard they are even talking about cementing over the pool and building a tennis court on top. Apparently they think tennis is more popular with their tenants."

He said that it wasn't certain, but that it was looking likely.

"I'm so sorry," Rosemary said. "Your lovely children."

Geoff had pictures of his children, a boy and a girl of eight and ten, stuck to a noticeboard behind the reception desk. They swam there every weekend, often running to hug him straight out of the pool and getting the legs of his trousers soaking wet. He never seemed to mind.

"Will the council find you other work?"

"I am hopeful," said Geoff. But he didn't sound like his hopeful self.

As Rosemary swam that day she tried to shut out the images of her lido filled with cement and closed forever to the public. It was only when she got home that she let herself cry.

A few days later, she had made the leaflets at a nearby library. She placed photos from her album on the photocopier beneath the paper where she had written her message. She had to wait quite a long time for the hundred copies to come out. As she sat she read all the flyers that were on display — adverts for events at the local cinema, yoga classes, and a very informative pamphlet on sexual health. Once the copies were finished the stack of paper was as hot as freshly ironed cotton. It strangely smelled like it too.

She decided to leave a couple in the library. That was the start of her scattering flyers like breadcrumbs tracing a route around the lido. She pushed them through the doors of the houses on her street and left a pile in the pool's café and in the changing rooms. The men looked a little surprised when they saw her sticking flyers to their mirrors.

"I'm eighty-six, don't you think I've seen all of that before?" was all she said, with a vague hand gesture.

Rosemary rises from her seat on the balcony and moves back inside, keeping the door open so she can hear the rain. She heads to the kitchen and takes down a black notebook from the top of the microwave, flicking through pages of handwritten notes until she finds the recipe she is looking for. Her hand rests on the page for a moment, tracing the curve of the familiar writing with her fingertips. Then she takes her paper bags from the market out of the fridge and starts cooking George's famous vegetable pie. As she cooks she takes a memory from the back of her mind and plays it over in her head like a well-loved record. The smell of cooking fills the flat and Rosemary remembers the day she first met George.

The whole city was celebrating, joining the

rest of Europe in a party that spanned streets and borders. On the street where Rosemary and her family lived, the mothers assembled a long table that went right down to the junction at the other end. Bunting hung from trees and Union Jacks were flung from windows. Families stood on either side, throwing tablecloths over to be caught by their neighbors and pulled tightly over the table. The mothers wore their curtain scrap tea dresses and cheerful sweaters made from the spare wool of their children's old ones, and today they wore them with pride. They had made do and mended, and it had got them through.

The doors were open and food came out of houses like suitcases out of hotels. The crockery was mismatched: blue and white plates from number twelve, dainty rose-patterned from number fourteen, and glasses collected from every cupboard along the street. Jugs held scruffy bunches of flowers picked from the park.

It was a day for splurging the rations: pork faggots with onion gravy and mash, homity pie, and dripping sandwiches. There was silent competition for the best eggless fruitcake. Of course, they all had the same ingredients so they tasted exactly the same. But perhaps Mrs. Mason's was slightly moister (or less dry)? Or was Mrs. Booth's sweeter?

Rosemary has a photograph from that day and all the children look clean and tucked in and buttoned up. The photo shows her crouching down with her arms around her neighbors' children. She had just turned sixteen and so was roped in to help the mothers with the little ones. The boys' socks were pulled up, knobbly knees peeking out of their shorts. Bows clung to little girls' curls. Toddlers toddled in their playsuits with puffed sleeves. In the photo she sees smiles and dainty teacups on the table behind them, and the pretty ginger cat from number twenty-one feasting on corned beef dropped on the pavement.

But she remembers it differently. She remembers the bonfire.

The tables were eventually cleared away, with only a few crusts left in the street for the foxes. The little ones went to bed, not quite understanding the importance of the day they had just experienced and instead feeling tired from the noise and the flag waving. When they were older they would look back and pretend to remember.

For the older children it was their chance to escape — brief, urgent freedom until the ten-thirty curfew would have them back to their beds. They headed to the park. Rosemary didn't know who set out there first, but after a while you just had to follow the smoke and the sparks falling from the sky to know where you were going. She remembers the heat of the fire hitting her in the stomach and reddening her cheeks. It was like a heart pumping blood; it looked alive and it made her feel alive. People were gathered in a messy circle, some throwing branches into the flames. Several girls had flags draped over their shoulders and danced the conga.

The smell of the smoke filled her throat. She felt buoyed up with it, like it could take the knees out from underneath her or lift her up and carry her away. In the darkness behind the fire she could see the shape of her lido. She wondered if the pool water would taste like smoke.

Her friends held her hands and they spun one another around on the grass. Their lips were stained with beetroot juice stolen from the pantry and their cheeks were pinched pink by the heat. As she danced she saw the scene in flashes: a flag waving above the flames, a couple kissing, the swish of gingham skirts. The fire sang inside her.

She was spinning and spinning when she noticed a boy who was still. As she became aware of him she couldn't stop seeing him standing there, like the spot a ballet dancer focuses on to ground her pirouette. When her friends let her go she wobbled dizzily in the grass. He was watching her with all the confidence of a sixteen-year-old who knows he will now not have to go to war.

He waved. She didn't turn to look for the prettier girl standing just behind her, because somehow she knew he was waving only at her. He moved toward her around the fire and she waited for him to reach her. He was a scruffy shadow with untidy hair, long legs, a straight nose, and a pink-and-white mouth smiling in the dark. His hands were thrust into the pockets of his wide brown trousers.

"I'm George," he said, and there he was.

They talked all night. Rosemary learned that he lived three streets down from her but had only just moved back from Devon where he had been evacuated at the start of the war.

He talked about his parents who ran the greengrocer on the station road and said that his father had escaped the front line because he worked as an air-raid warden, handing control of the shop over to George's mother. He told her about receiving a letter from his mother telling him the house across the road had been hit and their neighbors were dead. He knew the boys who had lived there — they were still in Dorset with a relative and he wondered if they would ever go back, if he would ever see them again.

He had no brothers and sisters, and they both confessed that they had never met another only child before. The house he was sent to in Devon had five boys living in it. Every room you went into had at least one person in it, he said, and the only place where he could be on his own was the air raid shelter. Unless one of the younger boys was using it as a hiding place during a game of hide-and-seek, which they often were.

He told her about helping in the gardens in Devon and all the things that they grew. He told her about the night that the families in the village came out of their houses to watch the sky turn red as Exeter burned.

Rosemary told George that she had never left Brixton. Her mother hadn't wanted her to go.

"I'm your mother, how would you manage without your mother?" she had said, although Rosemary wondered whether maybe she just didn't want to be left on her own.

Her mother used to work in the laundry,

but during the war she spent most of her time looking after the handful of children who also hadn't been sent away. When the school was taken over as a temporary fire station, Rosemary helped her set up a makeshift classroom in their kitchen. Instead of washing, they hung maps of the world by pegs to the line that ran above their stove. Rosemary loved the sound of chalk crunching under her nails, she said, and the smell of the books that belonged to her father.

She told George what it had been like to stay in the city. She described the air raids and huddling with her mother and neighbors in the Anderson shelter in the shared back garden. She told him about the whistling of the bombs and the terrible sound as the explosions that followed came nearer and nearer, but then the relief as they grew farther away again. They hit all across Brixton, ripping down homes and demolishing the theater. The bombs and the deaths became a new and terrifying kind of normal.

But she also spoke about the sense of freedom that came once the Blitz was over; walking alone into buildings that had their fronts blown off but still had furniture inside, not having to go to school because there weren't enough children or teachers left to keep one open, and going to the lido whenever she could, diving into the water and forgetting for a while that there even was a war on. Sometimes, she told him, if she lay on her back in the pool and looked at the empty sky, she could imagine that her neighborhood was exactly the same as it had been before the fighting started.

George talked about Devon; she had never seen the sea and she listened with admiration to his stories of storms and the feeling of having sand permanently under his nails and salt in his ears.

"And if you're out walking and you lick your lips, they taste like fish and chips."

The air was full of bonfire smoke but Rosemary could taste the sea.

"Rosemary, why aren't you dancing?" shouted her friend Betty, tumbling toward her, pigtails unraveling and her feet bare, her sensible shoes discarded in the grass in a pile of near identical pairs. She stopped in front of Rosemary and George and flashed Rosemary a look.

"Who's this then?" said Betty, hands on the waist of her collared knee-length dress, reminding Rosemary of her mother.

"This is George."

"Well, why doesn't George ask you to dance?"

64

But if they had been dancing, they wouldn't have been able to hear each other talk. Betty sighed and drifted back to the fire.

When they were alone again George turned to Rosemary and said, "I haven't been to the lido since I got back, let's go together — next Saturday?"

It took Rosemary a moment to realize she was being asked on a date and that she had never been on a date before. She felt nerves lacing her insides like a sweet kind of poison. But she was sixteen and the war had just ended; there was no way she was saying no.

CHAPTER 9

Everyone is equal when they are nearly naked. Dentists, lawyers, stay-at-home mothers, and an off-duty police officer enter at reception, but in the water they are all just bodies in varying amounts of Lycra. The men are full of surprises: Who wears briefs and who wears trunks? You might think you could guess from seeing them in their dry-land clothes, but you can't.

Sometimes the most unlikely people are the fastest swimmers. Like the fat man with the hairy back and the too-tight swimming trunks who is a bullet in the water. The opposite is true, too: there is a man who confidently says hello to everyone and stretches like a professional on the side but swims like a butterfly with a crushed wing.

The cold water wakes up a young doctor who has just finished a night shift. Her body is exhausted but she needs this. The morning sun shines on her face. Later, she will go home and shut her curtains on the day. She swims a fast front crawl, tumbling at each end before beginning another length. When she swims she lets it go. Everything is water.

Next to her a bus driver is on his ninetieth length; his muscular arms scoop up water and throw droplets like stars behind him as he swims. He listens to Mozart on an underwater MP3 player.

Jermaine from the bookshop is here too. His partner, Frank, is running the shop today so he has the morning to himself. Last night they argued about their finances and his body aches with tiredness. They were up late but he still woke early. In his dressing gown and bare feet he came down from their flat upstairs to drink an espresso among the books and the life they had made for themselves.

It was Frank who persuaded Jermaine to leave his job at his family's accountancy firm and start the shop together. Frank had worked in bookshops most of his life, first as a Saturday job in an antique bookshop in York, where he grew up, and then on the weekends when he moved to London to study philosophy. His classmates had thought of him as a party animal — and it was true that he enjoyed the freedom of

London, particularly the gay clubs that his friends took him to where he felt he could openly be himself for the first time. But weekends were sacred because that's when he worked at the Waterstones on Piccadilly. When he graduated a full-time job at Waterstones was the only thing that made sense.

Jermaine thinks about Frank while he swims — about his untamable optimism that Jermaine calls naïveté in their tensest moments (like during their argument last night) but that he loves all the same. He had fallen in love with Frank with a fierceness that surprised him; he had always been quiet, as if living in a circle that no one entered. When he met Frank it was as though he stepped over the line he had drawn around himself. Once he realized there was room inside for someone else he never wanted to let go.

Jermaine's parents had been distraught; they were religious, traditional, and had no idea that Jermaine was gay. His mother cried and told him he had broken her heart.

"I won't tell your father," she had said. "You know he has a weak heart. This would kill him."

Jermaine didn't want to argue. Instead he went home to his boyfriend who held him and said he should leave his job and they should start a business together. Frank's conviction about the idea, and about him, moved Jermaine. Coming from a family of religion, Jermaine knew something about faith. He had just been putting it in the wrong people. For once he didn't feel cautious: he said yes immediately.

Jermaine twists onto his back so that he can see the sky as he swims. He lets the water flow over him, hoping it will wash away some of his worries and clean him of the angry words he shouted last night to the person he loves more than anyone in the world. An airplane rips a tear through a cloud, dragging strips of white behind it into the blue.

CHAPTER 10

There are no cubicles free in the communal changing room so Kate peels her clothes off behind her towel. Fear of being seen naked brings out flexibility she didn't know she had. The Panic sits on her shoulders as she changes. She focuses all her energy on staying calm and holding her towel tightly around her as she wriggles out of her clothes.

Other swimmers are better acquainted with nudity, it seems. An older woman walks from the shower to the changing area naked except for a towel crowning her head. Her locker is next to Kate's. She stands by the open locker door, reaching for her swimming bag. Unraveling her towel crown, she starts brushing her short gray hair. She doesn't seem in any rush to get changed.

But it is not just the older women. Two women Kate's age chat as they change, their skin shining with the moisturizer they share, throwing it back and forth between them. Kate finds herself looking at their wonderful, heavy breasts. It's not attraction; it's something simpler — curiosity. She realizes she hasn't seen another naked woman since she was a child.

"Does anyone have a fifty-pence piece I can swap for change?" a woman asks. There is something about addressing a room so directly while naked that Kate finds incredibly impressive. She wants to be that woman. But she doesn't have 50p, or that confidence, so instead she pulls on her swimsuit, wraps her towel back around her, shoves her clothes in the locker, and buckles the key to her wrist.

Stepping out onto the deck she holds her towel around her self-consciously. She looks around her, checking to see if anyone is looking at her. No one is looking, but she feels their eyes on her just the same. She remembers swimming at school as a teenager and how much she hated her body — and still does. She walks quickly to the poolside. At least in the water no one can look at her.

As she approaches the ladder and prepares for her first swim at the lido she worries whether Rosemary was wrong. What if she has forgotten how to do it?

It was her sister, Erin, who taught her how to swim. Kate was six and Erin was twelve. When she was young Kate never thought the six-year age difference between her and her sister was unusual; she thought big sisters only came in the glamorous and incredible variety. As she grew up Kate came to realize that she had been a failed attempt at saving her parents' marriage.

Erin could ride a bike with no stabilizers and no hands, was friends with math and knew her periodic table, understood clothes and makeup, and she had the longest hair that bounced in perfect auburn curls. And she could swim like a seal.

It was a Saturday during the school holidays and Erin had (reluctantly) agreed to take her outside so their mother could work. The living room was plastered with A3 sheets of photos and words that Kate couldn't read.

"But I don't know how to swim," said Kate when Erin suggested the swimming pool. She had started lessons at school but hadn't yet been able to create the necessary magic to swim unaided across a width of the pool.

"It's easy," said Erin. "It's just like the splashing we do at the beach only you're splashing on top of the water and with your arms as well as your feet. I'll show you."

It was too late for Kate to object; Erin was already packing their swimsuits into a bag and heading out of the back door, checking to see if any school friends were nearby before taking Kate's hand.

"I won't let go, I promise," said Erin in the pool, holding her arms under Kate's stomach as she kicked vigorously. Chin in the water, Kate looked up at her older sister in her big girl's bikini, smiling down as only a big sister can smile at you.

"Promise?" said Kate.

Erin promised — and then removed her hands. For a moment the world and Kate's belief in it slipped away as she sank beneath the surface, water in her eyes and in her mouth and rushing up her nose. But then she climbed back up again, clawing at the water until she was floating, then moving forward.

The first thing she saw when she opened her eyes and blinked away the chlorine tears was Erin, smiling proudly.

Their mother was furious when the two girls arrived home with wet hair.

"You took her to the pool?" she shouted. "She can't swim!"

"Don't pretend you care where we are as long as we're not here!" shouted Erin.

"I can swim!" shouted Kate.

Everyone is right of course: once you know how to swim you don't forget. As Kate slips into the shock of the water she remembers her sister's reassuring smile and that first feeling of flying. The cold makes her heart jump. She feels it in her blood, in her toes, in her nipples. She yelps and ducks under the surface. Water rushes around her and then there is silence. Her hands look pale stretched out in front of her, searching into the blue. Another kick and then her arms pull her up for air. There is splashing and the sound of children shrieking with unashamed joy and then the relief of quiet as she sinks underwater again.

Her heart slows slightly as she gets used to the temperature and finds a rhythm. The cold is painful but it wakes her up. It prickles her skin. It's delicious to feel after so much time feeling numb. As she swims Kate takes deep breaths.

Her lengths are slow. Her right leg kicks upward when she swims breaststroke as though there is a string attached to her right foot and a puppeteer is tugging it as she swims. Despite her teacher's instructions at school, she has never managed to correct her corkscrew kick.

She knows she is not elegant or graceful

or strong. But she is swimming. And in the water she feels calm.

When she climbs out, shivering, she reaches immediately for her towel that she left on the side and pulls it around her body. In the changing room one of the cubicles is free and she rushes for it, locking the door behind her with relief. She sits for a moment on top of her towel on the bench catching her breath. She feels a sense of accomplishment but is also exhausted with emotion. She remembers the classmates at university who seemed to think the world was for them, and she thinks about her sister and how much she misses being a child with her — being taught to swim in a time when worries were small and her big sister was always there to catch her. The Panic that she left on the poolside creeps back until it overwhelms her. She puts her head between her knees and cries, holding her hand over her mouth so no one in the changing room hears her.

CHAPTER 11

The pool was theirs at night, and they were each other's.

"Meet me by the park gates tonight when it gets dark," said George into Rosemary's hair as he kissed her on the cheek one hot afternoon. Since meeting several months ago they had seen each other most days. They snuck out on their lunch breaks — George from working in the fruit and vegetable shop and Rosemary from working in the local library — and cycled to Brockwell Park. If they cycled quickly, they usually had as many as twenty minutes together. Their bicycles lay against the tree, his basket filled with newspaper that carried their lunches — jam sandwiches and a rare apple that they would share and savor.

Rosemary made daisy chains without realizing she was making them and chatted without really noticing what she was saying. He listened and practiced his handstands.

He was better at handstands in the pool, but George was determined to master them on land too. He started with headstands, his head at the base of the tree as he kicked up, resting his legs on the trunk and watching the world upside down.

"You have to see the world from this way round!" he said. She abandoned the string of wilted flowers in the grass and kicked herself into a headstand next to him. A young mother pushed a perambulator down a gray river that snaked through the park and birds swam in the sky.

"You'll be there? Won't you?" he said as they parted.

She never broke the rules and she was a little afraid of the dark.

"Okay," she said after a moment, "I'll come."

At dinner that night she was restless. She wasn't hungry but didn't want her parents to suspect anything so she ate more than usual.

"A healthy appetite for a girl," her father said, as she shoveled another potato into her mouth. She helped her mother clear their plates and wash them at the sink. They stood next to each other, elbows almost touching as they tried to get a lather with the soap flakes, silence standing between them with an arm placed gently on each of their shoulders.

Rosemary wanted to say something to her mother, to remind her of some happy memory or funny story to make her smile and say "Rosy" in a way that would make Rosemary feel like a little girl again. She couldn't think of anything to make her mother laugh like that though. She could only think of the park gates in the darkness.

After the table was cleared and the plates were stacked neatly in their shelves for the night, Rosemary kissed her father and mother and told them good night. They went to their chairs by the fire to listen to the wireless, and she disappeared to her bedroom to read.

Except she couldn't read, she could only brush her hair again and again and look out of the window waiting for the sun to go to bed so that she could leave hers.

Her room went from golden to gray to dark as the light fell. In the darkness she changed into her nicest dress. The print was faded but still pretty — white flowers on a navy blue background. It had pockets she had sewn on to hide tears in the front, and a ribbon she had tied around the waist.

As quietly as she could she pushed open her window. A warm breeze rustled the curtains. She gripped the window frame, swung up her legs, and stepped outside into the flower bed. It was good that they lived in a ground-floor flat. The heads of the flowers tickled her bare legs as she hopped across the border, leaving shoe prints in the dry soil.

The sound of the wireless drifted along the street. Everyone's windows were open that night, letting in the summer air. When she reached the park George was waiting for her, leaning against the gate with one knee up and a foot on the rails. His hair seemed combed for a change. Despite his stance he looked nervous, or at least she thought he did. But maybe that was just how she felt. When he spotted her he smiled. His smile was always a hello in itself; it was broad and open and extended directly to her like an open hand or a happy wave.

"Come on then," he said, putting his hands together in a cup shape and kneeling in front of her. She put her foot in his hands and reached for the railings, lifting herself up and onto the top of the fence as he stood up and took her weight.

Once up, she swung her legs over and jumped down onto the other side. Her dress billowed as she jumped.

"I hope you're not looking at my knickers,

George Peterson."

"I wouldn't dare, Rosemary Phillis."

He scaled the fence in a spiderlike motion, leaping down and immediately taking her hand.

They walked together into the park. The lights from the houses disappeared as they walked farther, but the moon was bright and George knew the way. Rosemary didn't look back.

He held her hand tightly as they made their way down the path, the trees creating patches of heavy dark and pale light.

They usually talked about anything and everything, their voices like young birds. But not tonight. She listened to the sound of their footsteps and her racing heartbeat in her ears. She watched his face in profile as they walked. She recognized the shape of it even in the darkness. She had kissed every part of it, discovering what a man's face tastes like with fascination.

Soon they reached a darker shade of blackness, which as they approached became the brick walls of the swimming pool. There was an old tree whose lowest branches hung just above the lido wall on the far side. In the darkness it looked like a giant with open arms.

Suddenly they were running down the

bank toward the tree. They tripped on grassy bumps, loose blades sticking to their muddy knees like flour to sticky fingers.

The tree looked taller once they were standing beneath it.

"I don't think I can," she said.

"Yes, we can," he said.

Again he helped lift her, this time to the first branch of the tree, which was damp with moss. Her fingernails sunk into the green flesh as she crawled along it, gripping tightly. For a moment she was afraid, but she was too embarrassed to ask to turn back. So she eased herself off the branch down the other side, face to the wall and feet flailing until they met the reassurance of a wooden picnic bench.

She turned and hopped off the bench onto the deck of the pool.

Everything was as quiet as a secret. The moon was high by now, bathing the enclosure in a silver light. A canvas cover was rolled over the surface of the water, looking in the darkness like a sheet of ice that could be skated over. At the far end of the decking she could make out the empty lifeguard's chair, watching over the nighttime lido in silence. She could just make out the face of the clock and the coils of rope curled up on the decking underneath like a sleep-

81

ing snake.

There was a light thud and George was beside her, brushing his knees and rubbing his hands on his shorts.

She stayed still, feeling her heart like a balloon that if cut loose would float out of her throat and into the sky.

Without speaking she edged to the side of the pool and peeled back one corner of the cover that tucked away the water. A glimmer of silver winked. George walked to the other side and took the other corner; together they peeled back the cover until the pool was exposed, its surface perfect and fragile.

They were on opposite sides of the pool now. In the dark it was hard to make out each other's faces.

Rosemary bent down and carefully untied the laces of her brogues. She placed them neatly next to her and rolled down her white socks. On the other side she saw the shadow that was George do the same.

Then they both looked at each other, barefoot but clothed. And they jumped. Perhaps she jumped first, or perhaps he was a second ahead of her, but their splash was one exclamation mark of water.

Under the surface she was a tangle of dress and hair. It was perfect night as though she had jumped down a hole into the dark and cold beneath the earth. She could make out movement on the other side of the pool — someone else was down the hole with her.

She bobbed up to the surface like a cork. George was floating on his back with his toes poking out of the water. Shaking with golden torrents of laughter.

She swam across to him, pulling the night through her fingertips. Then she twisted until she was floating too. The moon looked like a child had drawn it in the sky and the stars as though they had been hung there with pegs. She looked at the sky and imagined it watching her. It made her feel sad, and the sadness beat at her chest.

Rosemary ducked underwater, washing her salty tears with chlorine ones. She swam a steady breaststroke for two lengths and then pulled herself out of the pool.

George was still floating. He was quiet except for the splashing of his fingers as he dragged them through the water at his sides, making circles in the darkness.

"Do you think I'll be a somebody, Rosemary?"

She sat on the edge with her knees up to her chest, watching him and dripping.

"What do you mean?"

83

"Do you think I'll be someone important?" he said.

"Why are you asking?"

"The sky is so big when you look at it like this. It seems so important."

"I think you are important."

"So you think I'll be someone then?"

"Yes," she said. "Yes, you will, I know it."

The concrete deck was gritty against her bare feet. Her hair dripped down her face and her heart battered her insides. Her stomach ached. She wanted to crawl inside his body and try it on for size, to feel what it would be like to be him, to be running through his blood and swimming in his brain. She couldn't imagine wanting anything more.

She could feel him smiling even though she couldn't see him. He rolled onto his front and swam to the edge of the pool. As he climbed out he took her hand and pulled her up until they were standing on the side, wet arms tight around each other. She shook like a child as they kissed like grownups.

No one tells a tiger to hunt, but still it growls. Her body growled as they kissed, exploring each other's mouths with their tongues. There was a fire inside her, burning her up. She didn't feel afraid of the dark anymore.

They broke away from each other, the complex origami of their bodies unfolding just long enough for them to tug at their clothes.

Undressing they felt like they were meeting for the first time. Two nervous, naked bodies stood opposite each other on the side of the pool.

"I don't want to hurt you," he said.

"You won't."

They placed their wet clothes on the ground and lay down together, her warmth becoming his warmth and his warmth becoming her warmth. He kissed her cheeks and her eyelids and her mouth. The ground was hard and rubbed their skin, and they were all elbows and skinny knees and it hurt and she cried and her heart swelled and he held her tight and she felt alive and wild and swimming and falling.

Losing her virginity didn't feel like a loss. In the darkness they found each other and held on tight.

When Rosemary arrived home she climbed quietly back through her bedroom window. She hung her dress on the back of her chair to dry and slipped into bed, pulling her pink daisy covers around her. As she fell asleep she thought of the moon watching her and wondered if she should feel ashamed, but then she remembered that it had probably seen it all before for thousands and thousands of years.

CHAPTER 12

That night, Kate phones Erin for the first time in weeks.

"Hello, stranger," Erin says as she picks up.

"I know, I'm sorry," replies Kate, sitting in the corner of her bed with her knees tucked up to her chin, "I've been busy."

"Too much partying?"

"Something like that."

Kate can hear clattering in the background: she imagines Erin walking around her modern open-plan kitchen making dinner for her husband, Mark, the phone held to her ear with her shoulder. She pictures the gleaming work surfaces and the tidy living area behind with the spotless cream sofas. Perhaps Mark is pouring them both a glass of wine, passing it to Erin with a smile that says everything both of them ever need to know. When Kate thinks about Erin's life — about her senior role at a PR company in Bath, her husband's new business, and their friends who are wealthy and beautiful — she feels left behind, as though Erin has run off into the distance and Kate is left frozen on the starting line terrified by the sound of the gun marking the start of the race.

"What have you been up to?" asks Kate, sitting down on her bed.

"Well, I'm just back from a run — third one this week."

"Wow, that's great — good for you."

"It keeps me sane."

"You seem pretty sane to me."

Erin laughs.

"That's because you don't live with me. Mark might disagree. Work is exhausting, I can't remember the last time I had a proper weekend, the flat needs repairs and God knows how much that's going to cost, and we're still not pregnant. I barely manage to put on clean clothes on some days. But I'm glad I look sane."

Kate doesn't know what to say. She believes in her sister and her sister's happiness like she believes in the strength of bricks to keep the wind and rain out of her house. Erin must be happy, for her own sake but also for the smooth and natural running of the world as Kate knows it. But what Erin is saying now — is this the first time she has hinted at a less than perfect life, or is it the first time Kate has listened? Kate doesn't know what to say, so with shame caught in her mouth she says nothing.

"But I'm sorry, I didn't mean to rant at you," says Erin. "What about you — what's going on with you?"

Before she can even register the words coming out of her mouth, Kate says, "I've started swimming. At a lido. I'm writing an article about it."

"Wow," says Erin. "A lido, that's outdoors, right? Well, you're braver than I am!"

Curled up on her bed, the door firmly shut to avoid any interaction with her housemates, Kate wants to cry. Instead she stays silent.

Erin pauses, too — the clattering in the kitchen stopping. For a moment the phone line carries nothing but the quiet sound of the two sisters' breath.

"Is everything okay with you, Kate?" Erin asks after a moment.

Kate knows this is her opportunity to confide in her sister — the hand reaching out to her. But there is so much to say that somehow there is nothing to say.

"I'm fine," she replies brightly. "I better

have some dinner now, though — talk again soon?"

"Of course. You know where I am."

Once they've said goodbye and Kate has hung up, she shifts across to her desk and flips open her laptop, bringing up an internet tab. She turns instinctively to her door, checking that it's closed, and then types into Google: "exercise and anxiety." As the results come up she feels her heart rate quickening and a knotting in her stomach, like she's looking up things she shouldn't be on her parents' laptop.

"Swimming outdoors in cold water gives you a euphoria like nothing else," says one article. "Whenever I feel low, I try to go for a swim outdoors. I always come out feeling better," she reads.

Kate closes her laptop and quietly gets ready for bed, thinking about her conversation with Erin. She thinks about crying in the department store and in the lido changing room. The truth is, she has no idea what can help her, but as she pulls the duvet tightly around herself she decides it is at least worth trying to make the lie she told her sister become the truth. Surely she can try just one more swim — and then she'll see. *Just one more swim,* she thinks as she falls asleep.

CHAPTER 13

The next morning Ahmed, a tall young man in a Brockwell Lido fleece, sits behind the reception desk and smiles at the swimmers as they arrive. He has short hair that is spiked at the front, a shadow of a beard on his chin, and a pen behind his ear. In front of him is an open book. Ahmed reads his textbooks in between serving customers. He needs to get three Bs to get into university to study business. In his last practice exams he got two Cs and a D. He pretends that he doesn't care about his grades but he does. He cares so much that sometimes he is scared of even trying in case his best efforts aren't good enough.

"Good morning," he says cheerfully to the swimmers, some of the regulars stopping for a brief conversation. He watches them push through the turnstile and toward the changing rooms, checks no one else is on their way through the door, and focuses again on his book, his back to the perfect blue water outside.

A few years ago he never bothered with schoolwork. He had fallen into a group of friends who would have teased him for it. It was his older brother, Tamil, who convinced him to change his ideas. Tamil had already left for university and one weekend when Ahmed was fifteen their parents finally relented and let him go and visit. Tamil took Ahmed to the student bar and ordered two pints. "Don't tell Mum," he'd said, sliding one of the pints across the table to Ahmed. Tamil had talked about how much he was enjoying his courses, living away from home, and his new sense of freedom. Every now and then someone would come into the bar and nod at Tamil. He raised a hand at them and smiled, but stayed with his brother.

"You know, your friends aren't really your friends," Tamil had said suddenly. Ahmed had started to argue, but his brother interrupted.

"I know you think they are now, but they just want you to be like them — pissing their lives away because they can't be bothered to do anything else. If you keep on doing that, you'll be stuck living at home forever. You won't get to do any of this. Is

92

that what you want?"

Ahmed had looked sullenly into his pint glass, his gangly body hunched over as if he was a child and not a teenager close to becoming a man.

"I'm only saying it because I love you."

At that Ahmed had looked up at his brother. He'd never heard him say that before. Tamil's cheeks were flushed and he looked around him, perhaps checking if anyone had heard. He was clearly embarrassed but had said it anyway.

"Okay," said Ahmed. Because although he couldn't say it, he realized his brother was right.

"Can I have another pint?"

"I'll get you a half. But if you tell Mum, I'll kill you."

Sometimes Ahmed's old friends come into the lido reception and try and get him to join them smoking weed and drinking beers in the park after his shift. But whenever Geoff spots them, he comes out and asks them to leave if they're not going to go for a swim or use the gym.

"We're really lucky to have you," Geoff often says to Ahmed after they have gone, and Ahmed's whole body fills to bursting with a warmth he only later recognizes as pride.

CHAPTER 14

Rosemary's swimming bag is always packed. It sits on a chair by her front door with her raincoat and umbrella. Inside there is a swimsuit; she has three of the same navy one from Marks and Spencer. It always surprises her when she sees the number in the label. She was always slim. She is a slim young woman wearing a fat old lady's clothes. In the bag there is also her towel, goggles, a purple swimming cap, a comb, a pot of Astral moisturizing cream, and a Colman's mustard tin full of 50-pence coins. She rattles when she walks.

This afternoon, though, she leaves her swimming bag by the door as she exits her flat and heads to the lido. On her way to the Lido Café she stops to say hello to Ahmed at the lido reception desk.

"How is the studying going, Ahmed?" she asks him.

"Slowly, Mrs. P," says Ahmed, "slowly."

"Well, we all know what happened to the hare."

Rosemary pushes through the turnstile and out of the door that leads to the lido decking. After crossing alongside the pool she reaches the Lido Café. Tables face the water and she picks an empty one and sits down.

Kate emailed her first thing that morning. "I swam yesterday," she said. "It was so cold! So will you let me interview you now? I could do this afternoon if you are free?"

Rosemary has arrived early — she likes to just sit and watch her lido nearly as much as she likes to swim in it. As she watches children splashing in the shallow end she thinks about when she first learned to swim, just after the lido had opened with a celebration in which the mayor threw a young woman, fully clothed, into the water. (The young woman's father was proud that his daughter had been the one to get chosen for such an honor.)

"I promise I won't let go," said her mother as Rosemary kicked vigorously.

"I won't let go, you'll be okay." Her mother did let go that day and Rosemary sank and swallowed a mouthful of water. But she'd been okay.

"I'm sorry I'm late."

The sound interrupts Rosemary's day-dream and she looks up; Kate is standing above her, smiling.

"You're not late, I'm early," Rosemary replies.

Kate sits down and pulls her notebook and Dictaphone out of her rucksack.

"Thank you for meeting me, Rosemary," she says. A waiter comes over and Kate orders them both tea.

"So how was your swim then?" Rosemary asks.

Kate's mouth twitches into an almost smile.

"It was very cold!" she says. "I don't know how you do it every day."

Rosemary laughs.

"You wait and see. It becomes addictive."

"I did enjoy it — after the shock of the cold," Kate admits.

Rosemary raises an eyebrow and smiles. The waiter returns with two small teapots. Once they are alone again Rosemary reaches into her handbag.

"I've got a photograph to show you," she says, digging around in the contents. She pulls out a book; the photograph is slipped within the pages.

"It's just me left now," says Rosemary, her thumb leaving a print on the photograph as she passes it to Kate.

There are three rows of girls, some with their arms around each other, others with hands on hips or arms crossed tightly over their flat chests. The swimsuits are plain one-pieces that sit low over their hips like shorts. They must be between ten and thirteen years old, all grinning in black and white. The children in the photograph look so energetic that Rosemary still can't believe that she is the only one left alive.

"The oldest were at the back and the little ones at the front," she says.

"Which one is you?"

Rosemary smiles and points at a little girl in the front whose short hair is spiked with water and whose face is dirtied with freckles.

"Hello, Rosemary," says Rosemary. She looks at young Rosemary with the affection a mother might show for her child. As she looks up she catches Kate watching her.

"When you're my age you'll understand," she says. "You begin to miss yourself."

Kate looks at the photograph and then the old woman sitting in front of her.

"Do you have any brothers or sisters, Kate?" asks Rosemary.

Kate laughs and then covers her mouth as though the noise has surprised her.

"I'm sorry," she says. "It's just that I'm

supposed to be interviewing you! But, yes, I have an older sister, Erin."

"Do you love her?"

Kate looks startled for a moment, but then she smiles. "I love her more than anyone."

Rosemary turns to her.

"I wish I'd had a sister," she says. "Or a brother. I was an only child."

Kate scribbles in her notebook.

"And you say you've been coming to this lido as long as you can remember? Tell me something about it from when you were a child."

There are so many things to say, but it is hard to make words work. Pictures and sounds and sensations fill Rosemary like helium until she begins to feel dizzy.

"When most people tell you about their childhood, the sun is always shining," she says. "In their memories we were angels too. I'll tell you now that they are lying."

She flashes Kate a smile. Kate looks up from her notes and smiles back.

"There were beautiful sunny days, of course there were, but it's swimming in the rain that I remember. I remember coming here for swimming lessons at school before the war. Even though we were only very little then, our teachers would make us go in whatever the weather. Most of the time we didn't mind it because we loved the lido. We loved getting out of the classroom, we loved the walk through the park — although often we would run it.

"So most of the time we were happy to swim, even if the sun wasn't shining. But there was one day . . . . I think it was a Thursday because we were all feeling that sluggish end-of-week feeling but weren't cheerful enough for it to have been a Friday . . . . Anyway, one day when we had swimming in the afternoon it was really raining. It had been raining all day. The tarmac in the playground was flooded and we could hear the roar of buses making waves out of puddles outside our classroom.

"We begged the teachers not to make us go. Some of the bolder girls told them we'd get hypothermia or trench foot. The teachers just gave them a telling off for joking about the trenches.

"That afternoon no one ran. We trooped under umbrellas and huddled into our raincoats, the puddles soaking our shoes. When we got there, we got changed slowly, our teachers waiting under shelter.

"I can't remember who it was, but someone suddenly had an idea to get back at the teachers. When we came out of the changing rooms, we were all wearing our raincoats over the top of our swimsuits. Before the teachers could do anything we ran and jumped into the pool, our coats spreading like dresses around us. The whole class started swimming their lengths like that.

"The teachers went mad, of course. They dragged us out and told us we were a disgrace. We were sent home, dripping, to our families and the mothers were furious at all the sodden raincoats. But my father found it hilarious. He didn't stop laughing all evening."

"That's wonderful," says Kate. "And what about now? There are other pools in the area, so why here?"

Rosemary turns to watch a mother and child in the shallow end. The child is swimming a determined doggy paddle toward the mother who holds open her arms, beaming. Above them is open sky. Watching them she wonders why Kate needs to ask. She can't begin to say everything so instead she says the start of the truth.

"It is familiar," says Rosemary. "It is special and it is familiar and nothing else would be the same. The way the sun shines on the water in the morning. The view of the lido from the top of the hill in Brockwell Park. Even the smell is familiar. When I walk through the park toward it, I can smell

100

it before I see the brick building. It's the wet concrete that smells like storm, but mixed with cut grass from the park. And the chlorine . . . my skin always smells of chlorine."

Rosemary lifts her forearm to her face and breathes deeply. It is there, the scent of chlorine that permeates her skin like campfire smoke seeping into tent fabric. She closes her eyes. George always used to say that he never had to give her perfume because she had the lido. Chlorine was her perfume, he'd say.

After they married they didn't go away for a honeymoon. They couldn't afford one and the weather was so perfect in Brixton that summer that they didn't need to. They took a week off work and spent every day swimming at the lido, George stretching out in the sun and going brown like stained wood, and Rosemary sitting in the shade and watching him as though he was a snowflake that might melt away any second. When they were both warm they would dive into the water and swim up and down — George in the fast lane and Rosemary in the medium. It didn't matter that they weren't swimming together because they knew they were sharing the same experience of cool water on their hot skin and the way the light made a checkerboard of the bottom of the pool. With George, swimming felt like flying.

Once they were both tired they would clamber out of the pool, tug their clothes on over their swimming costumes, and walk back to the flat. As soon as the door clicked shut they peeled each other out of their swimsuits as though greedily peeling ripe fruit. Sometimes they didn't make it to the bedroom and they would collapse on the sitting room floor, kissing the chlorine off each other's bodies. He kissed her everywhere, breathing deeply her smell, their smell, of the pool and the summer and their passion for the afternoons.

Rosemary opens her eyes.

"Are your children big swimmers too?" asks Kate. Rosemary feels a shiver run through her.

"That is," says Kate anxiously, "if you have any children?"

"Next question."

"Is that a no?"

"Yes. That's a no."

"I'm sorry."

Rosemary looks at the pool and back at Kate.

"What's your next question?" she says.

"Why do you swim?"

Rosemary laughs.

"Asking me why I swim is like asking me why I get up in the morning. The answer is the same."

They talk for another thirty minutes. After their conversation Kate has her profile piece and Rosemary walks home smiling.

"See you in the pool next time?" Rosemary had said to Kate as they parted. Kate's face had softened into the suggestion of a smile.

"Maybe," she'd replied. "And I'll send you a copy of the article when it's finished."

Arriving home, Rosemary locks the door, takes off her clothes, and pulls on her swimsuit. Then she reaches for her raincoat, pulls it on over her shoulders, and sits like that while watching television until it's time to go to bed.

CHAPTER 15

Later that week Kate keeps her promise to herself and tries another swim. She has come prepared this time and is wearing her swimsuit under her clothes. Anything to avoid the stomach-twisting feeling of being naked in front of strangers.

She disrobes in a corner and listens to the conversations in the changing room, focusing in and out of them as though she is tuning a radio. Listening to them helps her to stay calm.

An older woman with a strong Caribbean accent: "I haven't seen you here for a while. Where have you been?"

Another older woman: "Don't laugh . . ."

"What is it, where have you been?"

"I went on a singles holiday. In France."

"Girl! Good for you! So did you meet a handsome Jean-Marc?"

"Well, we exchanged email addresses . . ."

The two women look at each other, raise

104

their eyebrows, and laugh.

Alongside the conversations is a backing track of showers running, the toilet flushing, and splashing that gets louder every time someone opens the door and steps outside.

Kate shuts her clothes in a locker, wraps her towel around herself again, walks quickly out, and lowers herself into the slow lane before she can change her mind. The cold is less shocking today. She is prepared for it and feels an unexpected sense of pride as she hears the yelp of a swimmer entering the water next to her. Again, Kate senses that her body is waking up like a sleepy dog pricking its ears up at its name. She lowers herself under the surface, takes a deep breath, and kicks off.

As she swims she looks around her. The lifeguard is drinking from a thermos and talking to a middle-aged woman, perhaps a regular swimmer, who holds the hand of a young boy in shark-patterned swimming trunks. At the deep end a man with a sculpted chest and shoulders and wearing a white swimming cap and streamlined red goggles dives neatly and begins heaving his arms out of the water. Waves surge and heads turn in respect of the man who has become a butterfly.

The sky stretches above her and for a moment Kate feels completely free. She rolls onto her back and tries backstroke so she can watch the birds crossing back and forth and the spring buds waving on the arms of the trees around the lido building. She stops swimming for a moment and floats; for the first time in a long time she lets herself relax. The water holds her. She breathes deeply, the water lapping at her cheeks. She feels almost like she might cry but it's okay.

Eventually she rolls back onto her front and goes back to her slow breaststroke, swimming toward the shallow end. That's when she spots Rosemary. The old woman is swimming elegantly toward her. She is wearing a navy swimsuit and a purple swimming cap. As she swims closer, Kate notices that her eyes are the same color as the lido. Rosemary recognizes her and smiles.

"Hello!" says Kate, putting her feet down and raising her hand in a wave.

"So you came back," says Rosemary.

"I came back."

Rosemary swims to the poolside and rests her neck on the wall, kicking her legs gently in front of her. She gestures at Kate to join her, and after a moment's hesitation, she does. For a while they stay like that. Kate leans her head back and looks down the

106

pool at the other swimmers. The sun is warm on her face.

"So how are you finding it?" says Rosemary. "Have you gotten used to the cold yet?"

"It's strange, I know, but I quite like the cold," says Kate. "It wakes me up."

"Why do you think I come in the mornings?"

They both laugh.

"I think I'm starting to understand it," says Kate, looking around her. Her heart beats fast but she feels calm. "Why you love it here so much, I mean," she says.

"There's nowhere like it," Rosemary replies, leaning back a little farther until her toes poke out of the surface of the water.

Kate watches her, this old woman in her navy swimsuit who has swum here all her life. She imagines what it might feel like to see your city changing around you like that and to lose the place that feels like home. As she thinks it she is reminded of her conversation with Erin, and how she had listened to her sister tell her things weren't perfect, and she herself had said nothing — done nothing.

"You really want to save it, don't you?" Kate says after a moment.

"Oh, I do."

"Maybe I can help you."

As soon as she says it she realizes that, without knowing exactly how or why, this is something she needs to do. She needs to keep swimming, and she needs to help Rosemary Peterson save her lido.

Rosemary looks at her for a moment, the wary expression that Kate had noticed the first time they met returning for a moment. But then she smiles.

"Okay then," says Rosemary.

"Okay then," says Kate.

CHAPTER 16

In one corner of the men's changing room a boy of fourteen is pulling on a swimming cap. He watches himself in the mirror as he tugs the cap over his ears, a serious frown on his face that looks too old for his young, skinny body. He rolls his shoulders and stretches his arms across his chest.

Once on the deck he dives quickly into the water and starts a smooth front crawl.

No one noticed him leaving his house. The night before, he came downstairs for a glass of water and saw them in the sitting room together drinking wine. They didn't notice him so he watched them for a while, enjoying the rare moment of calm. And then he heard a conversation that he wished he hadn't: he heard them agree that they would divorce once he had left home. The scene looked remarkably calm for something that made him feel sick. They drank their wine quietly and sat close to each other on the sofa, staring ahead at the fireplace that was topped with family photos. Perhaps they were too tired to shout, like two old lions with too many scars, but the quiet somehow disturbed their son more than the fighting.

He should be at school now. He has never skipped it before; he has never missed a homework deadline or been late to a lesson. When he woke up that morning he did his usual two hundred sit-ups in his bedroom and counted the hairs on his chest (eleven). Then he went downstairs in his pajamas and made himself breakfast in the kitchen. He ate alone, reading his way around the breakfast table from the back of the cereal box to the carton of juice. As he ate he listened to the muffled sound of his mother crying upstairs. She sounded like a wounded animal when she cried. He wanted to go up and comfort her but he realized he wouldn't know what to say. Words knotted inside him like a ball of string that wouldn't untangle. He wanted to help her fix her marriage; he wished he was a hundred years old so that he might have some advice from all that living that he could give to his mother. But he only had eleven-chest-hairs' worth of life inside him, and he knew that wasn't enough to help her.

The words on the back of the cereal box

110

jumbled until they didn't make sense and his eyes filled with tears. The table was a confusion of semiskimmed orange juice and whole-grain spread. He wanted to scream like a toddler and to empty his lungs of all the rage that lived inside his chest. Instead he neatly cleared away his breakfast things and padded quietly up the stairs. In his bedroom he changed into his tracksuit and a hooded sweatshirt, throwing his school uniform into his wardrobe. He reached for his swimming bag and slung it over his shoulder. On the way to the lido he phoned his school and told them that his son was sick.

"I hope he feels better soon," said the school receptionist.

Once he has finished a length he dives underwater and sits cross-legged on the bottom. He holds his breath and counts to ten. Looking up, the sun makes a crisscross pattern on the surface as though it has caught the pool in a net. The water presses his chest and fills his nose; he blows a stream of bubbles and watches them dance in front of him. His parents think he is at school; his teachers think he is at home with a fever. No one who knows him knows that he is sitting on the bottom of the pool.

The lido greeted him like the kind of

friend you can sit with in comfortable silence; here was a place where he could be himself.

Every now and then thoughts of his parents slip into his head. He wonders if it is his fault and whether they would still be in love if they had never had a son. His eyes are sore, but he tells himself it is probably just chlorine seeping into his goggles.

He wishes he had gills so that he could stay there forever, lying on the gritty bottom and staring up at the sky. Down there no one can find him, nothing could hurt him, and he isn't a boy but a fish.

CHAPTER 17

They were a couple, like the quotation marks around a sentence. They fit together and made each other feel less afraid and less alone. George was afraid of being a nobody: he was a somebody with her. Rosemary was afraid of being left behind: he held her hand and took her with him.

Their friends knew them as Rosemary and George, George and Rosemary. They came in a pair like salt and pepper.

In five years they had swum thousands of lengths, walked hundreds of laps around the park (walking extra slowly just so they could have longer holding each other's hand), and grown up together.

He proposed in his swimming trunks. The pool had only just opened again after the winter and they were going for their first swim of the season. It was still cold; the lifeguard was wearing a thick wool coat with the collar turned up against the chill.

It was a Sunday, so the greengrocer shop that George had taken over from his parents was closed. They had the morning to themselves before the deliveries started coming in for the next day.

They swam together like seals and then sat on the decking wrapped in their towels and sitting close together for warmth. They ordered two cups of tea from Mr. Fry's snack shop, holding hands and watching the steam rise off their tea and off the surface of the water.

The calm was like an umbrella, sheltering them. They breathed in the smell of the lido and the possibility of rain. Rosemary thought about the first time they made love on the cold decking close to where they sat. She thought about how she had first met him on the day that war ended and her life began.

And then he turned and looked at her. He didn't get down on one knee. There was no music and the sun didn't suddenly smile from behind a cloud. In fact it was a thoroughly normal, gray day — the sky the color of concrete.

"Marry me, Rosy," he said. There was no question mark. No question mark was needed. She already knew that the answer to every question was him.

CHAPTER 18

"How are you getting on with the story?" says Phil several days after Kate's talk with Rosemary. Kate pulls her typed-up interview with Rosemary, and the news story she has written to accompany it, from her bag and hands them to him. He sits at his desk and reads, stroking his vast stomach — a habit that Kate finds disconcerting. It makes her feel as though he is digesting her words and that they are giving him heartburn. She hates waiting for people to read her work — it makes the Panic climb into her throat.

Jay is in the office today and she catches his eye. They smile at each other.

After a while Phil nods.

"Good," he says. "People — that's what this newspaper is about. Our readers like to see the human side of everything."

Kate smiles, feeling like she is at school again and she's being praised by the teacher. It still feels as good, even if she feels ashamed for taking pleasure in such a small compliment. Phil gives his stomach a little pat.

"We should do a series on this — follow any developments, speak to some other lido users. The council — have you spoken to the council yet? Well, do that next. In fact, do that now."

Kate nods and packs up her things, her mind racing, not trusting herself to speak. She has never written a series before and feels excited and terrified by it. She waves goodbye to Jay and heads outside.

As a journalist she should be used to council offices and town halls, but Kate still finds them intimidating. Just like banks and churches, they make her feel small. That's probably the point, she thinks.

You can see the clock tower of the town hall from a distance. Its face watches the busy junction opposite the cinema and the McDonald's that is still remembered for a shooting in the queue. The clock has seen it all. Tall columns and a stone shield guard the entrance at the top of steps that lead to the town hall, steps that are often covered in confetti.

Once inside, she is asked to wait. An elderly man is sitting at the end of a bench opposite Kate. His hands shake in his lap.

He is wearing a long coat, gray trousers, and trainers. Kate notices that the laces don't match. The man reaches into his pocket and takes out a bag of Fisherman's Friend.

"Would you like one?" he says in a strong South London accent.

"No. Thank you though."

"I'm getting evicted," says the man. "In case you're wondering why I'm here. It's like the doctors, isn't it? You wonder but you're not supposed to ask. You try and guess which one's faking a cold and which one's dying. I particularly like to pick out the pregnant ones. They always look fucking terrified, the poor cunts."

Kate raises an eyebrow. The old man laughs and sucks on his sweet. It makes a popping noise.

"Sorry, I know the ladies hate it when I say cunt."

A woman comes out of one of the rooms along the corridor and crosses the hall. She looks at them before pushing open the door to the bathrooms. Kate and the man are silent as she passes.

"I'm being kicked out," he says again. "They're knocking down the building I live in. Putting up some swish new place with a gym and all that. The flats are old but they do their job, you know? I've been there forty years. It's my home."

He shuffles and puts another Fisherman's Friend in his mouth. Kate looks at him and wonders at his story — where he will go and who will be there with him when he goes.

"I'm sorry," she says after a moment. "I'm so sorry about your home." And she means it. He sniffs and nods his head.

"Do you remember the name of the company that are building the new flats by any chance?" Kate asks.

The man laughs.

"Paradise! Paradise Living is their name. I'm being kicked out of my home to make way for 'paradise.' "

Kate feels a jolt run through her, thinking of the lido.

"I work for the *Brixton Chronicle,*" she says. "I'm sure they'd be interested in your story . . ."

She reaches into her bag and takes out her business card, handing it to the man. He holds it for a moment, then nods at her and slips it in his pocket. A door opens and a woman holding a folder opens it and looks at the man.

"If you'd like to come through."

He stands up slowly and heads to the door.

"It was nice to meet you. I hope you're not pregnant, or dying." He winks at Kate and follows the woman down the corridor.

"Hello?" Kate calls into the house, knowing that she won't get a response. The door clicks shut behind her and she squeezes past the bicycle in the hallway to reach her bedroom.

The meeting did not go well. She tried to be authoritative, but she looks younger than she is. And she is a woman. She is used to not being taken seriously.

The councillor was middle-aged and wore a faded gray suit. He offered her coffee and got up to make it himself from a machine on the other side of the stuffy room. As they talked she heard the phrases she had expected: "redevelopment," "cash-strapped," "nonprofitable," "we've tried."

"I'm sorry," said the councillor. "We don't want to do this, either, but the offer from Paradise Living — well at the moment it seems like it might be the only option. It's unfortunate, we know that. But these things happen. Neighborhoods change, cities change. That's just the way it is."

She took notes and asked the questions

she had prewritten in her notebook, but as she talked she couldn't help thinking of what she had said to Rosemary: *Maybe I can help.*

She wasn't going to be able to help. She was hardly even going to be able to write another article. She was a terrible journalist and a weak person who looked thirteen years old and felt the same age a lot of the time. She lived in a dirty house with people who didn't care if she'd had a bad day at work or drowned in the canal.

She had felt her skin prickling and the room shrinking as she sat and listened to the councillor. The coffee smelled burnt and it made her feel sick; everything made her feel sick.

She reaches into the cupboard by the desk in her room and pulls out a pot of peanut butter and a spoon.

At the end of the meeting she had been ready to go and she could tell the councillor was ready for her to leave. But just before she left the room he said the first useful thing all conversation.

"We will be having a meeting in the town hall in two weeks' time. Local residents are invited to attend and voice their concerns."

Kate raises the heaped spoon to her mouth, then stops. She will go to the meeting, she decides. And she won't be alone. Maybe she can't help, but she can try. And with a smile she swallows the smooth spoonful of comfort.

Brockwell Lido Threatened by Closure

Lambeth Council announces struggle to keep local lido afloat

By Kate Matthews

Private bids have been made to acquire Brixton's outdoor pool and gym for redevelopment, as Lambeth Council announces rocky finances at the lido. The most notable offer is from property development firm Paradise Living, who want to develop the pool into a private gym for residents of their new flats.

Dave French, a spokesperson from Lambeth Council, said, "I can confirm that we are currently looking at our options with regards to Brockwell Lido and its future. At the moment nothing is decided, but it is true that running costs are high. We are considering offers, including from Paradise Living. It is uncertain whether the pool will remain open."

During the summer the pool welcomes hundreds of visitors every day, but the colder months are less popular.

Geoff Barclay, Brockwell Lido manager, said, "We are all naturally concerned by this news. Brockwell Lido is a special place within our community."

"A private gym would add real value to our properties," said a Paradise Living spokesperson. "Tenants and purchasers in our buildings would have exclusive access to the top-end facilities."

The council is currently reviewing proposals and more news will be announced in the coming months.

CHAPTER 19

It is dark and a fox is nuzzling a garbage bag outside a house on a street in Brixton. The fox pushes her nose farther into the plastic until it bursts like a balloon and dinner comes spilling out. On the menu tonight: a half-eaten bagel, the smeared leftovers of a can of mackerel, and the final dregs of a pot of peanut butter. The fox dines well but quickly. She makes a final check of the bag to make sure she hasn't missed anything and then trots down the path and back onto the road. The street is made up of two rows of terraced houses. Some have cars outside them but most don't. There are gates and low hedges outside some, paved driveways outside others. Some have pots outside the doors where flowers are just starting to burst into life.

The fox detours left to make a quick investigation of a toppled-over plastic bin in a garden overgrown with weeds and old bicycle parts. She makes a good discovery: a not-quite-empty box of fried chicken.

As she continues along the road the street-lamps catch her in their glow every few paces. But this city fox isn't afraid of the light. Instead she hurries quickly and steadily down the street until she meets the busy road. She joins it at a bus stop where a couple embrace against the stop sign. The woman wears one shoe. One leg is bent and resting against the pole and her lover presses into her. Next to them a woman dressed in a nurse's uniform tries to peer around the entwined bodies to find her bus number on the sign.

The fox passes them without being noticed and follows the direction of the buses that roar down the road. She tries some bins outside shops that have metal shutters pulled down to the pavement. One shop is still open: a hunk of meat rotates on a metal rod in the window and a queue lines outside the door. The fox feasts on chips that have been discarded like cigarette butts in the street.

Just past the kebab shop she turns a corner into a quiet square fenced with metal railings and a hedge. Tall houses face onto the square and from a window she can hear a baby crying and a father singing. She follows a path through the small garden alongside benches where the dark shapes of bodies lie still, only occasionally shuffling position under sleeping bags and blankets that are wet with dew. Beneath one bench is a rucksack with half a loaf of bread poking out the top. The fox pulls the bag into her teeth, dragging it to the other side of the square where she quickly eats, leaving the empty bag behind.

The night is turning to morning in the lower corners of the sky. Shapes that were black are turning to indigo blue. The fox leaves the square and makes her way quickly down the road, tail flicking behind her like a white comma as she runs.

A small group has gathered around a young man who has fallen into the road. Two men in high visibility jackets, on their way to work, are pulling him up by the shoulders and sitting him on the pavement. They sit next to him, put their arms around him, and ask him if he is okay. The fox skips over the young man's wallet, which he has dropped in the gutter.

"Don't lose this mate," says one of the men, reaching for the wallet and pushing it into the young man's pocket.

The fox makes her way past the bus stops and the sleeping schoolyard and then loops back down another road lined with houses until she reaches the edge of the park. She wriggles her full belly under the fence and disappears into the dark that is slowly becoming light with morning.

CHAPTER 20

"I don't understand," says Rosemary on the phone.

"The meeting is in two weeks. It's our chance to have our say about the plans to close the lido," Kate says.

Rosemary is in her living room, the balcony doors open and her body warm with the late morning sun. Her swimsuit hangs on the washing line, nearly dry after her morning swim. She had been contemplating a nap — just existing could be exhausting these days.

"This is our chance to try and persuade the council not to sell to Paradise Living — not to close the lido," says Kate. "But we need more people; do you think you can help get more people?"

One of the things about getting older is that you find your circle of friends shrinks. They keep dying on you. Rosemary thinks about the funerals she has been to over the past ten years. She remembers Maureen, one of the other children who had stayed in Brixton during the war and who had helped Rosemary and her mother with the make-shift "school" in their kitchen. Losing her, that last remaining link to that specific part of her childhood, had shaken Rosemary. Maureen's husband, Jack, had followed a few months after — and Rosemary got out her black skirt suit again. There had been less expected ones, too, like her old friend Florence, whom she met in the library when Florence was a teacher and would bring children in to choose books. Except that funeral wasn't for Florence — it was for her daughter. Rosemary hasn't seen Florence in a long time now — she lives in a nursing home in Dulwich and wouldn't recognize Rosemary anymore even if she did come to visit.

Rosemary sighs deeply.

"But you've lived here all your life," says Kate. "You must know people who care as much as you do."

"I don't want to ask for help."

"But it's not asking for you," says Kate. "It's for the lido."

Rosemary pauses. She pictures George opening his eyes wide when they were both underwater, smiling at her. She thinks of

128

the people she knows in Brixton: Frank and Jermaine at the bookshop, Hope, Ahmed, Ellis and his son, Jake . . . And she thinks about the lido as a tennis court, filled with cement.

"Yes," she says after a moment. "Yes, you're right. We have to save the lido, Kate." As she says it Rosemary feels an aching in her chest. With one hand still on the phone, she puts the other on the edge of the sofa and looks over at George's photo on the bookshelf to strengthen her. *I will try not to let you down,* she says silently, looking at the face she has loved since she was sixteen.

"I think I know what to do," Rosemary says to Kate. "Are you free later?"

They meet outside the underground station, Kate carrying a notebook and a stack of flyers, Rosemary leaning on an empty plastic shopping trolley.

"Hello," says Kate, balancing the flyers and notebooks on one arm and waving as Rosemary approaches. Kate's hair is down today and tucked behind her ears. Rosemary thinks again how young she looks and can't help but smile.

"Are you ready to meet Brixton?" Rosemary says.

Kate nods and they set off, Rosemary and

her shopping trolley leading the way and Kate following slowly.

They start on Electric Avenue, weaving their way through the market stalls.

"Rosemary!" says a man in his late forties with a touch of stubble and a dusting of gray in his black hair. His shoulders are broad and his arms strong from years of carrying crates of fruit and vegetables. He wears a green fleece, jeans, and heavy leather boots, even in spring and summer, a black money bag tied around his waist. He smiles broadly.

Ellis owns one of the many fruit and vegetable stands in the market, the stand that Rosemary visits each week to pick up her food. He moved to Brixton from St. Lucia when he was a little boy. He and George knew each other — it was Ellis's father, Ken, who introduced George to okra and cassavas. Over the years Ellis helped out more and more, until he finally took over Ken's stand when it became too hard for him to manage. Ken and his wife, Joyce, have since returned to the Caribbean, and when trade is particularly hard Ellis sometimes talks about doing the same. But Rosemary is not sure he ever will — Brixton is his home. And then there is Jake — Ellis's teenage son who often helps him with the stand, just like Ellis used to help his own father. Ellis and Jake are alike in both appearance and temperament, and Rosemary has always had a soft spot for both of them.

"Ellis, how are you? How's the family?"

"Can't complain, can't complain. And how are you Mrs. P?"

"Still standing!"

"Who is this then, Rosemary? You didn't tell me you had a sister."

Rosemary turns to look at Kate who is still standing at her side, smiling at Ellis and the piles of brightly colored produce.

"This is Kate," Rosemary says. "She's my journalist."

Kate smiles and introduces herself, shaking Ellis's hand across the fruit and veg stand.

"Rosemary is campaigning to stop the closure of the local lido," she says. "Here, take one of her leaflets."

Ellis catches Rosemary's eye and raises an eyebrow, smiling warmly.

"Well, well. I always thought you had a rebellious streak, Mrs. P," he says, winking. She smiles back at him as he takes the leaflet and looks closely at the diver on the front.

"I heard about that," says Ellis after a moment's pause. "I remember when I was a

131

lad watching your George swimming at the lido; he always used to splash us kids by jumping in right next to us. He did these handstands, too, that I couldn't believe."

Rosemary smiles. "He certainly could do a handstand." They both laugh.

Kate tells Ellis about the meeting at the town hall.

"I'll be there," he says. The three of them say their goodbyes and Rosemary turns to leave.

"Wait, before you go," says Ellis.

He hands Rosemary a bag of cherries and Kate a bag full of tomatoes that smell like sunshine.

"My favorite — you are too good to me, Ellis," says Rosemary, bending to put the bag of cherries in her shopping trolley. When she stands up Kate is blushing fiercely, her arms cradling the bag of tomatoes as though she is holding a baby for the first time and doesn't know quite what to do with it.

"Are you sure?" she says.

"Yes, of course, on me," replies Ellis.

Rosemary watches Kate's blush reaching her ears and her hands carefully protecting the tomatoes as they turn and walk away. It looks to Rosemary as though she is not used to handling fresh fruit and vegetables and a

132

wave of worry rocks through her. But Kate is smiling so she smiles too.

For the rest of the afternoon they walk slowly down the main street and the roads that flow off it like tributaries. The pavements are full of people queuing for buses or walking quickly down the street, and it is with difficulty that they maneuver Rosemary's shopping trolley through the crowds.

They go to the charity shop, where Rosemary is offered a chair to sit down and something from the shop of her choosing. She doesn't take anything and instead leaves them with a small pile of leaflets.

"I filled their shop a while back," Rosemary says. "It's nice that they remember it though."

After George died, there were lots of things she'd had to get rid of. Without anyone to give them to, she donated it all to the shop.

"This jacket is as good as new," she'd said to the manager. "I even kept the spare buttons, I have them somewhere in my purse if you'll just wait a minute."

She'd pulled out a small pouch filled with buttons from her handbag, then slipped it inside the jacket pocket.

"And this shaver," she'd said. "I promise you it still works."

Rosemary had looked around the shop until she spotted an electrical socket by the counter. There was a click in her knees as she crouched then unpacked the shaver from its box and plugged it in. A whirring noise filled the shop. A baby in a pram by the door started to cry.

She kept the books, his swimming cap, and a few of his clothes. But she gave away seven bin bags filled with shirts, ties, trousers, and shoes. The next day she had headed back to the shop to look for the jacket. She'd forgotten that George would need something smart for the funeral.

"I'm sorry, but the jacket was sold yesterday afternoon," said the shopkeeper.

"I suppose it was a very good jacket," said Rosemary. "Good as new."

In the end George was dressed in a shirt and sweater and was buried without a jacket.

It is still hard to be in the shop, but Rosemary is thankful for the chair and the conversation.

After the charity shop they visit Frank and Jermaine's bookshop.

Rosemary breathes in the smell of the paper as they push open the door and strokes Sprout who is in her usual spot in the window. Her tail wags heavily as she spots Kate — a new friend. Kate bends to rub the dog's ears and pat her back.

"What a lovely dog," she says, and as she stands up and looks around. "What a lovely shop! How have I never been here before?"

Rosemary looks around the familiar space and tries to imagine it as if seen for the first time: the comfortably messy stacks of books, the community noticeboard spilling over with flyers and business cards, and the stools scattered around the shop in corners that are perfect for reading.

"How indeed?" says Frank, hearing Kate from his spot behind the counter. He is dressed casually, wearing faded jeans and a checked shirt open over a T-shirt. His smile is wide and bright, his cheeks reaching right up to his green eyes when he grins. Jermaine, who is standing next to him, is taller and slimmer than Frank and more smartly dressed in black jeans and a pale blue mandarin-collared shirt. He has a well-kept beard that is the same color as his short dark, gray-flecked hair.

They both nod at Rosemary as she and Kate head toward them.

"So, this is Kate then?" says Jermaine.

Rosemary blushes, not wanting to admit how much she has talked about Kate since they met.

135

"We feel like we know you already," says Frank, reaching his hand across the counter to Kate. She shakes it and then takes Jermaine's hand too.

"This is Frank, and this is Jermaine," says Rosemary, and the couple nod.

"I know we're on a mission, Rosemary," says Kate. "But do you mind if I look around for a bit? This place is the best."

Rosemary is secretly glad of the pause. She pulls up a stool opposite the counter and sits down heavily.

"You can come back!" shouts Jermaine, as Kate disappears down one of the warrenlike rows of books.

Frank turns to Rosemary, leaning forward over the counter.

"So we heard about the lido," he says. "Ahmed was in earlier this week and told us. It's just awful."

Jermaine shakes his head, his usual composure breaking away as he says angrily, "Paradise Living! As if Brixton needs more million-pound apartments — and an exclusive gym for their tenants only? Oh yes, that's really what a community needs. But lidos, libraries, bookshops . . ."

He trails off and Frank wraps an arm around him. Jermaine looks blankly around the shop. Rosemary watches him, noticing

136

how tired he looks.

"How are things here?" she says. "Has business picked up at all?"

Jermaine sighs. "Not much. Who convinced me to open a bookshop? Oh, that was you, Frank."

He turns to Frank, shakes his head, and kisses him gently on the cheek. Frank smiles.

"There's still hope yet," Frank says brightly. "Just like there's hope for the lido. We'll help you, Rosemary. Won't we, Jermaine?"

Rosemary watches the pair smiling at each other. Her knees hurt and she feels tired suddenly. Jermaine nods and they both turn to face Rosemary.

"Yes, of course we will," Jermaine says. "We'll do everything we can."

As they talk Rosemary is half aware of Kate, bending down to pull a book off a bottom shelf, tilting her head to read the titles or simply casting her eyes around the shop, a look of wonder on her face. Eventually she returns to the counter, a pile of three books in her hands.

"It really is a lovely shop," she says.

"I'm glad you think so," says Frank, looking pointedly at Jermaine. "See? There is hope. We have a new customer!"

As Kate pays, Jermaine takes a "Save our

lido" flyer from her stack and pins it right in the middle of the community board.

"There," he says, stepping back. "Hopefully that will do the trick." Rosemary wants to hug him.

"Well, we'd better be off then," she says, rising slowly from the stool, her knees shouting at her. "Ready, Kate?"

Kate nods and turns. "I'll be back soon," she says as they both leave the shop, Sprout watching them from the window.

They visit Morleys, the independent department store, where a security guard helps Rosemary with her trolley up the steps. They go to the pharmacy and the shop that sells everything from colanders and clothes dryers to fancy dress outfits. On the way they pass several people Rosemary knows and greets, either by name or simply with a nod of recognition after a life lived alongside them.

They stop for a moment in the post office to speak to Betty, one of Rosemary's childhood friends, who is posting a pile of letters to her many family members.

"How's the brood?" Rosemary asks. Betty has two children, a son and a daughter, three grandchildren, and one great-granddaughter. Unlike Rosemary, Betty was evacuated during the war, to Wales. She came back with a slight Welsh accent, but it disappeared quickly once she started working in Bon Marché, the upscale department store by Brixton Station, and hanging out with her friends at the lido every weekend. Several years after she returned to Brixton, a Welsh boy called Tom arrived in the neighborhood. It turned out they had met during the war (he was the next-door neighbor of the family she stayed with) and he had promised to marry her. She didn't believe him, but they kept writing to each other and when they were both nineteen he'd come to Brixton and gotten work on the building sites in South London. Two years later, they were married, and have been ever since.

"I told you that you must have plenty of friends here," says Kate as they say goodbye to Betty.

Rosemary thinks about the people she knows in Brixton, placing them like colorful pins on the map she has in her mind of all her favorite places.

"I suppose I do have a few," she says.

Before too long they are out of flyers.

"Don't worry, I can always print some more at work," says Kate.

Rosemary is leaning heavily on her shopping trolley. Kate offers to walk her home but she refuses, even when Kate tells her it's not out of her way.

"It is, you live on the other side of Brixton, you already told me that. Just because I'm eighty-six it doesn't mean I'm senile."

"Okay then," replies Kate. "Thank you for today. I think it will help with the meeting. But I just really enjoyed it too." Her cheeks are flushed and she is smiling. She looks completely different when she smiles — less mouse and more woman.

They say goodbye and Rosemary turns for home, walking slowly down the streets she has known all her life.

CHAPTER 21

Kate has been to Electric Avenue many times but has never bought anything. Shop-keepers don't sell frozen microwave meals and wine there. As she unpacks the paper bag of tomatoes into a bowl, she thinks about Ellis's stall — how she took deep breaths through her nose and how the smell reminded her of her mum's spaghetti Bolognese. Her mum always made spaghetti Bolognese and a tomato sauce from scratch. When Kate was still at home she would help her sometimes. She loved peeling the skins off the warm tomatoes and feeling their plump flesh in her hands. It has been a long time since she's had the energy to peel tomatoes.

She opens cupboards and drawers, thinking about all the people that Rosemary knows in Brixton. In the Bristol suburbs Kate was used to knowing the staff in the shops and saying hello to people in the street. Since coming to London she has met people mainly through interviewing them. Today she had immediately liked all Rosemary's friends — Ellis, and Betty, and Frank and Jermaine — they made her notice something about the place where she lives that she hasn't seen before. Perhaps it really wasn't so different from her home after all.

As she takes out a pan and places it on the cooktop she remembers the secondhand bookshop and wonders why it has taken her so long to find this place. She supposes she wasn't looking before: it is hard to notice much when you have your eyes on the ground.

Kate boils water in the kettle and pours it over the tomatoes. Then she reaches for the shopping bag on the table — the bag she had filled in the supermarket after saying goodbye to Rosemary. For the first time in months — or if she is being honest, years — she had properly looked while she shopped, not just heading to the frozen-food aisle but picking up onions, mushrooms, ground beef, and garlic.

She wipes the grease and stains from the kitchen surface, piles her housemates' dirty dishes in the sink, and sets out the ingredients for spaghetti Bolognese on the table. Then slowly and tentatively she tries to remember her mum's recipe.

She forgets the garlic and adds too much salt, to the point that by the time she is finished, it is barely edible. The kitchen is even more of a mess than it was when she started and the plate of food looks much less appealing than the home-cooked dinner she remembers. She still sits down to eat it, though, drinking three glasses of water to combat the too-salty taste. It is certainly not her mum's spaghetti Bolognese made from scratch. But it's a start.

She suddenly wants to text Erin a photo of the meal, but admitting its significance to her would also admit how badly she's been eating recently. So instead she sends her a photo of the lido that she took the other day and asks her how her running is going. Then she puts her phone back on the table and continues her meal.

As Kate eats she feels tired from the day, but calmer than she has been in a while. She thinks about the lido. Hopefully the fly-ers will mean a good turnout at the council meeting in two weeks' time. She has written an article for the *Chronicle* about the meet-ing, too, calling residents to come and have their say about the future of the lido. She hopes it goes well, and as she thinks that, she realizes how much she is starting to care about the campaign. Like trying to cook for herself and learning to swim again, this is something she needs to do.

CHAPTER 22

Rosemary and George decided to marry in the registry office at the town hall. It would just be a small group: their parents, a few old school friends, and some colleagues of hers from the library. Her mother made her wedding dress. It fell just above her ankles, revealing white shoes with a low heel and small bows. The day before the wedding Rosemary and her mother spent all day covering the wedding cake in paper and decorations — there wasn't enough sugar for icing but from a distance it looked perfect.

Their parents tried to persuade them to hire a car to take them to the town hall but they didn't see the point when it was such a short walk from their homes. They wanted to arrive together, holding hands.

Rosemary dressed in her childhood bedroom. It was piled with boxes: George had found a flat in one of the new buildings sprouting up in Brixton, just opposite the lido, and they were moving there the day after the wedding. After unpacking and a honeymoon at home they would start their lives — George running his family's green-grocer and Rosemary continuing to work at the library. It was never a question for Rose-mary that she would work — her mother had, George's parents had, and so would she. She had friends who were moving to Canada or who were engaged to rich men. None of them had jobs but a few of them had refrigerators. Rosemary thought she would prefer a job to a refrigerator but she didn't tell them that. A small life was more than big enough for her if it had George in it, and if they could live in a flat by them-selves where no one would bother them and they would be in each other's arms if they got woken by rain or dreams in the night.

"Do you feel nervous?" asked her mother as she adjusted her daughter's hair, lifting the veil over her face. Her father leaned on a pile of boxes watching them, holding his daughter's bouquet while she adjusted her veil.

But she didn't feel nervous.

In front of the small group that sat on foldout wooden chairs in the registry office they promised to love each other for richer, for poorer, in sickness and in health. George needed no prompting to kiss his bride.

They stepped out of the doors of the town hall into a cloud of pink and white confetti and into the rest of their lives.

CHAPTER 23

This cinema only sells posh popcorn with flavors like sweet chili and sea salt, but the smell still permeates the walls, the carpet, the air. Popcorn dust gets into all the corners. The young staff members behind the ticket counter wear tattoos and peaked caps, smiling as they sell tickets and bars of chocolate. They encourage customers to sign up for loyalty cards or to upgrade their seats to VIP ones.

A film has just ended and the crowd starts spilling out of the double doors, some heading straight through the foyer and outside, others veering into the bar. The foyer is suddenly noisy.

"Well, that was a waste of money."

"What do you mean? I loved it!"

"I didn't see that ending coming, did you?"

"That bit that made me jump."

"I jumped because you jumped!"

People walk mainly in pairs, some in larger groups as they talk together. Among them is Rosemary, alone in the crowd.

"Sorry, excuse me," says a woman as she bumps into her, pushed by the wave of people.

"That's okay," says Rosemary, thankful of something to say. She smiles at the woman, about to ask her if she liked the film, but she has already gone. Rosemary makes her way slowly through the crowd.

Rosemary loves the cinema. She goes once a month, stuffing her pockets with sweets and propping herself up with a cushion that she brings from home. She likes sitting beneath the big screen, looking up at the huge actors and feeling the sounds vibrate around the whole cinema and up through her feet. It doesn't even matter what she sees — she picks the films by their names and without reading the descriptions. If the title sounds interesting enough, she buys a ticket.

She chooses a seat near the front so she doesn't have to tackle the stairs. She always arrives on time but only feels truly comfortable when the lights dim and everyone joins her in being lost in the film. She cranes her neck up to the screen and watches whatever romantic comedy or thriller or spy film she has chosen this month, joining the rest of the audience in laughter or tears. Emotion flows through the room like the wave at a sporting event. When she watches the films she is not alone, she is part of something bigger, one nameless face in a large audience of nameless faces.

It is only when the film is over and the audience breaks off and she is left behind that she misses the company.

A man holds the door open for her; he is smoking with a friend, and Rosemary nods at him then turns right out of the cinema. As she walks she watches the buses, checking the numbers and testing herself by remembering their end destinations. 59: Telford Avenue. 159: Streatham Station. 333: Tooting Broadway. 250. What is 250? It begins with C. It's not Clapham, or Crystal Palace. 250: Croydon Town Centre. She never travels to Croydon, or any of the other end destinations in fact, but it is important that she remembers.

She wonders if George would have liked the film. She enjoys most films — she goes for the atmosphere and the big screen and the music. But George was more particular. He had certain actors he loved (Sean Connery, Michael Gambon, Judi Dench) and would watch anything they starred in, but

150

other than that he said the old films were the best films. Sometimes the cinema puts on screenings of the classics — he would always want to go to those. *No, he probably wouldn't have liked this one,* she thinks as she walks. *It was too gory.*

Rosemary continues down the road toward the underground. Tonight she doesn't want to go home to her empty flat just yet. There is somewhere she wants to visit. She turns right onto the station road.

The street is quiet: the shops under the arches have their metal shutters pulled down. Some of the shutters are painted. One is covered with the Jamaican flag but most are painted with slogans. "Save our arches," "Stop the evictions," "Say NO to rental increases." The signs make her think of her lido and she pictures its doors closed and the pool completely empty of swimmers. The thought makes a shiver run through her body.

She walks halfway down the street, passing a group of teenagers huddled in the entrance to the station smoking and playing music from a portable stereo. They are wearing a uniform that they would never acknowledge as one; she wants to laugh and tell them they are just the same as every other group of teenagers she has seen here over the years.

For most of her life she has never felt frightened walking alone in the street. Even during the war she enjoyed the freedom of being one of those left behind. She was young then, too: she had survived and she felt certain she would survive again.

When the riots of 1981 hit she was much older and age had chipped away at her teenage confidence as though scraping the solid mortar out from between bricks. It was early April, and walking home from the library she saw the half-burnt shells of cars parked in one street as flames rose into the sky and a wall of police officers huddled behind plastic shields. Behind the blaze and the smoke she couldn't make out quite what was happening, but she heard shouting and saw people facing the line of police, their arms raised as though about to throw something. She walked home quickly and told George what she had seen. He didn't want her to leave the flat and on the worst day he shut the shop. From their balcony they could see clouds of smoke rising over the Brixton streets, reminding her of the war. Their living room was piled high with boxes of vegetables. He was worried they'd loot his shop. "Who's going to loot a fruit and vegetable shop?" she said. "I think they're after televisions and things, not piles of potatoes."

She ignores the teenagers and keeps walking until she reaches the arch she is looking for. It is the only one that is not closed; it glows with light and noise, crowds spilling out onto the street and sitting outside on benches. Paper lanterns hang from the entrance and a plastic flamingo stands guard outside the fence that runs around the outside seating area.

"Excuse me," she says, struggling to make her way through the crowd of twenty- and thirtysomethings.

Groups sitting at tables pull their chairs in to let her past. They watch her with raised eyebrows and then go back to their jugs of cocktails. The room is loud with laughter and music that Rosemary can't quite hear apart from the regular thumping of the bass. The crowd gets denser closer to the bar. A young man spots Rosemary and elbows his friend in the ribs, pushing him off his barstool.

"Hey, dick, give this lady your seat."

"I'm sorry, I didn't see her. I'm sorry, I didn't see you," he says, turning to Rosemary and giving her his arm to help her into the chair. She climbs in slowly.

"You can apologize by telling me what you

young people are drinking these days. It's been a while since I've been in a cocktail bar."

"Got it — I'll order for you."

He raises a hand and catches the barman's eye. A few minutes later a short, wide glass half filled with orange liquid and ice is put on a paper napkin in front of Rosemary.

Outside a group of workers in suits, wearing loosened ties, turn out from the station and scatter into the night, some going home and some heading to the pub. As they walk down the station road they see one glowing arch where an old woman sits at a bar drinking an old-fashioned. Around her crowds of young people laugh and drink from jugs filled with ice, sipping brightly colored cocktails with retro paper umbrellas. She is flanked by two couples in deep conversation, their backs to her. If they looked up they would see a faded green sign above the cocktail bar that says FRESH FRUIT AND VEGETABLES: PETERSON & SON.

CHAPTER 24

After Kate's first article about the lido runs Phil gradually gives her more assignments, this time not just planning notices, but proper stories. First is the story about the tenants being evicted from their homes to make way for the Paradise Living high-rises, which she pitched after meeting the man at the town hall. The next stories take her all across the neighborhood and show it to her from all angles: pretty and ugly.

She writes about a new bar opening and an old fishmonger closing, about a primary school raising money for charity and about a teenage boy who overcame his upbringing among drug-dealing parents to become a local sports star set to compete in the next Olympics. She suddenly finds herself busier than she has been since starting work at the *Brixton Chronicle* — heading across the neighborhood each day for interviews and research.

Each time she sees her name in print she feels a glow of pride. One evening her phone buzzes: it's a text from Erin.

"Loving your articles K. I'm so proud. E x."

Kate reads the text again. Although the *Brixton Chronicle* does have a website, not all of the articles go online.

"I didn't know you'd read them? It's a local paper! K x."

A moment later her phone buzzes again.

"I get it delivered! E x."

Kate pictures the *Brixton Chronicle,* delivered from South London to Bath, landing on Erin's doormat each week. How much must that cost her? She didn't even know it was possible to get it delivered that far. Perhaps Erin has an arrangement with Phil — although he has never mentioned it. She imagines her sister reading her words, tucked up on her sofa, and she wishes some magic could transport her instantly to Bath so she could give Erin a hug. Instead she sends a reply, "Thank you — that means a lot. Hope you are ok. K xx."

The next day Kate is sent on assignment to the Norwood and Brixton food bank, where she meets local volunteers and families who use the bank to stock their empty cupboards. She interviews a woman, Kelly, not much older than herself, who is relying on the food bank to feed herself while her daughter is unwell and in hospital.

"She's only six and she is really frightened of hospitals," says Kelly as she sits at a table inside the hall where the food bank is operated, drinking a cup of tea she has been handed by one of the volunteers. "So I've been going to see her every day. But it means I haven't been able to work for a few weeks. I've gone through our savings, and I have thought about trying to go back to work but she cries so much every time I leave and I'm just so exhausted all the time too. And I need to be around in case anything gets worse."

Kelly's eyes fill with tears and Kate wants to reach across the table and take Kelly's hand. Instead she focuses on taking notes, trying to remain professional.

"One day after visiting her in hospital I realized I hadn't eaten anything all day. But there was nothing in the house. There's nothing worse than that feeling — suddenly realizing you are starving and there is nothing there to eat. It terrified me and there was nothing I could do. So that's why I'm here."

Kelly looks around her as though she can't quite remember where she is. A volunteer smiles at her, gives her a gentle wave. As Kate watches Kelly, exhaustion and sadness knotted on her forehead, she feels a sinking sense of shame. She remembers all the nights she has gone to bed without dinner, all the times she has skipped a meal rather than bothering to go to the supermarket and buy food. She has felt plenty of fear, but never that specific, horrifying fear that Kelly just described.

"It feels like the biggest failure," says Kelly, looking up and meeting Kate's eyes, "not being able to feed yourself. That's the most basic, important thing, isn't it?"

Kate feels a lump invading her throat and her eyes filling with tears that are dangerously close to spilling over. She forces them back and thanks Kelly with what she hopes comes out as warmth and sincerity, for doing the interview.

"I hope things work out for you, and that your daughter gets better soon, I really do."

That evening, back in her flat, Kate cooks for herself again. Nothing complicated — just pasta with chicken and pesto — but she focuses carefully on preparing it, thinking about Kelly as she does. A feeling of helplessness washes over her — a helplessness to change any of the big things in the world or to make a difference in any meaningful way. On her worst days it is not just her own worries that consume her, but a gnawing fear at the state of the world, a terror at the huge sadness she knows is out there. In those moments it is as though she is a black hole and all the anxieties in the world around her are sucked inside until she is completely filled with darkness.

As she eats she avoids the rising tide of worry by thinking about the lido, focusing on the upcoming meeting and what else she can do to help Rosemary save her pool. Perhaps that's why the lido has become so important to her, she thinks. It might just be one thing, but it's something. And the darkness, although still there in the background, retreats.

CHAPTER 25

At first they didn't have enough furniture to fill their flat. To begin with they used a table made from a piece of wood balanced on wooden vegetable crates. George's parents gave them two chairs. They didn't match, but it didn't matter. For a while they were the only things in the living room aside from piles of books that they stacked against the walls. They would get to the bookshelves later. Both of them had a large collection of books, books that had nursed them through their childhood and comforted them as they became teenagers. They eagerly read through the titles as they unpacked together.

"When we get the bookshelves how shall we organize the books?" Rosemary asked. "Shall we have a shelf each?"

"No," said George, "I want to mix them all up."

When the bookshelves eventually arrived they took great pleasure in mixing up their

books: his Dickens cheek to cheek with her
Brontë.

George saved up any spare money and
used it to buy things for the house. One day
he came home from work with a potted rose
that he bought from the market. He put it
on the windowsill and put crosses on the
calendar in the kitchen to remind him when
to water it. For their first Christmas in the
flat they both chipped in for a gramophone.
Their record collection started with just
one: Nat King Cole's "Mona Lisa," which
they listened to over and over.

Rosemary liked seeing their two tooth-
brushes next to each other on the bathroom
shelf. They brushed their teeth at the same
time, both standing barefoot on the bathroom rug, he with an arm around her waist
and she looking at him in the mirror and
wanting to smile but being too full of
toothpaste and toothbrush. He pulled faces
at her in the mirror, trying to make her
laugh. They took turns spitting into the sink.
Once they were finished they wiped their
mouths with the same towel and kissed each
other, the mint making each other's lips
tingle.

For the first few months of their married
life they slept on a mattress on the floor with
curtains made from spare sheets and hung

up with pegs. They went to bed straight after dinner, sometimes when it was still light outside, sometimes leaving their dishes on the table, waiting until the morning to wash and dry them. They had to scrub the plates extra hard the next day but they didn't mind.

Their bed was the only place where they stopped their constant chatter, preferring silence but having whole conversations with their bodies. Their bodies whispered as they touched each other gently and screamed while their tongues met inside each other's hot mouths. They understood each other's language and knew how to reply.

Sometimes they were polite, sometimes they were bold, but they always kissed. Soft kisses, hard kisses, kisses on eyelids and cheeks and collarbones and at the soft skin behind the back of ears.

Once the sex was over they collapsed into the mattress, loving the feeling of not knowing whose arm or leg was whose. Her leg flung over his stomach, his head cradled in her arms. His body heaped over hers, heart to heart and his face in her hair. Side by side, with his arms around her stomach and cupping a breast, hers resting on his backside. They lay quietly, separate in their

162

thoughts but knotted together with their bodies.

"I love you," said George, on a cool summer's night several months after their wedding. They lay in each other's warmth on the mattress and beneath tangled sheets.

"And I love you," said Rosemary. She tucked her body under his arm, curling her head into his armpit and putting an arm across his stomach.

"I'm sorry we haven't got a real bed yet," he said. "I promise we'll get one soon."

She would have slept on a stone floor every night if it meant sleeping next to him. She thought she told him that, but perhaps she fell asleep before the words could come.

CHAPTER 26

Rosemary and Kate meet at the lido at seven a.m. Ahmed unlocks the glass door to the noticeboard and helps them pin up posters about the hearing, moving the advert for ukulele classes to make room.

"Who actually plays this thing anyway? It's basically a children's guitar," he says.

Once the posters are up, Rosemary and Kate go for a swim. Rosemary invited her, and Kate had been surprised by how pleased she was at the invitation. She can't remember the last time someone asked her to do something with them.

In the changing room Kate takes her clothes off to reveal her swimsuit underneath. When she turns around, Rosemary is naked, talking to another woman whom Kate guesses is in her late sixties. This woman is naked, too, except for a pink swimming cap. Rosemary and the woman start to laugh, holding on to each other's arms as their wrinkled naked bodies shake with laughter.

They see Kate watching them, hugging her arms awkwardly around herself.

"Sorry, Kate, this is Hope," says Rosemary. "We used to work together."

"Lovely to meet you," says Hope, reaching out to shake Kate's hand with both of hers.

Kate never thought she would find herself shaking hands with a naked sixtysomething woman. She doesn't know where to look.

"Rosemary has told me all about you," says Hope as Rosemary turns to change.

"It's lovely to meet you too," says Kate.

She waits while Rosemary gets ready. Eventually she turns round in her swimsuit, holding her cap and goggles in her hand.

"Come on, we'd better go."

"And I'd better get dry and dressed," says Hope. "Enjoy the water, it's cool this morning but lovely."

"See you soon, dear," says Rosemary. Kate says goodbye to Hope and follows Rosemary onto the pool deck, making sure to stay at Rosemary's side.

"You don't need to wait for me," Rosemary says.

"I sprained my ankle recently, I can't walk any faster."

"I don't believe you."

"Then don't believe me."

They arrive at the edge together. Rosemary holds on to the ladder for support.

"I'd prefer it if you didn't watch," she says.

There is a creaking, a pause, and a slight splash. When Kate turns around Rosemary is in the water, putting her cap and goggles on and splashing water onto her shoulders. Kate climbs down and joins her. Hope was right: the water is chilly but deliciously so. As the cold surrounds her body Kate takes a deep breath and feels something inside her stretching and coming to life.

In the pool it is Rosemary who has to slow down to wait for Kate, which she does after every few lengths, the two of them pausing for a moment. They swim together but apart, only occasionally breaking the silence to talk at the shallow end. The sun peers through the trees.

Rosemary watches Kate as she swims, struggling to keep her head above the water like a dog chasing a ball in a river.

"You should really get some goggles," says Rosemary during one of their breaks in the shallow end. "It's exhausting me just watching you keep your head up like that."

"I don't know how else to do it," says Kate. "And I hate getting the chlorine in my eyes."

"The goggles will help with that. I've got a spare pair you can have. Kick your legs and your arms separately — you'll find it less tiring. And let your head get pushed under with your stroke."

As Kate swims she feels safe, and free. She imagines her Panic sitting at one of the picnic tables on the lido decking. *You can't get me here,* she thinks as she ducks under water, the cold embracing her like an old friend.

167

After a half-hour's swim they climb out and wrap their towels around themselves. The changing room is busy with people getting ready for work. Women pull on tights and button-up shirts, their wet swimsuits hanging on the locker doors or piled on the floor.

Rosemary watches the line of women at the mirrors, some queuing for the hair dryer and others applying their makeup. They peer into the glass, pulling strange faces as they put on mascara. One woman is leaning into the mirror and drawing over her eyebrows with a pencil, her face creased with concentration. Next to her a young woman puts on another layer of foundation, each layer making her freckles fainter until eventually they disappear.

When she is dressed Rosemary rubs moisturizer onto her face and brushes her hair.

"See you outside?" she says to Kate, who is joining the line of women at the mirror.

Kate nods and reaches into her makeup bag. Rosemary watches her for a moment as she searches for the right thing to cover or highlight the right bits of her face. She wonders how much of a woman's lifetime is given to these rituals. And what for? She has seen all these women barefaced in the pool and naked in the changing rooms and they are perfect. Of course, she did it herself, too, when she was young. She didn't wear as much makeup as some of her friends, or some of the women who came into the library with a different haircut every week, but she did still make an effort. It used to take her at least five minutes.

Outside, Rosemary sits on a bench opposite the lido and waits for Kate. After a few minutes Kate appears and sits down next to Rosemary.

"Tell me about where you used to work, Rosemary," she says, as they wait for the sun to dry their hair.

"I worked at the library. I worked there for thirty-five years, until it closed."

"Oh," says Kate, "the Old Library."

The library is now a bar and café — Kate has been there before.

"It's stupid but I always thought that was just the name. How silly of me."

"I used to scan the books where the cof-

169

fee bar is now," says Rosemary. "I don't know what happened to all the books. I rescued a lot of them — it's why my flat is so cramped — but I don't know about the others. I desperately hope they were given to local schools. The thought of them getting thrown away . . ."

Rosemary winces, her bright blue eyes retreating into the deep creases of her skin.

"The problem was, we never really saw it coming," she continues. "One day there was a poster up announcing that there would be some cost-cutting schemes coming from the local council, and the next minute Hope and I were on the street looking up at the closed doors. It was just so sad.

"I took my job there very seriously. I was happy to work — I always thought women who didn't must have been dreadfully bored. I know I was just a librarian but I preferred to think of myself as the Keeper of the Books. It was my job to keep the shelves organized so that 'Romance' was tucked discreetly away from fiction, and so the twelve-year-old could find *The Body Book* without asking. We were also somewhere to go when it was raining outside. I remember a young lad called Robbie who used to come in with his rucksack and sleeping bag and leave them on a chair while he headed to the Languages aisle. He always said 'Bonjour' to me and told me he was going to walk and swim to Paris. I wonder where he is now . . ."

Rosemary sighs and looks up the hill at the park she has known all her life. She thinks about the library — about the children laughing in the children's corner, about people studying and using the computers to apply for jobs. On the library's last day several people spoke to Rosemary. Mrs. Lane talked about her delight at watching her young daughter Megan choose piles of books. "This is the only place where I let her get exactly what she wants," she had said. "How can letting her read all the books she likes be a bad thing?"

Mr. Gudowicz had actually hugged Rosemary. His eyes were shiny and wet and he told her that because of the library he had been able to study for the qualification that helped him get a job.

"I can be a husband and a father again now," he had said.

She turns to look at Kate. "The lido has to stay open. It just has to."

"I know," Kate replies.

Rosemary looks closely at the young woman next to her. Kate's brown eyes look serious but for once they aren't afraid.

171

They've nudged open like windows and Rosemary sees a peek of a very different woman inside. A woman who is strong, and who, Rosemary suddenly realizes, can help her. Will help her.

"That reminds me," says Kate, "the council phoned me with more details about the meeting. Apparently we need one nominated speaker who can best sum up the views of the other residents — what the lido means to them. I can't think of anyone better than you. You will do it, won't you, Rosemary? We'll all be right there with you."

Rosemary thinks about how Geoff first described her to Kate as their "most loyal swimmer." She hopes that she will be able to find the words to even begin to tell them what the lido means to her.

"I'd be honored," she says. Kate smiles, letting out a little sigh.

Together they watch the people with wet hair and bags over their shoulders leaving the pool and heading into the park.

Kate suddenly looks at her watch, "Oh no, I'm running late. I need to get to Brixton Village; there's a new shop opening and I'm interviewing the owner before it opens. I'll see you soon though?"

Rosemary nods and watches as Kate leaves, her slender figure moving quickly through the park. Rosemary reflects on the upcoming council meeting, trying to imagine what she might say when she is called to speak. She thinks about how much Brixton has already lost and how badly she wants to get it right this time.

CHAPTER 28

On the last Saturday of the month Brix Mix Market comes to Station Road and the street fills with local traders selling vintage clothes, printed African fabrics, homemade ceramics, and vividly painted wooden animals. The smell of jerk chicken fills the air as it sizzles on the grill outside a small van parked on the road.

A typical Saturday finds Kate inside her flat watching boxed sets. Sometimes she ventures to the coffee shop at the end of her road to sit and read a book, watching the street outside behind the safety of the window.

Today she steps out her front door into a bright spring day. She smiles as she walks down the road, letting the hopefulness of the blue sky buoy her. It has been days since her last panic attack. She has started swimming regularly, sometimes with Rosemary if she makes it to the pool in time, and sometimes after work. When she swims she is reminded of the articles she read about how exercise can help with anxiety. But there is more to it, too — the lido campaign has given her something to believe in, and to focus on. She feels more in control than she has in months.

As soon as she steps onto the main street she is shaken by the sound of the buses and the crowds that she can see spilling out of the station farther down the road. But instead of turning back as she normally might, she keeps going, trying her best to keep her head level rather than looking down at her feet. She weaves in and out of the other people on the pavement, careful not to bump into anyone.

She feels her phone buzz in her pocket. Pulling it out, she sees it's a message from Erin. Kate clicks on it to see a photo of Erin beaming, a medal around her neck. "I did my first 10k!" reads the text. Kate stops in the alcove outside a shop to look at the photo properly and reply. Erin looks so happy, her face pink and her red hair pulled back in a scruffy ponytail — one of the only times Kate has seen her with messy hair. It makes Kate smile, and the noise of the buses and the heaviness of the crowd seems to disappear.

"So proud of you sis," she replies, then slips her phone back in her pocket.

At the cinema she turns right onto Coldharbour Lane and follows it until she reaches the shop front with books and a golden retriever in the window. She pushes open the door and steps into Frank and Jermaine's shop.

Jermaine looks up from the counter where he is leaning and reading a book.

"Kate!" he says. She feels a rush — he seems happy to see her.

"I told you I'd be back again soon," says Kate.

"Frank is just on a break. He'll be so pleased to know you came by."

"Say hello to him for me. I'm just going to have a look around."

"Make yourself at home."

Jermaine goes back to reading his book and Kate explores the shop. There is a whole section dedicated to female writers and she starts there, browsing the spines until something speaks to her and she pulls it out to read the back cover and the first page. Then she moves on to foreign literature, then a stand given to cheerful holiday reads, then to the children's section at the back just for the nostalgia of picking up books she read as a child. She kneels and flicks through them, remembering the happiness of discovering reading and how it could take her to a different time and place, a different world. She could be whoever she wanted when she read a book. As she wanders she picks books up here and there, her pile growing until she has a stack of five. She feels content, the smell of the shop soothing her.

"I need to stop now before I have more than I can carry," she says as she places her pile on the counter. "It really is a lovely shop."

"Thank you," replies Jermaine, his tall body towering over the counter as he checks the prices penciled on the inside covers. He rubs his beard absentmindedly as he continues talking.

"It's a great thing you're doing by helping with the lido. Rosemary might have mentioned it, but we've been in a bit of trouble here in the shop. Not that you need me to tell you that — you could easily guess it. It's so hard to run a bookshop these days."

Kate looks around. The shop is messy but cozy, books piled everywhere and stools placed in nooks between the shelves where people can sit and read.

"We'll do whatever we can to help," Jermaine says, looking at Kate again. "Some things are worth fighting for."

"Thank you," she says, resisting an urge to hug him. She heads to the door, giving Sprout a quick stroke before opening it. "So I'll see you at the meeting then?"

"We'll be there."

As she leaves a smile spreads over her face. She and Rosemary may have a hard fight ahead of them, but at least they have people joining them. Hope, Ellis and Jake, Ahmed and Geoff, Betty, and now Frank and Jermaine too. And Kate is sure there will be more — there are so many other people who swim at the lido, surely they must care. *Maybe,* she thinks to herself, *maybe it will be okay.*

CHAPTER 29

"Are you sorry that we got married?" asked Rosemary.

She looked up at George as she said it, his hands clenched tightly on his knees, his back bent as he sat on the chair next to their bed. He was still wearing his leather apron over his clothes. Normally when he arrived home from work he hung the apron on the back of the front door so it was ready for the next day.

He had called in at the library and told them she wouldn't be in for a few weeks. She hated to imagine that conversation but she did it anyway: she imagined their pity and that is what she hated most.

"Why would you say that?" he said, reaching for her hand and squeezing it tightly. It ached as she moved to take his hand, but she tried not to let it show on her face. The warmth of his skin filled her whole body.

"If we hadn't got married, this might not

have happened," she said. "You might be with someone else. You might have a baby."

The word made her flinch. She thought again of the conversation George must have had at the library. Perhaps laughter had come from the children's corner as he spoke to Hope and the others and he had flinched too. She wondered what they would have said, what they could have said. She imagined going back to work. She would be able to lift the crates of books again, at least, and fit between the tight rows in the reference section. But it was little consolation.

He looked down at her and his face was sadder than she'd ever seen it before, and frightened like a child's. Rosemary felt she might break like a dry branch in a storm. She closed her eyes.

"You can't say that," he said. "Don't ever say that. I might be with someone else but it wouldn't be you. I might have a baby but it wouldn't be yours."

She opened her eyes again and there he was, loving her with everything he was. She never doubted that.

"Maybe this one wasn't ready to be born, but the next one will be," he said. "And we still have each other. I still have you."

George attempted a smile but it didn't quite work — it made his face twist and it made her even sadder, him trying to smile for her. Watching George she remembered a time at the lido when a nest had fallen out of the branches of a tree. They were still teenagers then but George swam out to the nest and was crying before he reached it because he already knew what had happened. He scooped the drowned nest out of the pool and dove to the bottom to collect the tiny bodies that had fallen out. She watched him diving again and again and she started crying too. She pretended to him that it was the birds she was crying for but she cried for him. He kept ducking under the water until he had collected all the birds and lined them up on the side.

George's eyes were filling up now and he let them spill over. They stained his apron in dark droplets.

"It's okay," she said.

And then he sobbed. His tears were never polite or quiet, they poured out of him like a dam had burst. From looking at him with his strong hands and wearing his muddy greengrocer's apron, you would never expect those kind of tears.

"Come into bed with me," she said.

He crossed to the other side of the bed and climbed in behind her, wrapping his arms around her body, resting his hands on her stomach. He held her and he cried and she cried too. She wasn't sure if she was crying for the baby this time or for him. He was still wearing his apron and his shoes when they woke up the next morning.

CHAPTER 30

On the day of the council meeting Kate feels the Panic creeping up on her. She doesn't want to fail the people she has met. She doesn't want to fail Rosemary.

At work she is quiet, typing up a story while thinking about what will happen at the meeting and whether enough people will come. And if them coming will even make a difference.

She is tired too. In the night she dreamed she was on her way to the lido, her swimming bag over her shoulder. But when she got to where the lido should have been it wasn't there. Instead she was in an unknown part of the city, at the bottom of a tower of flats that blocked out the sun. The streets were unfamiliar and the people were walking too quickly to stop them and ask for directions. A sign labeled SWIMMING POOL pointed left, but the map on her phone told her to go right.

She walked around the bottom of the building, leaning back to try and see the top. As she walked she started to panic. How could the lido have moved? How could it be on the map but not here? She walked down streets she didn't recognize and checked her phone. It told her she was two minutes away from her end destination, but where was it?

Then the panic and fear bubbled over into hot, angry tears. Her breathing came in gulps and gasps and she was frozen to the pavement, tears running down her face as she struggled to breathe.

People walked quickly past her like she was a misbehaving child. She imagined what she must look like to them: a young woman with makeup smeared down her face, crying impolite tears for no apparent reason in the street. Eventually a teenage boy came up and asked if she was okay.

"You don't need to cry, please stop crying," he said.

And then she woke up, feeling just as exhausted as she does after every panic attack.

"I thought you might want a coffee," says a voice as a mug is placed gently on her desk. She looks up and sees a mess of strawberry blond hair, and a smiling face.

"Thank you, Jay. You read my mind."

"Photographer slash mind reader. It's a burden I have to carry."

She sips the coffee, the smell alone reviving her slightly.

"I've been asked to come along to your meeting tonight to get some photos for the paper. I hope that's okay."

Kate pauses; she doesn't know Jay well, but his strawberry blond hair and kind face are part of the fabric of her days at the paper and somehow soothing.

"It's not really my meeting," she says, "but of course that's okay. I'm not sure you'll really get anything that useful, though — it's just in the council offices."

"We'll see," says Jay, hopping down from the end of the desk where he had been perching, and picking up his camera bag. "If I'm as good a photographer as I am a mind reader, you might be surprised. Right, now I'm off to photograph that new Mexican restaurant. I can probably get you some free nachos if you want? They don't know yet that we're only giving them two stars."

"That's okay, the coffee is hitting the spot. Thank you."

"No problem. See you later."

As Jay leaves Kate realizes that it has been a long time since she has had a conversation with a man who isn't her boss or interview subject. She also notices she has stopped feeling quite so anxious.

CHAPTER 31

After Rosemary's third miscarriage, George suggested a holiday. "I want you to feel the seawater between your toes, Rosy," he said one evening, and she smiled, imagining what it would feel like. He was sitting in the armchair by the fireplace and opened his arms. She crossed the living room and climbed onto his lap. She still remembered his descriptions of Devon so vividly that she could taste the salt water on her lips and hear the sound of the waves whenever she thought about it, but she had never seen it for herself.

"I want to go away, just us," he said. It was always just the two of them but she understood what he meant; she also longed to escape the memory of that person she had never met. She wanted to feel like they were teenagers again. So they decided on a holiday and were suddenly swept up in the excitement of it.

187

It was the first and only time that he had closed the shop for a whole week since they were married. He put a sign in the window announcing the planned closure several weeks before they were due to leave and every conversation he had with his customers during those weeks was about the holiday. He talked proudly about the planned trip, using the American word *vacation* occasionally. Rosemary and George were not vacationing people. They had never been on a holiday before in their lives.

Devon was too far away so they opted for Brighton, booking a week in a B&B and saving for the two shillings six pence extra to travel on the *Brighton Belle* from Victoria, the chocolate-and-cream-painted Pullman train known for its beautiful carriages.

"You're my Brixton belle," George said into Rosemary's ear as he helped her onboard at the crowded platform, carrying the small suitcase that they had borrowed from one of Rosemary's friends. Once they had found their seats Rosemary took in the carriage around her — the brown art deco wallpaper, the soft glow of the table lamps and the faint smell of toast, coffee, and kippers.

Rosemary tried to hide her nerves — she had never left London before and felt an ache in her stomach as she watched the station platform drifting away. It felt like an untethering and she was floating free. George squeezed her hand.

"What do you think that's for?" asked Rosemary, pointing at a bell push on the wall.

"It's for the waiter," said a woman opposite them, raising an eyebrow. George and Rosemary looked at each other and smiled. He pressed the button. A few moments later the waiter was there, showing them the menu and addressing George as "sir" (Rosemary covered her mouth with her hand to hide her laughter). They could only afford a pot of tea, but it could have been champagne. The journey was rickety and the seats uncomfortable, but they didn't care.

When they arrived Rosemary wanted to see the sea straightaway, so they followed the families and couples down Queens Road to the waterfront. Everyone was dressed for the beach — dark round sunglasses on the faces of men and women and sunhats on children's heads. They passed by ice cream shops and tea shops and jazz bars, but Rosemary barely saw them, she was so focused on getting to the sea.

She walked faster as they got closer. She could hear seagulls screeching as they wheeled above her in the sky. Then she finally saw it: the vast expanse of green water that seeped like ink into the blue horizon. Jutting into the water was the Palace Pier, with its mismatch of buildings and domes and the two helter-skelter spiral slides at the end facing the water.

A sea wind blew against them as they walked down to the beach. Rosemary licked her lips: they tasted like fish and chips.

On the beach, striped deck chairs held reclining families and young couples. A man in briefs ran after a woman in a one-piece and swimming cap and together they dove into the water. A child sat on the pebbles pointing at seagulls and eating a sugar sandwich. A group of teenagers lay in the shade of an upturned boat, smoking.

Rosemary and George took off their shoes and socks and placed them on top of the suitcase. Then they walked over the pebbles and down to the water, fingers locked together. The seawater was as cold as the lido. They stood at the edge, looking out at the sea that seemed to go on forever. George, watching her, seemed to smile with his whole body.

At the pier they bought baked potatoes dripping with butter and ate them leaning against the railings, seagulls circling them hoping for scraps. Rows of men in white caps fished for mackerel at the sea end of the pier; women in summer dresses walked arm in arm and children queued at a stand for freshly fried doughnuts. The stallholder passed a small girl a greasy paper bag and she grinned with delight.

George turned away from the sound of the children's laughter and leaned back against the railings. Rosemary turned to him and smiled, hoping that he saw enough in her face to fill his life.

They spent the week investigating the town, roaming the beach, eating cake in Lyon's tea shop, and exploring the smoky jazz cafés in the evenings, before returning to the B&B, their skin sticky with a layer of tar from the sea.

"You just need to rub yourselves with butter and it will come right off," said the B&B owner, so they took a stick of butter to their room and rubbed each other up and down with the pale fat, laughing like teenagers as they did. They fell asleep smelling of butter, their soft bodies a muddle of bare limbs in the sheets.

After their last day at the beach, when their faces were brown and sore from the salt water and the sun, they headed to a café to drink hot chocolate and listen to the jukebox. The room was foggy with smoke and steam from the coffee machine. George paid for a song, and the sound of Elvis Presley singing "My Wish Came True" filled the bar.

"Dance with me?" he asked. They pushed aside their table and held each other in the middle of the shop. Rosemary rested her face against his chest and listened to his heartbeat, thinking that it sounded like home. She loved the sea, but now she wanted to be back in her lido. She had enjoyed feeling for a week as though they were young again, hiding from each other in the maze of mirrors on the pier, making love on a squeaky bed in the B&B, and escaping thoughts they both wanted to forget. But she wanted to be home in their small flat. Even though their shared sadness was dislodged every now and then with a surge of billowing emotion, it was their home and their life and it was enough for her.

Elvis Presley sang to them as they danced and George kissed her.

CHAPTER 32

Rosemary stands on the steps of the town hall, looking at the confetti at her feet. A breeze blows a paper heart onto the toe of her black Mary Jane with the low heel. She stares at it clinging there.

"Ready?" asks Kate, reaching and squeezing Rosemary's hand. Rosemary looks down, surprised by the contact. Kate smiles before quickly letting go.

The others wait behind them on the steps. The lido and café staff sped through closing up in order to be here in time; the barista is still wearing his apron. Ahmed and Geoff, Ellis and Jake, Hope, and Frank and Jermaine stand in clusters close to Kate, Sprout at their feet. Betty is there with her granddaughter. A woman is there with her new baby, who sleeps in a fabric sling across her chest, and her husband who holds her hand. A yoga instructor who teaches in the studios at the lido is there, too, with some of her students gathered around her. There is a skinny teenage boy and two people who stand close to him but slightly apart on the pavement who Rosemary assumes are his parents. The department store security guard is there, along with several local teachers and a group of children from the swimming club, their parents, and the coach. And at the back there is Jay, his camera strap slung around his neck as he takes photographs of the group gathered on the town hall steps.

"We're all behind you, Mrs. P," says Ellis.

Rosemary looks up at the columns that frame the door to the town hall, takes hold of the handrail, and slowly climbs the stairs. The others file behind her into the meeting room.

Behind a long table sits a group of men in suits; the councillor Kate met is in the middle and several others sit on either side of him.

"Welcome," he says as they arrive, his voice carrying over the scraping of chair legs as they pull up seats opposite the panel. "How good that so many of you could make it. We might need to get more chairs!"

Eventually enough chairs are dragged over and the group settles, Rosemary and Kate in the front.

"Let me help you take your coat off, Rosemary," says Kate, reaching across to help her. But Rosemary pulls away, tugging the belt on her coat tightly around her.

"No. I'm cold."

Once everyone has sat down the councillor starts the meeting. He talks quickly and his speech is peppered with jargon that makes the group of residents shuffle in their seats. He talks about cuts to funding and slashed budgets and says that the pool is "leaking money that could be spent on other valuable local amenities and resources."

"Surely you want that money to go to other services, like the local schools?" he says, looking across at the room of lido users as if to shame them.

"Now, it's time to hear from you. Who would like to share your thoughts on the closure? Sorry, the potential closure. Do you have a nominated speaker?"

Rosemary stands up slowly, using Kate's shoulder to help her up. She pulls her coat tightly around herself and adjusts the scarf at her neck.

"You have three minutes to speak, let's hear it," says the councillor.

Rosemary is aware of the faces of her friends, turned up to her expectantly, rely-

195

ing on her.

She thinks about her morning swims with Kate, coaching her on her corkscrew kick and then sitting together on the bench and talking. She thinks about George doing handstands on the bottom of the pool, the pale soles of his feet pointing up toward the sky. She thinks about the people she sees every day who have found somewhere to escape their problems, swimming out their tensions length after length. She clears her throat, and then she begins.

"When the old library closed down no one realized the importance of what we were losing until it had gone. It was a place for learning and also a center of our community. And it's the same with the lido. We all take it for granted and that is why it is so important. We rely on it being there for us. It is somewhere that you can go for a moment to yourself, whatever your reason might be for needing that moment."

She turns around and looks at the people sitting behind her, all carrying their own reasons on their shoulders.

"The lido holds so many memories for us all. For children who have never been to the seaside it is their summers and their freedom. For parents it is the memory of seeing their child swim for the first time — that moment when you just have to let go and let them fly. And for me . . . well, for me it is my life." She pauses.

"But have you thought about the colder months?" the councillor interrupts. "Yes, the lido might be busy on sunny days, but when the weather is bad, it loses even more money. People just don't want to swim in an outdoor pool when it's cold and raining, which, let's face it, is a lot of the time. Surely a woman of your age must understand the health risks of swimming in such cold water?"

As the councillor talks Rosemary slowly starts unbuttoning her coat. There is a flash of black as Rosemary unwinds her scarf from her neck. She shrugs her coat off her shoulders and her friends around her start to clap.

"As you can see, I am perfectly well equipped."

Her pale head and neck poke out from the top of the wetsuit that hugs tightly to her plump body. It stops at the knees and reveals her bent legs and the black Mary Janes on her feet. The councillor is seized by a coughing fit as Jay's camera snaps the picture that will make the front page of the *Chronicle*.

"We thought it would be worth diversifying the products we sell at reception," says Geoff, patting Rosemary on the arm of her wetsuit. "You're quite right that it can be quite chilly in the water — but now there are no excuses!"

Rosemary does a slow turn to better show off her outfit, and her friends cheer. She catches Kate's eye — she looks like she is trying not to laugh, but then she is failing and laughing with everyone else. The council members have obviously never seen an eighty-six-year-old woman in a wetsuit in the town hall before. The meeting is adjourned.

CHAPTER 33

The next day, Jay's photograph of Rosemary in her wetsuit makes the front page of the paper. Kate writes the story, mentioning that customers will now be able to buy wetsuits from the lido once the summer is over and the weather gets colder.

When Kate arrives at work she is greeted by Phil, who waves the paper at her. Jay is at his desk and lifts a second cup of coffee at Kate when he sees her.

"I heard people talking about this on the bus this morning," Phil says as soon as Kate is through the door. He points at the photo of Rosemary. "Do you know how often I hear people talking about the *Brixton Chronicle*? Never. It's there in every local newsagent and at the tube station but sometimes I just think people take it home to peel their potatoes into."

Kate and Jay look at each other, raising their eyebrows.

"But this — where did you find her?"

Kate doesn't reply. She's starting to wonder if it was she who found Rosemary or the other way round.

"That's what this lido story needs: more pictures. Kate, I want you to take Jay down to the pool, introduce him to the people you have met there. Jay, I want human interest pictures, a view of the 'beating heart of the community' as Rosemary Peterson says."

"Righto, boss," says Jay, picking up his camera bag.

Phil sits down at his desk, tears open a paper bag stained with grease, and starts work on a ham-and-cheese croissant. Pastry flakes fall onto the newspaper as though showering Rosemary in autumn leaves.

Kate is packing up to leave, when her mobile buzzes on her desk. She picks it up and reads a text from Erin: "I love Rosemary Peterson! She is amazing — that photo made Mark and me laugh so much this morning! So happy to see your article on the front page. E x."

Kate grins as she reads.

"Are you coming?" Jay says to Kate, his bag slung over his shoulder and a tripod under his arm.

"Yes, sorry!"

She sends Erin a swimmer emoji and some kisses and puts her phone in her bag. "Let's go."

As Rosemary eats her breakfast she reads about herself and looks at her photograph on the front page.

George would not believe that she has made the front page of a newspaper, even if it is just a local one. When she went to the newsagent to collect it this morning she saw several people looking at it.

"Look at this, this is amazing," said a young man to his girlfriend as Rosemary quietly walked past and paid at the till.

She hardly believes it herself. The wetsuit is hanging up on the back of her bedroom door as a reminder. When she saw it this morning she smiled.

It had been a struggle to get into it before the meeting. She put plastic bags on her hands and feet to push them through the tight arm and leg holes, and when she caught her reflection in the bedroom mirror she couldn't stop laughing. Then the laughing made her wheeze and she had to sit down for a moment, wetsuit half on and plastic bags still on her hands and feet. As she sat on the bed she had looked across at the photo of George that sat next to her pillow. It was one of him outside the greengrocer wearing his apron and holding the biggest pumpkin they had ever seen. He was grinning.

"What am I doing, George?"

Doing the zip up at the back by herself had been difficult. She spent a long time twisting and reaching for the zip and nearly fell over twice. Once she was zipped up she buttoned up her coat and wrapped her scarf tightly to hide the neckline of the wetsuit. There was not much give in the suit so she had to get onto all fours to reach for her shoes.

In many ways the council meeting had not gone well. The councillors looked down on them, she could tell, and made her feel as though she was at school again and they were the teachers. Halfway through her speech she remembered the teachers who'd made them swim in a storm, and the look on their faces when they'd jumped into the water in their coats. The memory made her smile: *Just wait until they see under this coat,* she'd thought.

It had been hard to tell what the outcome of the meeting was. Once Rosemary had put her coat back on and the councillor had stopped coughing he told them that their concerns would be submitted to the Board (whoever they were) and filed for consideration. The residents and lido staff would be kept informed, he said, but there was no date set for another meeting. Despite the uncertainty, for a moment her worries were put aside by the pats on her back and the laughter of her friends as they left the town hall. They even went for a drink afterward at the pub around the corner. Kate and Ellis helped her up onto one of the high barstools, which meant her feet couldn't touch the ground. Ellis bought her half a pint of cider. She got a few strange looks from the other customers as she sat there in her wetsuit and coat. She just raised her glass and smiled.

As she drank she watched the group of people around the bar. Ellis, Hope, and Betty laughed and shared a bag of peanuts and memories about Brixton. Frank and Jermaine slipped pork rinds to Sprout, who lay on the sticky carpet under one of the tables. They talked to Kate, whose eyes lit up as she told them about the latest book she was reading, her cheeks pink. Ahmed spoke with the nice photographer who had told Rosemary that she had a face for the front page.

Rosemary had watched them all and felt a great sense of contentment and warmth flow over her. The cider had helped too.

When she has finished her breakfast she opens a drawer and pushes aside a rolling pin, cling film, and a roll of tinfoil until she finds the kitchen scissors. Her hands shake as she slowly cuts out the front-page story. Once the story is detached she pins it to the fridge, moving Hope's postcard from the cruise she went on two years ago and a menu for the Caribbean takeaway shop on her street.

Then she phones Kate and does something she hasn't done for anyone in a very long time: she invites her to dinner.

Kate sounds surprised, but she agrees straightaway.

"Yes, of course, I'd love to. Thank you," she says. "Oh, and Rosemary, I know it's last minute, but what are you up to now? If you are free, we could use your help at the lido. Jay is taking some photos for another article — we're hoping the coverage will help. Ahmed has set up a 'Save Brockwell Lido' Facebook page that we'll mention in the piece too. I'll show it to you later but it's already getting a lot of support."

"That's wonderful," replies Rosemary, a smile spreading across her face at the thought of Ahmed helping and of others joining in and showing their support for the lido. "I'll be there in fifteen minutes."

"Can you bring your swimsuit?" Kate says. "Jay thought a picture of you in the lido would work well. And seeing as you've already been on the front page, I thought you might not mind?"

Rosemary laughs.

"Why not," she says.

Ahmed greets them outside the lido, he's so excited to show Rosemary the Facebook page on his phone.

"It has sixty likes already, and I only set it up this morning," he says happily. Rosemary wants to ask him what a "like" is, but doesn't want to seem ignorant. So instead she says, "That's wonderful, Ahmed; well done, you."

Then Kate and Rosemary show Jay around. He meets the staff and the swimmers, all the time taking photographs. The children from the swimming group ask him to show them his camera. He kneels down on the ground and tells them what the different buttons do and shows them some of the photographs on the screen. They reach out eagerly to touch the camera. When he stands up his trousers are dark with water at the knees. He looks like he is wearing kneepads and it makes Kate laugh.

"I'm sorry," she says, when he sees him laughing. "I hope you don't mind them playing with your camera?"

"I'm used to it," he says. "I have three nieces and two nephews."

Rosemary watches Jay and Kate talking and notices how different Kate looks compared to the first time she met her. Happy.

At the end of the day the three of them part ways at the park gates.

"See you tomorrow evening then, Rosemary?" says Kate, squeezing Rosemary into a hug.

"Yes, see you tomorrow," says Rosemary.

CHAPTER 34

"You have a lovely home, Rosemary, thank you for inviting me," says Kate as she steps inside Rosemary's flat and hands her a small bouquet of lilac tulips. The evening sun streams in from the balcony windows, casting the living room in a golden glow. It is a small room, but it is neat and ordered. There is a two-seater sofa, an armchair, and a coffee table with a record player next to it on the floor. Brightly colored cushions decorate the sofa and armchair: Kate recognizes the vibrant prints from the African fabric shop in Brixton Village. She thinks the room looks calm and cozy.

"You can put your coat on that chair," says Rosemary, pointing to the chair by the door where her swimming bag sits expectantly.

Rosemary disappears into the kitchen, leaving Kate in the living room. While she is gone Kate wanders to the balcony doors. She looks over the fence and across the road to the lido walls, the bricks a burnt terra-cotta in the evening sun. Beyond the lido the rest of the park stretches into a green haze of treetops and grass.

She steps back from the balcony and across to the bookshelf that runs the length of one of the walls.

"Oh, look at all the books!" calls Kate into the kitchen, tilting her head sideways to read the titles on the long bookshelf. *The Catcher in the Rye, A History of Brixton, Poems for Life . . .*

"Shall we put on some music?" she asks, as Rosemary comes back into the room carrying the dish of peanuts. She points at the record player.

"What would you like to listen to?" says Rosemary.

"It's hard to choose — you have such a great collection."

"They're George's mostly."

"May I?"

"Please do."

Rosemary sits down and Kate kneels on the floor and leafs through the records. Eventually she picks one and carefully slides it out of its sleeve and lifts it onto the player.

"I love Frank Sinatra. My mum and step-dad used to dance to him in the kitchen. It embarrassed me when I was a teenager but

I loved it really — the songs and the dancing."

"George and I danced to him on more than one occasion too."

"I'm sorry," says Kate, "I can choose another one if you prefer?"

"No, leave it. I like it."

From her seat on the sofa, Kate examines a framed photograph of George and Rosemary on their wedding day. They are in the park holding hands under a tree. Neither of them is looking at the camera; they are laughing and looking at something over the photographer's shoulder.

"You look beautiful," says Kate. "Both of you."

"Thank you. I know we don't usually use that word to describe men but I think he really was beautiful. He got so brown in the summer."

Rosemary smiles and closes her eyes for a moment. Frank Sinatra's smooth voice fills the flat.

As she listens to the music, Kate thinks about home. It has been some time since she went back to visit her mum and Brian. She used to worry that if she let herself go home, she might not come back. She might not have been home in a while, but she can still picture it clearly. It's the smell of home that comes to her now: orange-scented candles and the wood of the dining table that they have had for as long as Kate can remember, and an indescribable scent that is a mix of the hair and clothes of the people she loves most in the world. When Erin and Kate were young they both had the same patterned scarves that were given to them by their grandmother. To tell whose was whose they would simply sniff the fabric and then swap them, recognizing each other's smell instantly.

Kate looks up and realizes Rosemary is watching her. She glances at the wedding photo again, thinking how different Rosemary looks now, but also how similar in some ways too. Her face may have aged but her eyes are the same and there is still a certain confidence that can be seen clearly in both the photo and in the old woman in front of Kate.

"Tell me more about George?" asks Kate as she gently places the photo frame back on the shelf.

"Oh, where to start," says Rosemary, sinking back a little into her chair. "You have probably guessed by now that he was a very good swimmer. He was evacuated to Devon during the war and he even swam with dolphins once, if you believe what he told me, which I'm not sure I do."

Kate laughs.

"When I finished early at the library I would go and visit him at the fruit and vegetable shop. Sometimes he'd be serving customers and I'd stand and wait by the potatoes, watching him twist the paper bags in the air so they closed, or weighing tomatoes with real concentration. If there was no one in the shop he would often bring out a present for me: maybe a flat peach that he knew would be particularly sweet, or a twisted carrot from a sack of straight ones, or something I hadn't seen before, like a yam when he had visited his Caribbean friends at the market.

"He liked to read, just like me, and I'd bring us both books home from the library. We'd sit and read them together and sometimes he'd just start laughing at something that he had read and then he'd try to keep quiet so he wouldn't disturb me but often he couldn't help it and he'd laugh so much he started crying and there'd be tears streaming down his face. Of course that would make me laugh, too, and I'd just imagine what his customers would think if they saw this tall greengrocer laughing until he cried."

Kate sits and rests her chin in her hand as

she listens to Rosemary describing the man she loved. As she talks her blue eyes sparkle and her cheeks grow slightly flushed. Kate imagines the swimming greengrocer George. She pictures him sitting in this living room, sharing the two-seater sofa with Rosemary.

Rosemary looks up. "I'm sorry, I'm boring you."

"No, the opposite," says Kate. "I'm enjoying listening to you."

"I suppose it has been a while since I've talked about him."

"You must miss him," Kate says gently.

Rosemary looks around the flat. Kate wonders what she sees — whether George is sitting on the armchair, standing by the balcony, or smiling at her from the kitchen door.

"Oh, terribly."

"Time to eat," says Rosemary then, the brief shadow passing away from her eyes.

The table is laid for two and there is a vase of cut lavender sprigs in the center.

When the timer buzzes Kate helps Rosemary lift a steaming dish out of the oven. A roasted joint of lamb sits on a bed of crisp, honeyed vegetables.

"This smells delicious, Rosemary," she says.

Rosemary reaches above the fridge and takes down a black clothbound notebook that is nearly falling apart. Pages hang out of it and scribbled notes are stuck on scraps of paper that poke out of the edges. She passes it to Kate.

"George's recipes. They've been very helpful. He used to do most of the cooking."

Kate opens it and carefully turns the pages. Some have fingerprints and drops of food on them. Others have crossed-out notes and added comments. She turns page after page of recipes.

"You must have been very proud of him," she says, carefully handing the book back to Rosemary.

"Very."

Rosemary places the notebook gently back on the top of the fridge. Kate pulls the table out so Rosemary can sit down, and then tucks it back in.

"You cooked, I'll serve," she says.

Rosemary looks as though she is about to argue, but she is trapped behind the table so has no choice but to sit down and let Kate help.

"There's a salad in the fridge, can you get it out? Please."

As Kate goes to open the fridge door she notices her article and Rosemary's photo-

213

graph and smiles.

The fridge is full of colorful vegetables from Ellis and in the fridge door there is a bottle of white wine with her name on it. Kate reaches for the bowl of salad and the wine and closes the door.

She puts the salad on the table and holds out the wine with a smile and a raised eyebrow, turning the bottle with the "Kate" label stuck on it to face Rosemary.

"Oh, yes, I nearly forgot" says Rosemary. "Would you like some wine?"

"Glasses?"

"Top cupboard above the microwave."

The cupboard has two of everything. Kate takes down the two wineglasses and opens the wine. She pours Rosemary's well above half full.

"You deserve that," says Kate.

The meat and vegetables are perfectly cooked and even the salad is delicious, made with fresh leaves and drizzled with a dressing whose flavor Kate can't identify, but which tastes wonderful.

"I'm so impressed, this is amazing. Thank you, Rosemary."

"You're welcome," says Rosemary, smiling. "I'm very lucky — George was an excellent cook. He knew everything about vegetables, of course, but he was good with meat too. He learned from the butchers in the market — he would ask them to tell him their secrets in exchange for a sack of potatoes or some bags of fruit."

As they eat she continues to talk, telling Kate about George and their life together. Afterward, Kate quietly clears the table and washes the dishes. She is filling the kettle when Rosemary lets out a soft sigh.

"This has been a lovely birthday," she says.

Kate turns around quickly. "You didn't tell me it was your birthday!"

Rosemary shrugs.

"I would have brought you something more than tulips," says Kate, her eyebrows knotted and her voice full of concern. "I would have done something. And now I feel bad that you did all that cooking."

"This is my eighty-seventh. I have had more than my fair share of birthdays."

"Well, we should at least have another glass of wine," Kate says, turning the kettle off and reaching for the wine instead.

"Here we go," she says, pouring two full glasses. "Happy birthday, Rosemary."

The two women clink glasses and take a sip. They sink back into their chairs and into conversation. They talk about the lido and about George, and for a while it is as though he is there in the kitchen with them, squeezed at the table that is only really big enough for two.

CHAPTER 35

It looked much higher once she was up the tree. She wrapped her legs around it and gripped the mossy branch tightly between her hands, her feet dangling below her. George was already on the other side; she could make out the shape of his body standing on the picnic bench, arms outstretched and waiting for her.

"I'm much too old for this!" she called down to him.

"I don't know what you're talking about," he said. She couldn't see his face properly but she could tell from his voice that he was smiling. "Don't they say that sixty is the new thirty?"

"But I'm seventy-one!"

He laughed. "Well, we can't be more than the new thirty-five then."

"Well, my knees certainly aren't thirty-five."

On cue her knees sent a stabbing pain

217

down her legs.

"You can do it, Rosy, I know you can do it."

A cloud rolled away from the moon and lit up his face for a moment. He smiled broadly up at her. *That face,* she thought as she looked at him. *I have always been a sucker for that face.* She swung one leg over the tree branch and hugged it tightly between her arms, reaching her legs out beneath her, searching, searching for a solid surface. Lower, lower, she went until her feet met the safety of the bench. As she set herself down she slipped slightly and landed with a thud.

"Ouch," she said. "Have I always been this graceful?" She brushed herself down and took his hand.

"Oh, and more," he said, laughing.

Together they both climbed slowly off the bench, examining themselves quietly for injuries. No blood, no broken bones, no torn clothes. Once they had established that they were both in one piece they looked up at the same time.

A dappled light from the moon shone on the decking of the lido, the clock glowed white, and the lifeguard's chair stood empty in the shadows. Above the lido it was patchy with clouds. Stars lined the pockets of clear

218

sky. The trees stood to attention around the lido walls, their branches even darker than the sky behind them. It was still and quiet and cool.

"Shall we?" said George, looking at his wife's face and not seeing the lines that had crept there over the years.

They let go of each other's hand and walked to either side of the pool. Rosemary took one corner and George took the other. Together they peeled the cover off until the water beneath was revealed. They turned and headed together to the picnic bench, where they sat down next to each other. Rosemary kicked off her shoes. George leaned to untie his laces.

"Ow," he said, straightening and holding his lower back.

"Back?" she asked. He nodded and pulled his left shoe off with his other foot. She put a hand on his shoulder and rubbed it. They undressed slowly, Rosemary helping George with the buttons on his shirt, George helping Rosemary with the zip on her skirt.

"It's the one that gets stuck halfway," she said. "You need to pull it hard, remember."

Eventually they were naked. Their pale bodies were paler still in the moonlight. They looked at each other as if looking in a mirror — they knew each other's bodies as well as they knew their own. That scar on George's left foot from dropping a crate of potatoes when unpacking a delivery into the shop; the purple scar on Rosemary's wrist from burning herself taking a pie out of the oven (it was no wonder that George only rarely let her cook); the curves of their stomachs were both softened and padded with the years.

They held hands as they walked to the pool.

She slipped into the pool first with a splash and a quick intake of breath. The dark water swallowed her up in its cold. He followed her, choosing to face the wall. Rosemary watched his pale backside as she floated, waiting for him, and couldn't help but laugh. He swore as he entered the water, doing a few quick strokes to warm up. But then he was laughing too. They floated on their backs for a moment, getting used to the cold that buoyed them up and filled their ears. Then they started to swim. They swam through stars and inky black patches of water where the clouds above blocked out the light. They stayed close to each other, matching each other's steady pace. Ripples spread out through the water as they kicked, each of them feeling the waves of the other's breaststroke.

Without having to mention it to each other they both had the sense that it would be somehow disrespectful to talk as they swam; it was so beautiful and so quiet. So they remained silent, wrapped in the cold and looking up at the sky.

After a few laps they headed to the shallow end again and pulled themselves out, their bodies so cold that they felt warm. They walked to the corners of the pool and pulled the cover back over the water as though they were tucking it in for the night. Back at the bench they pulled towels out of George's backpack and wrapped them loosely around themselves. Then they sat down next to each other.

"Do you remember what we did next?"

Rosemary laughed. "I hope you're not getting any ideas, George."

"Did we even put a towel down? I can't remember, I certainly had grazes on my knees."

"Ouch! What were we thinking?"

"Oh, I think we knew exactly what we were doing. It was one of the best moments of my life."

Rosemary turned to George. His smile was the same, just outlined now with deep lines that spread outward like waves. But he had wrinkles in all the right places — they showed the truth of his character. Some people she knew who would consider themselves optimists had been surprised when frown lines formed between their eyebrows. She had seen through them, though, remembering old arguments or bitterness. The lines didn't lie.

George's hair had long since gone — he'd started losing it in his late twenties and did an admirable job of laughing at himself about it. She knew it bothered him really and that he worried about staying attractive for her. She had caught him flicking through a copy of *Men's Health* in the supermarket once. But she didn't care if he didn't have a single hair on his head — he wore his baldness with grace. And besides, her hair had started to thin, too, and she knew she had put on weight over the past years. Her once slim figure had filled out. At first she minded terribly, hardly recognizing herself, now she only minds slightly.

"Fifty years," he said, sighing. They were both quiet for a moment, looking across at the dark lido.

"I hope you think it's been worth it," he said quietly, looking down at his bare feet. "I know we haven't traveled, that we've stayed in the one place all our lives. And I have never been exactly rich, and, well, it's only been the two of us . . ."

Rosemary watched her husband as he watched his feet.

"And I know I've never been a smart dresser, and that frankly I've gotten quite fat. And all these wrinkles. And I know more about cabbages than I do about politics. But what I mean to say is I hope this has been enough for you. I hope I have been enough for you."

He looked up from his feet and at her face. He looked like a teenager again, in those rare moments when he let his confidence slip and she saw straight through to the nervous little boy behind. She swallowed hard.

"You silly man," she said, reaching for him and kissing him hard. They held each other close, their bare arms wrapped around each other, their towels slipping slightly as they reached for each other. They stayed like that for a while, holding each other, feeling each other's heart beating against their chests. *It's always been enough,* she wanted to say, but she couldn't make the words come out and she knew she didn't have to. The way they held each other said that they both understood.

After a while they pulled apart a little, adjusting their towels and laughing at their naked bodies.

"And anyway," she said, "we're both fat and wrinkly."

They both laughed.

"Come on, we'd better get going," said George, passing her clothing from the bench. "Um, darling, I don't think this is mine . . ." George said, lifting up Rosemary's lavender bra.

"Oops, sorry." She laughed, swapping him the pair of boxers she held in her hand. He helped her fasten her bra, stroking her shoulders. They dressed slowly, struggling with buttons and zips in the darkness.

"Damn these laces!" he said as he reached for his shoes.

"Let me do it," she said, kneeling down to tie them.

"Ouch!"

"Knees?" he asked.

"Yep. They're real bastards these days." She tied his shoes and then stood up.

"What are we like?" he said, smiling at her.

"We're old is what we are."

"When did that happen?"

"Oh, I don't know. I think we were too busy living to notice it really."

"Yes, it has snuck up on us."

"Maybe we're not actually getting old;

224

maybe everyone else is just getting younger."

"Ah yes, that must be it."

"Come on, let's go home. I need a cup of tea."

George put his backpack on his shoulders and helped Rosemary stand up on the picnic bench, beneath the tree. She turned and took a last look at the lido. She imagined swimming there again tomorrow, keeping the secret of their night's adventure tucked behind her smile. The clock hands were standing smartly together — it had just gone midnight.

And then there was a terrible cracking sound like the splintering of a ship's belly against rocks. Rosemary turned around just in time to see the branch snapping and falling to the ground, showering leaves onto the decking of the lido. George stood on the bench looking up at the empty space where the branch should have been; his arms still extended in the air, empty. He looked down at the branch on the ground.

"Well, that wasn't supposed to happen."

They both looked up at the tree. Without the help of the branch to pull themselves up, there was no way they would make it over the top of the wall. They looked down at the branch again.

"This could be interesting."

The lido didn't open until 6:30 and they were both shivering. They looked at each other in panic for a moment — they were trapped.

And then they both started laughing. They giggled like children, holding on to each other as the laughter shook through them. They couldn't stop; it was infectious and ridiculous. Eventually George started wheezing and Rosemary helped him down from the bench, her eyes streaming with tears.

"Enough, enough," she said. They sat down on the bench and looked again at the mess of leaves. The moon winked from behind a cloud, a car sounded its horn, and a motorbike roared. Inside the lido walls everything was still.

"Well, we'll have to phone for help," said Rosemary eventually.

"But we've been trespassing, won't we get in trouble?"

They started laughing again.

"I'm serious!" said Rosemary when they had quieted down. "I'm not staying here all night, I'm freezing. We're much too old for this; we might not make it through the night. This was your idea; you need to get us out of here, George Peterson!"

So he reached into his backpack and

pulled out the mobile phone they had reluctantly bought a few years ago for emergencies. This wasn't exactly the emergency they'd had in mind.

"How do I turn it on?" said George.

"It's that big button on the top."

"I can't see it, it's dark!"

"Here, let me see."

George passed her the phone. She fumbled in the dark until the screen lit up. She handed it back.

"There."

"Thank you."

When the phone had turned on George tapped "999" onto the keypad.

The phone rang and Rosemary listened to George's side of the conversation.

"Hello? Police, please, or possibly fire brigade. We're at Brockwell Lido, Brixton, stuck inside."

There was a pause.

"We climbed over the wall but the branch broke you see and now we can't get out. My wife and I. Yes, my wife. Seventy-one. Yes, I said seventy-one. No, this isn't a prank call. Well, yes, I suppose we are old enough to know better."

Rosemary was laughing again, her hand over her mouth, trying to hide the sound. George gave her a look and slapped her

227

thigh gently with his free hand.

"What's that? Well, yes, I suppose we should have thought of that. Okay. Okay, thank you."

He hung up the phone.

"They'll be here soon."

They waited together in the darkness, sat side by side on the picnic bench like schoolchildren waiting to be summoned into the headmistress's office. Rosemary leaned her head on George's shoulder and they watched the clouds and the stars in the sky above them.

The fire brigade saved them the embarrassment of a siren, but they did see the blue light flashing over the wall of the lido, lighting up the branches of the trees.

"Hello?" someone called after a moment.

"Hello!" Rosemary and George called back.

There was the sound of metal on brick as a ladder was pushed up against the lido wall. After a few moments a fire officer was perched on the top, peering down at them.

"What's going on here then?" he said. George and Rosemary looked up from the bench, the darkness hiding their pink cheeks.

"Ready?" shouted someone else from the other side of the lido wall, and the fire officer turned to take hold of another ladder that was being passed up from below. He took hold of it and fed it down on the other side of the wall until it was resting on the decking near to where the tree branch snapped.

"Come on then," said the officer, his voice gruff but laughter tickling the edges. George took Rosemary's hand and helped her onto the first steps of the ladder. She climbed up to the top and the officer helped her swing her leg over the wall and down the ladder on the other side. George followed, taking one last look back at the water before crossing over the wall and down into the park.

The officers told them off for wasting fire brigade time, but left it at a warning, as this was their first offense.

"Oh, I shouldn't worry, Officer," said Rosemary. "I don't think my knees will be up for a climb like that again."

They were offered a lift home, but they told the officers that they lived just across the road. So they apologized again, then took each other's hand and walked back to the flat. Once inside their bedroom they climbed straight into bed, their bodies close enough to feel each other's breath on their faces. They fell asleep quickly, their towels hanging on the back of their bedroom door.

CHAPTER 36

When Kate wakes up she regrets the last glass of wine. She can feel it pulling her eyes closed and knocking at the inside of her head like a deliveryman at a front door. Rosemary may be eighty-seven, but Kate is the one who needs to learn how to handle her drinks.

She rolls over in bed and looks at her phone. There's a text from Erin and a missed call from her mum. She sends them both a short message — telling them about the dinner but leaving out the hangover. Then she throws her phone back on the side — the brightness of its screen is hurting her eyes.

She skips her swim and makes a detour via the coffee van outside the station on her way to work. The sound of the steam coincides with the sound of a bus pulling up in the road. She orders one for herself (with an extra shot) and one for Jay.

"Thanks. Late night?" he asks as she puts the coffee down at his desk and sits down quietly at hers.

"Is it that obvious?"

"So were you on a date?"

Kate laughs and takes a sip of her coffee. She sees Jay watching her over the rim of the coffee cup.

"Yes. It was wonderful, we had great conversation, great food, and drank lots of wine. Except he is a she, and she is eighty-seven and called Rosemary: you've met her."

Jay laughs, too, and drinks his coffee.

"Speaking of Rosemary, have you seen today's paper?"

He passes her a copy across her desk.

Jay's photographs of the lido and its swimmers take up a double-page spread in the middle of the paper. Surrounding the images is Kate's article, full of anecdotes about the lido from people of all ages who swim there. "Memories of Water," reads the headline.

"I like doing handstands with my daddy in the pool." Hayley, 7.

"I trained for a triathlon at the lido. It is close to my home so meant I could come before work. When I eventually completed the triathlon I came back here to swim a victory lap a few days later. It felt so good to be home where it all started." Reggie, 43

"My children learned to swim at the lido. My favorite photo of them is by the side of the lido covered in sunscreen. They look so happy and it makes me happy every time I look at it." Dawn, 59

"Through the good times and the bad the lido has always been there to jump into when I need it. I just want to say thank you." Ben, 55

"It's a beach in the city." Mel, 12

There is Ahmed caught looking up from studying, the start of a smile on his face. He is surrounded by scattered Post-it notes that have invaded the reception desk. A beam of light is coming in through the window behind him and shining off the surface of the pool, making stars on the reception ceiling. In the foreground a little girl with a dolphin backpack holds her mother's hand and looks up at the stars of light, her mouth slightly open and a perfect look of enchantment on her freckled face. She is wearing water wings over the top of her sweater.

Here is the lifeguard half standing in his chair, his whistle in his mouth and his cheeks puffed. He is pointing at the far end of the pool to where a line of young boys holding hands are frozen in midair, legs akimbo. The smallest one on the end is the only one with his eyes open as he looks down the line of children, his eyebrows raised in shock. Kate imagines them seeing this photo when they are grown men with families and job titles that their children don't understand, and she wonders if they will recall jumping into the pool with their friends.

There are several photographs of Rosemary. Rosemary standing on the decking clothed, carrying her swimming bag and looking defiantly into the camera. Even clothed you can tell that her knees are bowed but she stands as straight as she can. Behind her is the old clock and the pool fading into blue in the background. There is a picture of Rosemary in the water with her arms crossed on the side, her swimming cap pulled down over her hair. The camera does not hide the lines on her face or the moles on her arms, but she looks elegant. Light reflects from the surface onto her face. Kate thinks she looks beautiful. And then there is Rosemary sitting on a chair outside the café, holding a mug and gazing out across the pool, watching.

And finally there is one of Kate. It is a surprise to see a photo of herself in the paper, and at first she doesn't realize it is her. But there she is, sitting in the chair opposite Rosemary watching her watch the pool. Kate has never seen a photo of herself where she looks as unguarded as that, caught in a moment that she didn't even realize was happening.

"They're beautiful, Jay."

"Thank you. I actually think so too."

Kate is too absorbed looking at the photographs to notice that the whole time she is looking at them Jay is looking at her.

CHAPTER 37

Rosemary skips her morning swim that day, too, treating herself to a rare lie-in. She stays in bed until nine o'clock. She might be eighty-seven now, but she has not grown out of that feeling that tugs her out of bed in the morning — the feeling that she should be at school or heading to work in the library. It is the first lazing about in bed she has had in months.

It is shopping day, so she eventually heads to the market. The air is heavy with the smell of ripening mangoes and the sound of traders shouting today's deals. It is busy this morning, and she weaves her way slowly through the shoppers. Ellis spots her approaching and waves at her. Unusually, a frown crosses his face.

"Are you okay?" asks Rosemary as she reaches the stand.

Ellis shuffles on his feet. He rubs a hand over his short hair and looks at Rosemary.

"I'm not sure I should tell you . . ." he says anxiously.

"What is it?"

Ellis looks at Rosemary for a moment longer and then reaches into his pocket and pulls out his phone.

"I started following Paradise Living on Twitter when I heard about the potential closure," he says, "and this morning I saw this . . ."

He hands her the phone. She pulls her reading glasses from her handbag, perching them on the end of her nose. On the phone's screen is a cross-section drawing of a squat brick building. Inside is an image of a café with glass windows looking out onto a tennis court. It takes her a moment to recognize the building.

"They've released plans of what the lido might look like if they won the bid," Ellis says, taking his phone back from Rosemary, who is standing very still. "Of course, it wouldn't be a lido anymore . . ."

Ellis may have taken his phone away, but the drawing is etched in Rosemary's mind.

"I'm sure there's still hope though," says Ellis quickly. "You're still waiting to hear back from the council, aren't you?"

"Yes," says Rosemary, "Kate says it should be soon."

She is quiet, looking down. The strawberries have just come in, and small baskets of the juicy fruit take center stage on the stall.

"I'm sorry," he says. "Maybe I shouldn't have told you?"

"No, no, it's fine," she says, looking up and attempting a smile. "I'm glad I know, and I can tell Kate about it later too. It might make a good article for the *Brixton Chronicle.*"

"Ahmed's Facebook page is doing really well," says Ellis. "It's got hundreds of likes now, so I'm sure that will help. People certainly care."

"Yes, I'm sure," she says. "Well, I'll just take my usual and then I should be going."

Ellis packs up two parcels and passes them to Rosemary, who slips them into her bag. Ellis puts a hand on her shoulder before she leaves. They don't say anything; instead he nods at her then takes his hand away. She turns and heads away back up Electric Avenue. Normally she would meet Hope for a coffee, but she is busy looking after Aiesha today and Rosemary is secretly glad. She doesn't feel much like the company right now. Instead, once her shopping is done she walks slowly back home.

Kate looks at the plans on her computer at

work. It seems so strange to see the lido she has come to love filled with cement instead of perfect blue water.

"Are you looking at it?" says Rosemary down the phone.

"Mm-hmm," says Kate.

"And?" says Rosemary. "Do you think you can write an article about it?"

The sketches of the people don't look quite right either. They look too perfect, or too much like a fancy development firm's idea of perfect anyway.

"Yes, yes, of course I'll write about it," says Kate after a moment. "Thank you for telling me about it. I'll write the story to-day."

"See you tomorrow morning for a swim?" asks Rosemary.

"Yes, see you tomorrow."

When she puts the phone down Kate stares at her computer screen. She feels her heart knocking hard against her chest and her hands beginning to sweat. She looks up and across the room, instinctively looking for Jay, but he is out on an assignment. Her breathing quickens.

"Is everything all right?" asks Phil, crossing the room from the kitchen to his desk with a cup of coffee in his hand. When he reaches Kate's desk he leans slightly on the edge of it, threatening to topple over a pile of files and books.

She takes a deep breath and looks up at him, forcing the semblance of a smile onto her face.

"Yes, I'm fine," she says, "I have a piece for you — a development on the Brockwell Lido story."

"Great," he says, standing up. "Have it for me by two?"

"Yep, will do," she says, and he walks back to his desk, leaving Kate alone at hers.

She takes a drink of water and then a deep breath to try and calm herself. Her mind fills with thoughts of the lido: how the cold water soothes her in the mornings when she swims there, how she promised Rosemary she would try to help, how since discovering the lido she has started to feel truly at home in Brixton for the first time since moving here. She knows that Paradise Living releasing these plans is really just part of what they already knew was happening, but actually seeing the image of the altered lido makes closing feel suddenly very real.

Leaning over her computer, Kate focuses on the two o'clock deadline to help her stay in control. Her Panic presses its face up against the office window and peers in at her, watching as she types. This is the one place where she has never let it enter. It takes all her strength, but she is determined to remain professional and not to let her colleagues see a crack in her shield. She might seem distanced or worried at times, but never consumed by panic. She puts her head down and focuses hard on what she has to do.

She delivers the article at 1:45.

Paradise Living Releases Plans for Brockwell Lido

An artist's rendering shows the lido as a private gym for Paradise-only tenants and owners

By Kate Matthews

Brockwell Lido is up for sale and the property firm Paradise Living is currently in the running to make the winning bid. Today they share a first look at what the site could look like in the future.

"A private gym would add real value to our properties," said a Paradise Living spokesperson. "Tenants and purchasers would have exclusive access to the top-end facilities."

The plans include a gym, a sauna, and a café, but not a pool.

"Our research suggests that tennis is more popular in Paradise — or among our target demographic," said the spokesperson. As such, the plan would be to cement-fill the pool and build a tennis court in the center.

A Facebook group called "Save Brockwell Lido" is gaining support from local residents.

Ahmed Jones, who started the page and who is also an employee at Brockwell Lido, said: "Now that Paradise Living has released these plans we can all see what a loss it would be if the lido turned into a private members club. I encourage everyone to show their support by liking our page, where we will be posting developments of the story and ways you can get involved. We can't let these plans become a reality."

CHAPTER 38

The next day Rosemary rises early again.
When she wakes up the first thing she thinks
of is the image Ellis showed her yesterday
of Paradise Living's plans for the lido. It
makes her want to stay in bed, to pull the
covers high over her head and hide there
for a while. But she forces herself up, pausing to place a hand on the frame of George's
picture beside her bed before swinging her
legs round and stepping down. She dresses
as quickly as she can (which is not very
quickly) and takes her swimming bag from
its spot by her door.

It is only a short walk to the lido, but she
goes by a longer route this morning, taking
the time to walk through the park, veering
off the path and onto the grass. The dew
soaks through her canvas lace-up shoes but
she doesn't mind. She wants to feel the
earth beneath her feet. She remembers running into the park when she was younger

when it snowed. She wanted to be there first so that she could make footprints that shouted "I exist" to the morning sun and birds huddling for warmth on snow-tipped branches. She leaves footprints of flattened wet grass.

Passing the windows to the exercise studios Rosemary looks inside, watching the yoga class saluting the sun. They turn into their next pose and a few of them spot Rosemary. For a moment an image of the studio as a café with a view through to a tennis court flashes before her and catches her breath. But she smiles and continues walking, turning around the building until she reaches the lido's entrance.

Once she's changed and poolside, Rosemary looks for Kate's towel on the rail by the shallow end but it isn't there. She wonders whether to wait for her, but decides she will probably be here soon so instead she climbs slowly down the ladder. She braces herself for the bite of the cold and slips into the water.

Rosemary swims her lengths and tries not to think about the future and what it holds for her and the lido. She focuses instead on the sensations: the cold on her skin, the morning sun on her forehead, the water trailing through the slight gaps between her fingers as she swims breaststroke. Every now and then thoughts of George enter her mind — him diving from the high diving board that used to cast a shadow over the deep end — but that is too painful as well. All she can think about is the right now that is held gently within these four walls.

As she nears the end of her swim, Kate still hasn't appeared. Rosemary stops and looks across the pool, watching the other swimmers. Some make the lido look like a pond they cross it so quickly. For others it is an ocean.

Her eyes are drawn to the Lido Café, where one of the baristas is struggling to tie a bunch of colorful balloons to a sun umbrella. When one escapes, he jumps to grab it but the string slips through his fingers and it is free. Rosemary watches it bobbing up and sailing above the pool. She hopes it doesn't get stuck in one of the trees; she wants to see it fly. A gust of wind blows it away from the arms of the oak tree and up higher into the air. For a moment it drifts in front of the sun, making it look like the sun is a yellow ball with a ribbon for a tail.

Rosemary pulls herself slowly out of the pool, becoming mortal again as she steps on dry land. Her knees never give her any trouble when she swims.

By now the barista has secured the rest of the balloons and is back inside the café. Rosemary wraps her towel around her, tucking it in at the front.

"She's out!" shouts a voice. Suddenly Kate is through the café doors and onto the decking, followed by Frank, Jermaine, Hope, Betty, Ellis, Jay, Ahmed, and Geoff. They are carrying plates piled with pastries from the café.

"Happy birthday!" they call out in unison.

"For two days ago," adds Kate, standing in the middle of the group wearing a floral summer dress that Rosemary thinks is unusually colorful for her. "We're sorry it's a little late."

Rosemary stares at the balloons, only just realizing that they are for her. Jay has his camera around his neck and takes a quick photograph, catching her face as her eyebrows rise in surprise.

"Quick, grab her before she runs away," says Ellis, and Kate puts her plate down on the table and heads toward Rosemary. She puts an arm around her and leads her to the table. Rosemary doesn't put up much of a fight; she is stunned.

Jay pulls out a chair at the head of the table and Kate pushes Rosemary gently into the seat. Rosemary sits in her towel, the sun bright enough now to keep her warm without needing to go and fetch her clothes.

"I'm sorry I didn't swim this morning — I was busy getting this ready," says Kate. "Eighty-seven couldn't pass by without any celebration. And I know it's a little early for cake, but . . ."

Rosemary looks down at the table. A fluffy Victoria sponge oozes cream and jam. It is decorated somewhat haphazardly with slices of strawberries and sprigs of rosemary. A dusting of icing sugar covers the top.

"This is beautiful; did you make it?"

Kate nods, beaming. She stayed up late the night before making it. First she had to clear away her flatmates' dirty dishes and wash the surfaces. Then she had put some music on and carefully weighed out all the ingredients.

"Thank you, Kate, it's wonderful."

Geoff and one of the baristas come out onto the decking, each carrying a bunch of flowers.

"For our favorite customer," says Geoff, leaning down and kissing Rosemary on the cheek. She blushes and takes the flowers, holding them on her lap.

"I don't know what to say."

"You don't need to say anything," says Hope. "Just enjoy your breakfast."

No one moves for a moment, but then everyone is leaning forward and taking pastries and cutting slices of cake. As everyone busies themselves with breakfast, Kate shuffles closer to Rosemary.

"I know we had some bad news yesterday with the plans," she says, "but I was thinking about it, and I don't think it means anything. We shouldn't stop fighting, and we shouldn't stop enjoying it here. And we certainly shouldn't let it interfere with your birthday celebration. Okay?"

Rosemary is surprised — she has never heard Kate talk this confidently before.

"Okay," she says with a nod and a smile. "Now if you wouldn't mind cutting me a slice of that delicious-looking cake . . ."

Kate waves a hand over the cake. "Just one sec before you cut it," she says pulling out her phone. "I promised my sister I'd take a photo. I told her about this party last night — we used to bake together when we were little."

Rosemary smiles again, thinking how happy Kate looks. Kate takes a photo of the table with the cake in the center, then Rosemary raises a knife and cuts into the soft sponge.

They all laugh and talk, asking Rosemary to tell them some memories of the lido. She warms into her story about the lido when she was a child.

"It was even busier then; you had to try not to trip over sunbathing bodies just to get to the water. And once you were in there was barely enough space to swim a width of the pool. It didn't matter, though; all you wanted was to plunge in the water and cool yourself off — we were all too hot and lazy for real swimming. It was the place to be and to be seen — us girls would sit in a row on the side with the same knee crossed over the other. We'd hang our feet in the water. We pretended not to watch the boys diving and they pretended not to watch us watching them. I don't think any of us did a good job."

She laughs, and everyone laughs with her.

"It was just over there," she says, pointing to the lido. "I sat just there."

Everyone turns and looks at the pool, trying to imagine young Rosemary with her feet in the water watching the boys.

"I have been swimming here for more than eighty years."

Her friends smile at her. Every now and then a swimmer comes over from the pool to say hello to Rosemary and wishes her a happy birthday. Some pause for a longer conversation, Rosemary asking them about their children or their job or the campervan they are renovating.

Eventually Frank rests his hand on Rosemary's shoulder. "I'm afraid we have to get back to the shop now," he says.

"I left Jake in charge of the stand today," says Ellis, standing up too. "I better go back and check that I'm not bankrupt yet." Hope follows him; she is reading to children at the local primary school this morning.

"Jay and I have to get to work too," says Kate. "Do you want to head off with us?"

"You go on," says Rosemary. "I want to sit here for a little longer."

"Are you sure?" asks Jay.

"Yes, you go. I just want to enjoy the view for a moment. And thank you, Kate."

Rosemary takes her hand and squeezes it, looking fondly at Kate, who returns her gaze with a wide smile.

"You're welcome," says Kate, blushing slightly.

Once they are gone Rosemary stands up; there is a breeze rattling the trees and tugging on the strings of the balloons. They jostle against one another, knocking against the umbrella. With a little difficulty she reaches up. It is fiddly work and her hands aren't as easy to control as they used to be, but eventually she manages to untie the balloons. They are immediately released into the air, scattering in different directions. Her towel has become unknotted in her reaching and has fallen to her ankles. She stands in her swimsuit and watches as the balloons are lifted up over the pool. The swimmers in the water stop and look up, too, treading water or lying on their backs to watch them dancing in the air above the lido. Rosemary's heart soars with them, hope suddenly filling her. As she watches them, anything and everything seems possible. Eventually they are just dots and then they are gone completely.

CHAPTER 39

"There was a boy," says Kate as she sits next to Rosemary on the bench outside the lido the next morning. They have just been for their swim and now sit with cardboard cups of tea that they sip slowly before Kate goes to work.

Just that morning, Kate had seen a photo of Joe on Facebook, and remembering had made her heart race.

Kate looks sideways at Rosemary: she is stirring circles in her tea and looking at her with an eyebrow raised. For once Kate wants to talk. She knows that the boy, now a man living in Manchester, apparently with a girlfriend and two dogs, is just one of the things knotted up inside her, but if she can dislodge her memories of him — well, it is at least a start.

"There is always a boy," Rosemary says.

"I was just a girl too. Which makes what we had small, tiny in comparison to what

251

you and George had. I should be over it by now."

Kate thinks about seeing the photo on her phone this morning, and how she had flinched at his face.

"Love is love," says Rosemary. "Just like a tree is a tree. It can be a sapling or a hundred-year-old oak, but it still has roots and life and is at the mercy of the seasons."

"Yours was an oak, Rosemary. Mine was a sapling."

A cloud passes over the sun, creating a brief shadow, before it is blown away again as though the sun was merely blinking.

"Tell me about your sapling."

Kate unfurls a little, tilting her head to look at Rosemary. She is waiting.

"His name was — is — Joe. It sounds mad when I say it now. We had been spending a lot of time together but nothing had happened. One day at school I decided I had to tell him how I felt.

"I saw him in the corridor and told him I had something to talk to him about. Not knowing where to go, I took his arm and pulled him through the door next to us — it led to the wings of the school theater and I guess I thought it would be quiet there. I closed the door behind us and it was suddenly dark and we were pressed up against each other between some props and the costume cupboard.

"When I had opened the door, what I hadn't realized was that a drama class was rehearsing on the stage. But where we were, no one could see us, and we kept quiet. I remember these big clouds of dust in the air around us. I waited for the dust and my nerves to settle. I didn't know how to tell him, so I told him to close his eyes and when his eyes were closed I kissed him."

Kate sneaks a look at Rosemary. The old woman is smiling widely.

"I know!" says Kate. "You'd hardly think that I could be that brave. I can barely even believe it myself now. And the drama group kept on practicing their lines as we stood there in the darkness kissing. It was my first kiss. I'm not sure whether I actually enjoyed it or hated it — I felt sick and was sweating and his mouth felt alien, but it was still wonderful."

Kate stops.

"In the first few weeks that followed our kiss I felt like the floor was falling out beneath my feet. I had never felt like that before. I didn't care that I was falling, because I felt so alive.

"I'm sure my friends hated me. I used the word 'boyfriend' so often. 'My boyfriend'

253

this, 'my boyfriend' that. I'm sure I made them feel sick."

Rosemary laughs. "They don't call it lovesick for no reason."

Kate laughs, too, and for a moment their laughter reaches out across the space between them on the bench and embraces them both.

"Looking back, I suppose I was sickening, I felt like I was the first person to discover life's big secret. Love was suddenly this huge thing that took over my life."

"But," says Rosemary softly, "I think there is a 'but' coming."

"For a long time there was no 'but.' It was perfect. And then one day it wasn't. I knew he was going to university in Durham and I was staying in Bristol, but I guess I hadn't really thought about the future. I just felt so confident.

"Then he said he didn't want us to stay together when we left school. He had a life to live and so did I. I said I understood and that there wasn't much point staying together for the rest of the summer. He looked hurt when I said that but I still don't really know why. It should have been obvious that I couldn't bear to spend another second with him when there was a time limit on it like that. Maybe I was incredibly naive, but

254

I wanted all of him, always. That was the only way I knew how to love him.

"That day I walked home as usual. I spoke briefly to my mum and Erin, who was home for a few days. I don't know if either of them noticed anything was wrong, but they didn't say anything. I pretended to do some revision for my exams. I went to bed. And then I cried and cried and cried."

Kate stops. She remembers the feeling of holding on to her duvet like a life raft, trying to stay afloat as she cried her new kind of tears.

"I know it is stupid to still think about it," she says. "People break up all the time. I was so young and it was such a long time ago but I saw Joe's photo this morning, and I haven't really met anyone else like him. I haven't met anyone at all. And I think maybe it's one of the reasons why moving to London has been so difficult. Being in a new place, on my own. Realizing that's what he wanted when we broke up — but that for me it hasn't felt like an opportunity like it did for him."

Kate breathes deeply. "I'm sorry," she says, wiping her face.

Next to her, Rosemary shakes her head fiercely.

"Never be sorry," she says, a storm in her

eyes. "Never be sorry for feeling. Never be sorry for falling in love. I was never sorry. Not for a single day."

Kate watches Rosemary twist the wedding ring on her finger.

"And you will meet someone," Rosemary says, looking up and fixing Kate with her bright eyes. "You just need to be ready to find them."

They sit as the buses pull up and move off again on the other side of the park. In the silence loneliness is like a third person between them. They nod their heads to it, acknowledging it is there but never calling it by its name.

Kate lets out a sigh and closes her eyes for a moment, aware even with her eyes shut of the shape of the lido in front of her and Rosemary beside her. She feels a sense of relief after talking to Rosemary. Joe may have appeared on the screen of her phone this morning, but in reality he is in Manchester and she is in Brixton, a place she has recently learned to love. They are no longer part of each other's lives. And as she breathes deeply, the knot inside her loosens a little.

CHAPTER 40

They were together until the end. Rosemary didn't want to be apart from him and when one of the nurses who came to help suggested moving him to assisted accommodation she laughed out loud.

"Are you married?" asked Rosemary.

The nurse had looked surprised.

"Yes," she replied.

"Well then, you should remember your vows. In sickness and in health. Till death us do part. I've been married sixty-four years and I still remember that."

The nurse frowned and packed up her things quickly. Rosemary regretted snapping — the nurses were all very kind — but being with him was the only way she knew how to be. She couldn't bear to think of him alone in a hospital.

Once the nurse had left, Rosemary took George a cup of tea. She pulled the cushions around him and heaved his body up by hooking her arms under his armpits. She held the mug and tipped his head gently, helping him drink the warm liquid. When he was finished she climbed into the bed next to him and held his hand. Each breath was shallow and rattling and made her wince but she tried to hide it.

He was trying to say something.

"Ffff . . ."

"Food?" said Rosemary. "Are you hungry? You've just eaten."

George shook his head.

"Ffff. . . ." he started again. He was lifting his arm, pointing to the wardrobe.

She looked at where he was pointing.

"Photos?"

He nodded. Rosemary kissed his forehead and climbed out of the bed. She dragged a chair over and climbed onto it, reaching for the box on the top of the wardrobe. She took it down, stepped off the chair, and carried the box to the bed. Once she was back propped up against the pillows with the box between her legs she took off the lid and reached inside.

"Look at this one," she said, holding a photograph out so George could see. "Oh, you were so brown. Just like a walnut."

She reached for another photograph. They weren't in any particular order so both

George and Rosemary grew older and then younger again as Rosemary took out photo after photo.

"Look at me here," she said. "I loved that swimsuit. I wish I could still fit into it! And don't you tell me I wouldn't look the same in it! Oh, and look at this — the diving board was so high. You were such a good diver, dear."

She reached for George's hand.

"Here we are in Brighton," she said, leaning closer to him and holding the photograph up to his face. "Do you remember the doughnuts we ate on the beach? Mmm, I could go for one of those now. I remember the sound of the seagulls, and how did that song go? Elvis Presley . . ."

She remembered the jukebox and started to sing. She was out of tune but didn't mind.

As she sang, she felt his hand move beneath hers, squeezing her fingers. Her voice shook but she continued, growing quieter for the words she couldn't remember and louder for the chorus. Once she had run out of song she stopped singing and gently kissed his cheek. Then she wiped her eyes quickly.

"Enough of that," she said, her voice shaking. She took a deep breath. "Oh, look at this one, George . . ."

She showed him every photo in the box, laughing and pointing at them, talking to him about each one. Once she was finished the box was empty, her lap was piled with pictures, and George was asleep. She carefully placed the photographs back in the box and put it back on top of the wardrobe. Then she changed into her nightdress and slipped into bed next to George. She lay facing him, an arm across his stomach. She watched him sleeping for a while.

"Good night, dear," she said.

When she woke up he was still sleeping.

CHAPTER 41

The council won't return Kate's calls. In between typing up interviews and proof-reading articles she tries the town hall and each time is asked to leave a message. When she asks about the lido she is told the same thing: "Options are being reviewed by the Board." When she asks to speak to the councillor she is given a number that takes her to another answering machine message.

"No news from the council?" asks Jay as he arrives in the office.

"Is it that obvious? I'm supposed to be doing other work too."

"No, I was just wondering. How is Rosemary? How are her knees?"

"She didn't tell me about her knees."

"She doesn't want you to worry."

"Well, I do worry. Just like I worry about what's going to happen to the lido. I wish I didn't but honestly, I am worried."

Things have returned somewhat to normal

since the surprise party: Kate has been swimming most mornings with Rosemary before heading into work. She has been writing her articles for the paper — this week focusing on a story about preparations for the Lambeth Country Show — a fair that fills Brockwell Park every year with food stands, music, and farm animals. It is a fun article to write, reminding her of the contradictions and random bursts of sunshine in the city where she lives. But the worry is still there in the background — the fear of what is around the corner for the lido and for how much longer her morning swims with Rosemary can continue.

"It will be a real shame if it does close," Jay says. "Just like Rosemary said about the library: they protested it but it was only afterward that they realized what they'd lost."

"That's actually a really good idea," says Kate, glancing up from her computer. Jay looks confused, his light eyebrows scrunching up on his face. It makes Kate smile but she tries to hide it.

"Thanks, I have plenty of them," replies Jay. "But what was this one specifically?"

"A protest," says Kate. "We should hold a protest."

Jay is nodding. "Yes. The one thing that

would have improved that picture of Rose-mary at the town hall would have been if she was holding a placard."

"Come on, I'm being serious."

"So am I. If you're serious about a protest, you need to think about how it will look on the front page. Think of how it will photo-graph."

"So you'll help us then?"

"I don't remember you asking nicely."

"Will you help us, please?"

"Of course I will. We can brainstorm tomorrow over dinner."

Kate nods and turns back to her computer to hide the wide smile that is spreading across her face. She realizes it is the second time someone has asked to dinner recently.

The next evening while Kate gets ready she sprays perfume into her room and then dances through it in her underwear. She read in a magazine that this is the best way to put on perfume. It is not the most ele-gant.

"Help!" she texts to Erin as she opens her wardrobe and holds two different dresses up to her chest while taking a photo. "What should I wear?"

She watches with anticipation as the dots

move on her phone indicating Erin is typing.

"You'd look great in both," comes the reply, "but I'd go for the blue one."

Kate smiles with relief, at the same moment that the doorbell buzzes.

"Shit," she says, pulling the dress over her head. As she wriggles into it she slips her feet into the sandals that are by the door, knocking over a pile of her books as she does so.

"Shit," she says again.

She can hear Jay laughing through the front door.

"I'm coming!" she yells, pushing the books aside gently with her foot. Her denim jacket hangs on the banister at the end of the stairs and she reaches for it and shrugs it onto her shoulders. The pocket catches on the handlebars of the bike that is propped up in the hallway and she untangles herself before opening the front door.

"Wow, you look a mess." Jay laughs. He is leaning on the low wall outside the front door, the evening light picking out the strawberry in his strawberry blond hair. She straightens her dress.

"Charming!"

"I didn't mean it as an insult. You look scruffy but lovely. I like that about you."

Kate doesn't know what to say so she doesn't say anything. Instead she pulls the door shut and steps out into the street.

"I've got something for you," he says once they are outside. He hands her a flat package.

"I didn't know whether to give it to you now or later so thought I'd give it to you now. But maybe I should have given it to you later because you'll have to carry it now."

"Thank you. And it's okay, I have a bag," she says as she opens the wrapping paper. It is a frame; in the frame is the photograph of Kate and Rosemary by the pool. She holds it out in front of her and looks at it as if lost.

"I'm sorry, maybe I should have bought flowers."

"No, it's perfect. Thank you," she says, swallowing the lump in her throat.

They walk in silence for a while. A fox runs across the road in front of them and disappears through a gap in someone's garden fence.

"This is a nice street," says Jay, looking down the tree-lined road and up at the big windows of the town houses. Some are split into two or three flats; others are family homes with toy cars and swings in the small front gardens.

"It is. I can only live here, though, because I share a house with four other people."

"What are they like?"

"I don't really know. We don't see each other much. I didn't know that living with so many people could be so lonely."

They don't look at each other as they walk, but she is very aware of the shape of his body next to her on the pavement. She doesn't mean to be so honest with him but it happens before she can stop herself.

"Tell me about it," he says. "I have three sisters."

"Three? That's a lot of feminine energy."

"I know, right? My dad and I were ganged up on a lot of the time. We'd often sneak out together with our cameras just to escape from them. He was the one who got me into photography."

Kate finds it surprisingly easy to imagine a young Jay and his father with cameras around their necks and matching strawberry blond hair, escaping from a house full of women. She realizes she has worked with Jay for nearly two years but has never really asked him anything about himself before. The thought embarrasses her and she finds herself making up for lost time.

"And what about the rest of your family?

When we were at the lido the other day you mentioned you have nieces and nephews?"

As they walk Kate learns for the first time about Jay's family: his two sisters who still live in London with their husbands and children, and one who lives in Edinburgh with her partner. She turns to watch him every now and then, his face lighting up as he talks about his nieces and nephews. She learns he has lived in South London all his life, in Croydon and Peckham and now Brixton. She tells herself that the only reason she never asked before was that she already guessed this from his accent, but she knows that isn't entirely true. She just never thought to.

"How about now — do you live with flat-mates?" she asks him.

"Yes, just one, though, my friend Nick. He's a musician and works in a bar so we don't often see each other. Most of the time I have the place to myself. It's just a tiny basement flat that is constantly damp but I like it."

"I suppose toads do like the damp."

"Ouch!"

"That's getting you back for calling me a mess!"

"A hot mess."

"Is that better?"

They turn to each other and smile.

"Come on, we're nearly there."

They turn off the street and along the road that traces the perimeter of the park. When they come to one of the apartment buildings they turn into the parking area and small courtyard outside. Rosemary sits on a low wall by the entrance. She is wearing a pale green dress and a matching jacket. She holds a small handbag and looks at her watch and then up as she notices the pair walking toward her. As Kate reaches her she smells Lily of the Valley.

"Rosemary, you look beautiful," says Kate.

"A vision in green," says Jay.

"Oh, this; I haven't worn this in years. I'm surprised it still fits," she says, but she smiles.

"Thank you for inviting me."

"Think of it as a work meeting; we need you here, Rosemary," says Kate. "If it wasn't for you, none of this would have started."

"Still, it's nice to get out — and to have the company too."

"And besides," says Kate, "you cooked for me. I'm sorry I'm not a great cook but what I can do is take you to the best pizza place in town. Or at least that's what Jay tells me — I've never been before."

"You'll both love it," says Jay. "Best pizza

outside of Italy."

As the three of them walk, Rosemary between Kate and Jay, Kate wonders what they must look like. Perhaps they look like two children taking their mother or grandmother out for dinner. Or maybe they just look like what they are: three unlikely friends. And as she thinks it she realizes something for the first time since moving to London. She has friends.

They enter Brixton Village through one of the arches on Atlantic Road. It takes a while to cross the street, which is busy with traffic and a van making a delivery to the new Mexican restaurant on the corner. It is part of a chain but with its brightly painted façade and handwritten chalkboard outside it could easily be mistaken for a family-run business. They wait to cross outside a shop with pots, pans, and dustbins hanging outside its brightly lit window.

Their pizza restaurant is tucked into a corner of the Village opposite a butcher's. At the front of the restaurant is a counter where people buy individual slices of pizza. A cyclist in Lycra leggings and a jersey holds his helmet under one arm and orders a slice before his journey home. Next to him a mother holds the hands of her two children, their faces tilted eagerly to the counter.

Jay leads Rosemary to a seat on a wooden bench tucked under a long table. There are candles on the table and metal pots filled with flowers.

"Shall we order some wine?" says Kate. As they wait to order Kate looks around her, taking in the sounds and the smells in the market. It is noisy and busy with people laughing and talking. The smell of the pizza cooking in the wood oven makes her wonder how much good food she has missed out on with all her microwave meals.

The evening passes with wine and pizza. Rosemary starts eating with a knife and fork until she sees Jay and Kate picking theirs up and she does the same. She spills tomato sauce on the table but doesn't care. They drink two bottles of wine between them. Jay tops up their glasses without them noticing.

As they eat they plan ideas for the protest, Kate scribbling notes.

"I've decided to start an online petition," she says. "I'll share it on the 'Save Brockwell Lido' Facebook page. I should have done it sooner, but hopefully it will still help."

"Good idea," says Rosemary. "You can write about the petition when you write

270

about the protest too."

"We need something for the protest that will really make a splash," says Jay, "if you'll pardon the pun."

"It needs to be something that works visually," says Kate. "We could make banners and hang them at the end of the pool? But what could they say? 'Save Brockwell Lido,' 'Just keep swimming,' 'Don't pull the plug on our lido' . . ."

"I like that one," says Jay, and Kate writes it in her notebook.

"What about rubber ducks?" says Rosemary. Kate and Jay turn to look at her. Then the three of them burst into laughter.

"It's perfect," says Kate. "And I think I know someone who can help us too."

Rosemary's cheeks glow pink and she smiles. Kate feels herself smiling too.

Later in the evening a band sets up opposite the restaurant: a folk singer and two guitarists. The music is loud and at first Kate feels her heart rate start to rise with the noise.

"Will you make an old woman happy and dance with me?" says Rosemary suddenly, pulling herself up and reaching a hand down to Kate. Kate looks up, startled.

"Oh, I'm not much of a dancer."

Kate remembers school discos where she

271

would hide in a corner, watching her class-mates laughing and moving their bodies with such ease, and wishing she could do the same. After a couple of years she stopped going altogether. When she was at university she always made excuses when her fellow students went out clubbing. They quickly stopped inviting her.

"Neither am I," says Rosemary. "But that doesn't matter. I just enjoy it."

Kate looks up at Rosemary and suddenly thinks that maybe she is right. Maybe it doesn't matter. Any of it. She stands up.

"Okay, let's dance," she says.

The two women move away from the tables and into the passageway in front of the musicians. Then they reach for each other's arms. Rosemary is slow and Kate is clumsy, but they dance. The guitarist and singer smile at them, and people in the restaurants turn to watch. For once Kate doesn't notice them; she is too busy looking down at her feet and then up at Rosemary.

"I'm doing it!" she says, beaming.

"Yes, you are!"

They continue to dance on their own in the passageway, watched by the musicians, the customers, and Jay. They turn slowly and spin each other round and round.

Kate focuses on the music and the movement and blocks out everything else. Warmth fills her whole body. She feels like a balloon full of air, about to float away. Her body feels full to the brim with light but she feels empty and free at the same time. At first she thinks it must be the wine, but then she remembers the feeling. It is joy. As she dances she can't wait to phone Erin and tell her about this later.

"I'm sorry, my knees," says Rosemary, stopping. "Jay, come over here. I don't think Kate is quite done dancing yet."

Jay stands up and Rosemary heads back to the table, placing a hand on his arm as they pass each other.

"Take care of her," she says quietly. Jay nods and walks over to Kate, thinking she has never looked as beautiful. Her cheeks are pink and her eyes are bright, as though a cloud has rolled away for a moment.

"Let's dance," says Kate, holding out her arms and surprising herself with her own confidence. He takes her hand and pulls her closer to him with an arm around her waist. They dance out of rhythm with each other and the music. They bump into each other and step on each other's feet. But they laugh. And as they dance Kate feels joy filling her whole body and she holds on to it tightly. Rosemary watches them and remembers.

Tonight when they are in their beds alone both women will dream of dancing. Jay will too.

CHAPTER 42

The lido is full of rubber ducks. They float on the surface, a smiling sea of yellow. Some cluster in groups, nudging into one another as the breeze blows; others bob in twos, their orange beaks meeting as they float into each other. Two mallards swim among them, seeming confused.

"Help me with the other end of the banner," says Kate to Erin, passing her one end of a long sheet of fabric. They walk along the poolside in opposite directions, Frank and Jermaine helping them tie the banner.

Kate had called Erin after her dinner with Rosemary and Jay.

"We're planning a protest to help save the lido," said Kate. "And I thought that with you being a PR expert and all, you might be able to help." Erin had agreed immediately, saying she would be happy to help. But as Kate looks across the pool at her sister, her red wavy hair jumping in the breeze as she bends to help Frank and Jermaine tie the banner, she thinks there is probably more to it as well. For both of them. They catch each other's eyes for a moment and Kate remembers jumping from Erin's shoulders into the water of their local pool when they were young. She looks at her sister now, trying to spot the differences between the woman by the pool and her younger self. Her eyes are the same green, her hair is still the shade of red that Kate envied when she was younger but that she knew Erin hated; Erin is still taller than Kate but has grown into her height, no longer embarrassed by it. The angry expression she often wore as a teenager has softened, but there are traces of dark circles under her eyes — and Kate is reminded of the stress Erin spoke about around her job. Today she is wearing a bright blue fitted dress and pristine makeup. Erin has always said that dressing well is important for her job, but Kate knows that the clothes and the makeup are part of Erin's armor. Beautifully cut, colorful armor, but armor nonetheless.

Once the banner is secured, they all step back to admire it.

"Don't Pull the Plug on Our Lido," it reads.

"It looks perfect," says Frank, turning to Jermaine. They have left their part-time assistant in charge of the bookshop this weekend. As much as they love their shop and their home it is a relief to be away from it for a few days. They can't stop smiling at each other.

"It really does," says Rosemary, who is directing proceedings from a chair by the water's edge, an iced tea resting at her feet.

Kate had been strangely nervous to introduce Erin and Rosemary. But Erin gave Rosemary a huge hug and said, "I hope you don't mind, I just feel like I know you already. I've been so enjoying reading Kate's articles about the lido — and about you." Rosemary smiled at Erin first and then at Kate, who stood by Erin's side, hugging her arms around her and smiling sideways at her sister. Erin had been calmer with Jay, shaking his hand but smiling warmly.

"Kate has told me a lot about you," Jay had said, which wasn't technically true. But when Erin turned and flashed her smile at Kate she realized why Jay said it.

Erin also had chatted easily with all the others — particularly with Ahmed, who was delighted to learn she had studied business at university too. He proceeded to ask her a long list of questions.

Jay's camera shutter clicks as he takes photos of the sign and the rubber ducks floating on the pool. People crowd the decking around the lido. A teenage boy ties balloons to the umbrellas in the café; Ahmed strings up another banner at the end of the pool underneath the clock; a mother holds her baby on her hip, pointing at the rubber ducks. The baby giggles. In the café Hope orders teas and coffees for everyone, which the barista brings to one of the outdoor tables on a tray.

"It looks great, sis," says Erin once she has crossed over to her side of the pool. She stands close to Kate, their bodies almost but not quite touching.

"Thank you for coming," says Kate. "And for all your help."

Despite her smart blue dress, Erin had chipped in to help as soon as she had arrived, resting boxes of ducks on her hips and carrying them across to the water, but her greatest contribution had been her idea for the rubber duck distribution.

After the protest they will deliver a box of ducks to the local council and others will go to the offices of several local and national newspapers. Each rubber duck will have a tag around its neck reading, "Don't pull the plug on our lido." Sending the ducks had

278

been Erin's idea.

On the tags will be a link to the petition Kate has started. So far it has a hundred signatures. The number amazes Rosemary; Kate is disappointed.

"I don't know anywhere near a hundred people!" says Rosemary. Kate tries to explain social media to Rosemary without success.

There is a splash: the teenage boy has dived into the water and is swimming alongside the rubber ducks and the real ones that are flapping their feathers in one corner of the pool. Kate and Erin turn to watch him.

As the boy swims underwater he twists onto his back and looks up through the yellow shapes at patches of blue sky. He blows bubbles out of his nose, watching them climb to the surface like the fizz in champagne. As he bursts up for air a group of rubber ducks wobbles to one side to make room for him. He laughs, a short but loud laugh that escapes him with the unexpected suddenness of an engine backfiring.

Kate spots Jay kneeling by the poolside, taking a photograph of the boy with his head just above the surface, surrounded by yellow ducks.

"Come on, group photo time," he says to

the boy, who swims to the shallow end and pulls himself out, ignoring the ladder. The two of them walk along the length of the pool.

"I suppose we better head over," says Kate, and Erin nods and follows her to the side of the pool where a crowd has started to gather beneath the clock and the banner. Erin joins the group and Kate starts directing them like a photographer at a wedding.

"Rosemary, you go in the middle. Ellis and Hope, you go either side of her. Ahmed, can you go over there . . ."

Jay joins her, standing at her side and watching the swimmers huddling into a group.

"Do you think that looks okay?" she says to him. "Sorry, I know this is your job."

"Perfect," he says. "Now you get in too."

She gives him a reluctant look and he gives her a gentle push.

"I've already been on the front page," says Rosemary. "And it wasn't half bad. Now it's your turn."

She reaches for Kate and puts an arm firmly around her shoulder. Kate stands in the very middle with Rosemary on one side and Erin on the other, surrounded by the people she has met since the lido came into her life three months ago. As Jay takes the photos she smiles, not for the camera, but because of the warmth surging through her body.

By the afternoon they have all the photos they need and the pool has been cleared of rubber ducks. The others have gone to the café for drinks and Rosemary has headed home to rest, but Kate and Erin stay on the poolside. They have kicked off their shoes and trail their feet in the water. It is cold, but after a day on their feet it is just what they need. Kate trails her feet gently back and forth and watches Erin doing the same. Her toenails are painted bright red.

The sun is at its golden hour and it lights up the brick walls and Erin's auburn hair. It shines brightly off the surface of the water, making it look bluer than blue.

Kate feels strangely nervous in Erin's presence. They know each other well enough for silences to be comfortable, but this time there is so much that Kate wants to say.

"I'm sorry I can't ask you to stay," she says. "But I have work I need to do and I worry I wouldn't be much fun."

It is partly true — she does have work to do — but the image of her dirty house and the housemates she has implied are good friends makes the thought of Erin visiting terrifying.

"It's okay," Erin replies. "I have friends in Hackney I've been meaning to visit."

They are quiet again for a moment, the sound of laughter coming from the café and the gentle trickling of the water as they dangle their feet off the edge the only noises interrupting them.

"I should have asked this a long time ago," says Kate, "but is everything okay with you? A while ago you mentioned your job, and the fact that you're struggling to get pregnant. I'm sorry, I didn't really know what to say but I should have asked you about it. Are things any better?"

Erin sighs gently, leaning back on her arms and stretching her legs out of the water before plunging her toes back under again.

"I'm still not pregnant," she says, "but we've decided to go to a fertility clinic. Just deciding it has made us both feel better, I think — just more in control of the situation."

Kate leans back and feels good to hear Erin talking, even if she still feels guilty for not having asked her these questions sooner.

After she finishes, Erin looks at Kate, her green eyes shining in the sunlight.

"And what about you?" she asks. "How are you? And don't say you're fine. I mean, really, how are you?"

Kate knows she should have seen this question coming — seeing her sister looking at her like that, concerned but also open, ready to listen, makes her want to cry. She takes a deep breath.

"It's been hard," she says. "These last couple of years have been really hard."

As she says it she realizes she should have said it a long time ago. But she couldn't. The words had been locked up so tightly inside her that they were like a bolt holding her together. Admitting them to her sister or her parents would have broken her.

"I hadn't realized that moving to a new place would be so lonely," she says.

"You're much braver than me."

"What do you mean?" Kate asks, frowning.

"Don't you remember?" Erin says. "I was supposed to move to London for university. I got a place at University College London. But I didn't go — I was too scared about moving that far away to a city that big."

Kate shakes her head. She didn't remember that.

"I guess you were little then," says Erin, shrugging slightly. "I was probably embarrassed to tell you. But I didn't go. Since then I could have moved so many times. Lots of my friends are here now. But I never did it. I tell myself I'm happy in Bath — and honestly, I am. I wouldn't want to move anymore, especially now that Mark and I have our flat there and he's just set up his business. But I do know partly it's been due to fear. In Bath I have a senior role at a top PR firm. But trying to do the same job in London? There'd be so much competition. What if I ended up a nobody?"

Erin's words rock Kate. Erin isn't scared of anything. Erin knows all her times tables and shouts when she is angry, and flirts and gets her way when she's not, and lives in a beautiful flat. Maybe that's all still true, but it's also not true either. Just like it's true that Kate lives in London, has a job she enjoys, and has now found a group of people she would call her friends. But that's not the whole truth.

So, as they sit on the edge of the pool that Kate has come to think of as some sort of home, she finally tells her sister the rest of the story. She talks about her time at university and the crippling sense of inadequacy she felt around her classmates. She tells Erin about the housemates she doesn't know, and how despite having a nice room and being on a pretty street, she hates coming home to that house every day. For the first time, she describes her Panic: how it started, what it feels like, and how swimming seems to have helped. Then she talks about the lido — how she first heard about it and how she met Rosemary and has become invested in it, much more so than any of the other stories she has written for the paper.

And because there isn't much to say, Erin does the even more generous thing. She just listens.

After a while Kate has run out of words, and tears. Erin reaches into her handbag and pulls out a pack of tissues, which she hands silently to Kate. Once Kate has wiped her face and her breathing has calmed, she stops. She watches the light on the water and the reflection of the clouds. Erin turns to her, checking she is finished before taking her turn to talk.

"I spoke to Rosemary earlier," she says. Kate remembers seeing Erin pausing by Rosemary's chair while they were unpacking boxes, bringing her a refill of iced tea from the café. "She says none of this would have happened without your help — the articles, the petition, the protest."

As Erin talks Kate spots something yellow floating in the far corner of the pool. It is a rubber duck — they must have missed one. It bobs up and down on the water, a glimmering speck of yellow in the expanse of blue.

"You're doing a great job," says Erin. "It might not feel like it all the time, but that's okay. You're allowed to feel lonely, you're allowed to feel panicked. It doesn't make you any less of a person."

As Erin says it, Kate realizes that is how she has felt. In her darkest moment she has felt broken — like she is failing at just being.

"But next time you talk to me, okay?" says Erin. "We'll talk to each other."

When Erin reaches out her hand, Kate takes it. They sit like that for a while, holding hands and trailing their feet in the cold water of Brockwell Lido as the sun dips behind them and the lights inside the café shine like searchlights onto the water.

When Rosemary is home that night she thinks about George and how much the ducks would have made him laugh. Sometimes she has dreams where he is sitting in the living room with her and they have a long conversation — all the things that she has been holding inside her coming out in endless dreamy chatter — what she cooked for dinner or the new restaurant that has opened where the old fishmonger was, or gossip from the lido changing room. Sometimes she just tells him about a particularly beautiful sunset over Brockwell Park.

She hopes that she has a dream like that tonight — she will tell him about the protest and the ducks and how proud she felt standing with her friends underneath the banner and the lido clock. How she felt like she was a somebody.

CHAPTER 43

The lido is closed again the next day for a wedding. The park is quiet — it has been raining all morning, an unexpected summer shower that bursts the heat of the past week. White balloons are tied in the trees at the back of the building, droplets of water sliding down their round faces and dripping through the leaves. Outside the café entrance a member of staff drags a white umbrella outside the door, sheltering a chalkboard where the couple's names are written in looping letters. Silver buckets are propped next to the chalkboard, full of plump white peonies that look like the layered skirts of ballerinas. The ramp up to the café entrance is lined with small potted trees: today they all wear wedding outfits of winking white lights.

Rosemary and Kate walk toward the lido under the shelter of a large black umbrella that Kate holds over the two of them. Rosemary had resisted the umbrella. "It's bad luck to have black at a wedding!" she had said as they prepared to leave her flat. Rosemary had put on her only remaining smart dress, in a lavender-and-white floral print fabric that fell halfway between her knees and her ankles. She wore matching lavender shoes — flat but with a pointed toe. She even put on lipstick and combed her hair into thin waves.

"But it's the only umbrella you have," said Kate, adjusting the buckle on the ankles of her raspberry pink heels, "and I'm not going out in these shoes and this rain without an umbrella."

The dress is much more fitted and colorful than anything Kate would usually wear, but she fell in love with the vivid raspberry fabric as soon as she saw it. It has a high neck and capped sleeves but at the back falls just below her shoulder blades.

She had taken a morning off work so she could go shopping while it was quiet — when she handed over her credit card at the counter she had grinned, feeling proud of herself for her planning and for finding exactly what she wanted without getting overwhelmed. As she paid she silently counted the weeks since her last panic attack — it had been three. She beamed at the thought. The shop assistant looked at her strangely but she didn't care.

So the black umbrella had stayed and had kept them mostly dry on the short walk from Rosemary's flat to the Lido Café.

As they arrive Jay opens the café door, his camera around his neck. He is wearing gray trousers, a white shirt, and a pale gray tie, a navy raincoat over the top. His hair even looks as though it has been brushed. Kate has never seen him look so smart.

"Oh, it's you two!" he says, nearly bumping into them as he pulls the hood of his raincoat up over his head. He kisses Rosemary on the cheek and looks at Kate for a moment before kissing her too. She feels very aware of the curve of her hips in her pink dress. For once she doesn't mind the feeling.

"I'm just stepping outside to take a photo of the flowers and the chalkboard before the writing melts completely," he says. "Great weather for a wedding!"

As they step inside they are greeted by Sprout, her tail wagging and a white bow tied around her collar.

"Look at you," says Kate, kneeling to stroke the dog who brushes up against her, leaving blond hairs on the raspberry fabric of her dress.

"Look at this," says Rosemary, tugging at Kate's arm.

The café is transformed, small tables pulled together into two long rows lined with vases of white peonies that stand on top of piles of old books. White paper flowers hang from the ceiling like moons and candles flicker in glass lanterns along the window ledge. Beyond it is the lido, empty and gray in the now heavy rain. The room is full of guests talking and drinking from champagne flutes, and the sound of laughter.

Kate and Rosemary greet Jermaine and Frank by the bar. Jermaine wears a navy suit and Frank's is gray; both have white flowers in their buttonholes. Sprout finds them again among the crowd and sits at their feet, looking up at them with soppy brown eyes.

"This is beautiful," says Kate.

"We were going to say our vows by the pool but it looks like that's off now," says Jermaine, looking out of the window. "We thought a summer wedding would mean we'd avoid the rain! But I suppose this is England."

"It's cozy in here; I like it," says Frank, pulling Jermaine toward him and kissing the spot where his beard meets his cheek.

"The lido has never looked so lovely," says Rosemary, looking through the flowers and the candles at the rain falling onto the surface of the pool. Frank hands her a glass of champagne.

"Oh, I don't know if I should. I can't remember when I last had champagne," she says.

"We insist," says Frank, placing the champagne in Rosemary's hand with both of his around hers.

"Oh, go on then."

At the back of the room, Rosemary sits to soothe the aching in her knees.

"Are you sure you are okay?" Kate asks. Rosemary insists that she is, and Kate drifts back to the group, never moving too far away.

Rosemary happily observes Kate talking animatedly with Frank and Jermaine.

As the few children at the wedding run in and out among the adults and duck under the tables to play in their world of ankles and tablecloths, condensation gathers on the café windows, the warm bodies getting even warmer from the champagne.

Kate laughs with a group of Jermaine's friends, surprising herself with the sound and with her own confidence. She waits for the feeling of anxiety that usually comes when she is among so many strangers, but it doesn't come and they don't feel like strangers. She looks out at the lido and across at Rosemary every now and then — the two views grounding her. She lets herself get light-headed with champagne.

The wedding is small and informal and it is a member of staff who suggests that Frank and Jermaine should probably say their vows now, as the food is nearly ready to come out. The guests take their seats along the table and Frank and Jermaine move to the front of the coffee bar. Sprout seems to sense the change in mood and darts out from under the table to join them. Parents pull their children from the floor and sit them on their laps. Everyone is quiet.

"I take you as you are, loving who you are now and who you are yet to become," says Jermaine, his voice shaking. As he says the words he thinks about his mother, now dead, and how she had cried when she realized her son would never get married.

"I promise to listen to you and learn from you, to support you and accept your support."

He thinks about the bookshop and how much it means to both of them, despite the stress and sleepless nights that it often brings. The walls of their relationship are built with books.

"I will celebrate your triumphs and mourn your losses as though they were my own. I will love you and have faith in your love for me, through all our years and all that life may bring us."

Rosemary starts to cry, tears falling silently down her face like the rain dripping down the windows. She cries for George, for all their years and for all that life brought them. But she also cries a different kind of tears — tears that come from a place of being happy to be alive seeing the candles and the flowers and the empty lido in the rain and hearing vows that will last another couple's lifetime.

"What I possess in this world, I give to you," says Frank. "I will keep you and hold you, comfort and tend you, protect you and shelter you, for all the days of my life."

Frank and Jermaine are both crying now, too, as are most of the guests. Kate reaches for Rosemary's hand and squeezes it hard. Sprout barks loudly and the room softens into laughter.

Jermaine wipes his eyes and kisses his husband, thinking that he will never tire of calling him that.

CHAPTER 44

On Monday Kate misses Rosemary at the pool. She swims her morning lengths in silence, slipping deeper into her thoughts length after slow length. Afterward, she nods at a few of the regulars but they do not exchange words, each caught in their own thoughts this morning. Summer peeks in over the lido walls. The trees are heavy with green and the morning light is golden and hazy.

Kate remembers swimming as a child in the summer holidays. Before she learned to be self-conscious her mother dressed her in a Minnie Mouse swimsuit, which she wore all the way to Bournemouth when they visited the grandparents. Erin sat in the back of the car next to her, a blue bikini poking out from underneath her clothes. She spent most of the journey texting and listening to music, but joined Kate in the race to spot the sea.

"I can see the sea, I can see the sea!" they both shrieked, pointing at the silvery blue that sparkled with the sun. They parked on the cliff top, the children below like colorful pebbles in the sand, building sandcastles or skipping to the sea. The water was always cold, just like the lido. But the cold could be as delicious as a Mr. Whippy ice cream on a hot day.

Kate and Erin's grandparents buried coins in the sand for them both to find. Erin always forgot that she was a teenager in the ageless and unifying pursuit of pocket money. Afterward, if Erin was in a good mood, she would take Kate's hand and they would run to the sea together, Kate only occasionally tripping on account of her much shorter legs.

As they swam, their mother and grand-parents would sit behind a blue-and-yellow-striped windbreaker, their grandmother wearing an anorak and passing a thermos of tea between them, whatever the weather.

Kate and Erin would splash at the water's edge, sinking their feet deeper and deeper into the sand as the waves rolled in and out, until they had to make an effort to tug their legs out with a sound like jelly being scooped from a bowl. In the white foam they splashed and danced, jumping over waves or defiantly crashing right through them, tasting the salt water on their lips as the spray drenched their faces. Sometimes their grandfather would join them and swim a steady front crawl along the length of the beach, the two girls watching him in admiration until he was just a brown dot bobbing on the waves.

Remembering her grandmother watching them, Kate thinks of Rosemary. Kate realizes that her corkscrew kick has come back and she is missing the guidance and company of her friend. Once she is dry she asks after Rosemary at the reception desk.

"No Rosemary today?" she asks Ahmed.

"Not today," he replies.

Kate wonders if perhaps Rosemary drank too much champagne at the wedding. She phones her and leaves a message on her voice mail, then heads to work.

But the next day Kate swims on her own again. She asks Ahmed again at the reception whether he has seen Rosemary. He shakes his head.

"No, I haven't seen her. She's never missed two days in a row before — never. And Ellis came swimming here last night and said he hadn't seen her at the market, either, and Monday is her shopping day. Is she okay?"

As Kate leaves the lido she phones Phil and tells him she will be late to work and will make up the time this evening. She crosses the road to Rosemary's flat, fear making her walk fast and Panic filling her throat like a thick tar.

The summer Kate turned eight, during a visit to her grandparents, Kate's grandmother went out to an exercise class. Erin was upstairs reading a book, and Kate's mother was on a work phone call that seemed to go on all afternoon.

From her position curled up on the sofa in front of the television Kate could just see the top of her grandfather's head out of the window, in the garden tending to his busy Lizzies. Sometimes it would dip below window level as he bent to water the flowers. She watched *Tom and Jerry*, feeling the quiet guilt of being inside on a sunny day, but enjoying the luxury of solitude. In the heat of the living room she fell asleep, dreaming that she was a mouse chasing a cat.

When she woke up she looked up at the window, expecting to see the brown top of her grandfather's head. But he wasn't there.

She decided to visit him in the garden and walked dozily out of the patio doors. The maid in *Tom and Jerry* started to scream

298

and Kate heard the sound of her broom swiping at the cartoon mouse as she spotted her grandfather, lying faceup in the flower bed. His eyes were open and his trowel was abandoned in the dirt next to him.

The front door clicked shut and Kate heard her grandmother calling for her granddaughters.

"I've got Battenberg for you," she said, appearing behind Kate with a tray in her hands. She screamed and dropped the cake into the grass, crying and running toward the flower bed. That was when Kate began to understand and started crying too. She has never been able to eat Battenberg since.

Now Kate shields the sun from her eyes with her hands and looks up at the midrise, trying to spot signs of life on Rosemary's balcony. The flagpole is empty — there is no swimsuit waving in the breeze today.

Kate presses the flat number into the keypad by the door and waits. A young mother is pushing a crying baby in a swing in the play area outside the block of flats. Kate presses the buzzer again and waits.

After a few minutes a noise comes out of the panel and can just be heard above the baby.

"Hello?" it croaks quietly.

Kate breathes out heavily in relief at the sound of Rosemary's voice.

"Rosemary, it's Kate. Can I come up?"

There is a pause and then the door buzzes and clicks open.

The door to Rosemary's flat is already open when Kate reaches it and pushes inside. The curtains to the balcony are shut and the living room is dark. The room smells faintly of urine, but Kate pretends not to notice.

"Don't turn the light on," says Rosemary from the sofa.

It takes Kate's eyes a moment to adjust to the gloom. White piles of tissues carpet the floor and she can make out the shape of Rosemary's body curled under a blanket on the small sofa. Her head is resting on the arm. Tucked up like that she looks tiny, like a baby animal that hasn't grown its fur yet.

"What has happened, Rosemary?" asks Kate, closing the door and making her way across to the sofa, careful not to bump into any furniture.

"Nothing happened," says Rosemary. "I got old."

Kate kneels down by the sofa and puts her hand on Rosemary's forehead. Her skin feels dry despite the fever.

"When did you last have something to eat?

Or some water?"

Rosemary shakes her head but doesn't answer.

"Have you called the doctor?" Kate calls behind her as she heads into the kitchen, filling two glasses with water. She opens the fridge and looks inside — it is empty and she remembers what Ahmed said — that Ellis reported Rosemary hadn't been to the market. Back in the living room Kate lines the water glasses up on a small table. She helps Rosemary sit up and holds the glass to Rosemary's lips.

Rosemary avoids Kate's eyes as she takes slow sips. She doesn't answer the question about the doctor. Kate waits until Rosemary has finished both glasses of water before going to the phone and dialing the local doctor's office. She talks quietly but quickly.

"The doctor will be over soon," she says after hanging up.

In the darkness she scoops up the tissues and puts them in the bin. She boils water in the kettle and makes Rosemary a cup of tea with two sugars. While they wait for the doctor Kate takes Rosemary's keys from her swimming bag by the door and pops out to the local corner shop. Rosemary doesn't notice — she has fallen asleep.

Kate returns with cans of soup, a loaf of

bread, a pint of milk, and some eggs. As Rosemary sleeps on the sofa Kate boils her an egg, heats up some soup, and cuts toast into thin strips. Kate helps her eat, dipping the toast into the yolk of the egg and handing the slices to Rosemary, who eats them slowly, her hands unsteady. Rosemary drops a piece of toast onto the blanket. Kate picks it up and puts it on the side of the plate.

Kate wants to say something, to tell her that it will be okay, but Rosemary's embarrassment is clear, so she says nothing. She opens the balcony door and pulls the curtain back over it, a breeze blowing through the thin fabric.

"I'm cold," says Rosemary, pulling the blanket tighter around her.

"You're hot," says Kate. "And you need some fresh air."

Kate tidies around Rosemary as she drifts in and out of sleep. Eventually the doctor buzzes up. Kate lets him in and follows him to the sofa.

"Is this your grandmother?" the doctor asks.

"No," she replies, "she's my friend."

"And how long has she been ill for?"

"I can hear you, you know!" says Rosemary.

"I'm sorry, Mrs. Peterson," says the doctor, kneeling beside her and opening his bag. "How long have you been ill for?"

"Since Sunday evening. I thought it was just the champagne. We were at a wedding. I haven't had champagne in a very long time."

He does some checks and then stands up.

"It's the flu," he says to Rosemary. He turns to Kate. "She should be okay but needs plenty of fluids and lots of rest. She will need watching and taking care of — if her temperature rises, you should call the surgery again. Do you have any children, Mrs. Peterson?"

"No."

"I can look after you," Kate says to Rosemary, kneeling next to the sofa with her back to the doctor, who is now standing up and packing away his things.

"I don't want to make you do that," says Rosemary.

"I can look after you," Kate says again. She looks at Rosemary, who doesn't say anything else.

So the doctor leaves them and Kate makes a call to Phil explaining the situation and telling him she will need to work from home this week.

"I'm just going to go and get my things, okay?" she says to Rosemary. Before she leaves she heads into the kitchen and reaches above the fridge for the black notebook that she knows lives there. She walks quickly to her house, collects her laptop, sleeping bag, and a bag with some clothes and toiletries. Then she heads to the market to ask Ellis for help.

CHAPTER 45

While Rosemary is ill, Kate cooks, working her way through George's notebook. Ellis filled bags with everything she would need for a week of recipes and wouldn't let her pay for anything.

"Just get her better," he had said.

Kate has never cooked this much in her life. She gently handles the notebook, turning each page with care and deciding what Rosemary might like to eat. There are pies and puddings, stews and casseroles. One recipe just reads "Rosemary's favorite soup" so Kate starts with that. She painstakingly reads and follows every instruction. Every now and then she has to ask Rosemary to read a certain word where she can't quite decipher George's handwriting.

Rosemary eats hardly anything, but the smell of the cooking seems to revive her a little. She sits up slightly on the sofa and looks out onto the balcony, watching the bees on the lavender pots. When she was sleeping Kate dragged the pots closer to the door so that they would be easy for her to see. She keeps the curtains open and the door ajar so a breeze fills the flat. Kate eats, too, sitting on a cushion on the floor by the sofa. Rosemary doesn't talk and Kate doesn't want to force her, so she reads or types on her laptop as they eat in silence. Every day Kate checks the Facebook page and the petition. It has reached over a thousand signatures now, and she writes a short piece about the milestone for the paper. She also receives several emails from local businesses who want to show their support for the campaign by putting posters in their windows. Jay helps to make and distribute them while Kate works from Rosemary's flat.

It gives her hope, but something at the back of her mind makes her worry. She remembers the image of the lido turned into the private members' gym and fear enters her like a chill through a window.

At night Kate helps Rosemary to her bedroom. She turns away while she changes. The old woman's naked body looks very different in the dim light of her bedroom than it does in the fluorescent glare at the swimming pool changing room. It might be darker but she seems more naked here.

Rosemary wears button-up men's striped pajamas. The sleeves of her shirt are rolled up neatly at the wrists. Kate helps her onto the bed and pulls the covers over her, tucking them around her body. Rosemary rolls onto her side and faces the wall. Kate makes sure there is a glass of water and George's photograph on the bedside table, and then she softly closes the door.

In the living room Kate unrolls her sleeping bag onto the sofa and climbs inside. She considers taking a book from the shelf to flick through before falling asleep, but she doesn't want to disturb the pattern of titles — a pattern that only Rosemary knows the logic to. She keeps the curtain to the balcony open so she can see the sky and the glow from the streetlamps as she falls asleep.

Hope phones several times during the week; she hasn't had her flu vaccination so Rosemary doesn't let her visit in person. Rosemary takes the phone into her bedroom and closes the door while they speak. Kate can hear the hushed voices from the other side of the door as she washes up and makes Rosemary a fresh pot of tea. While she waits for Rosemary to finish her conversation she texts Erin, who is eager to hear about Rosemary's condition and whether she's getting any better.

"Honey and lemon," writes Erin. "Remember Mum making that for us when we were little? It did the trick. E x."

Kate adds a spoonful of honey and a squeeze of lemon to Rosemary's tea.

In the middle of the week Jay comes to visit. He arrives with coffee for Kate and flowers for Rosemary. He pulls books from the shelves that Kate can't reach for Rosemary to read, piling them around the sofa where Rosemary sits during the day, Kate's sleeping bag rolled up neatly and tucked away under the window.

"You're doing a great job," he says to Kate as he leaves. "The flowers are for you too." They are pink and white stock and fill the flat with the smell of summer.

After a week Rosemary's temperature is back to normal and she is eating again.

"Thank you," she says. They are sitting in the living room together, both reading, Rosemary on the sofa and Kate leaning against it on the floor. Rosemary puts down her book and puts a hand on Kate's shoulder. She squeezes.

"Thank you," she says again. "I'm lucky to have a friend like you."

"That's okay," says Kate, a surge of feeling running through her at the feel of

Rosemary's hand on her shoulder. "I'm glad you're feeling better."

Rosemary pauses for a moment, looking out the balcony windows.

"I think we're running out of time," she says softly. Kate looks across at her. She has lost a little weight during the week, but the color is back in her face and her eyes look blue again, not the dull gray they had seemed for most of the week.

"What do you mean?" she says.

"The lido," replies Rosemary, gesturing out the window. "I know you say the petition has more signatures, but it's been a week since the protest, and what, a month since the hearing? And still nothing. I think it might be coming to an end."

Kate doesn't know what to say. She is exhausted, but her need to reassure Rosemary, and perhaps herself, overwhelms her.

Despite her own fears, Kate says, brightly, "Don't worry. There's still plenty of time. The most important thing now is that you're feeling better."

With Rosemary recovered, Kate decides it is safe to pack up her things and head back to her house. Before Kate leaves for home Rosemary shuffles into the kitchen to get something.

"I want you to have this," she says. "I have

them all in my head really. You've cooked for me, now I want you to cook for yourself."

And she hands Kate George's black notebook of recipes.

CHAPTER 46

Back at work the next week Kate tries to chase away Rosemary's words about the lido coming to an end. Over the weekend several local groups, schools, youth groups, and even a band who formed when the members all lived in Brixton, shared the petition and it has now reached fifteen hundred signatures. On Monday Kate writes an article about it.

In the office, a rubber duck sits proudly on Phil's desk. Kate gave it to him after the protest when the image of the pool full of ducks made the front page. He was delighted and called the duck Debbie, chuckling to himself whenever he caught a glimpse of it.

The protest had certainly helped drum up some support, but they have still had no response from the council. Kate wonders what they must have thought when the delivery of rubber ducks arrived at the town hall. She imagines the middle-aged councillor opening the box and taking out a grinning rubber duck; the thought makes her smile.

"Good morning!" says Jay, arriving with three coffees, one for him, one for Kate, and one for Phil. They settle down to work, Debbie watching them from Phil's desk, a dazed grin on her plastic face.

At one o'clock Jay stops by Kate's desk and asks her to lunch.

"You read my mind again," she replies, taking her bag off her desk. They go to ask Phil if he wants them to bring anything back for him, but he is on the phone, a frown puckering his plump face.

As they walk from the office to the main street, the sun is warm on Kate's shoulders. She breathes deeply; she knows the air is full of exhaust fumes from the passing buses but in the sunshine it seems clean and sweet. They talk as they walk, about their families and how lovely London is in the summer.

"It's like everyone gets half a stone lighter," says Jay. "People don't walk, they bounce." He tells Kate what a London summer means to him: cider in Brockwell Park, lying on his back in the grass and watching airplanes and imagining where they are

312

traveling. She nods, saying she loves the long evenings that make you want to actually go out and do things for once rather than eating microwave meals in front of your laptop on your own. She stops, wondering if she should have told him that, but he just smiles. They walk quietly for a while — silence being as comfortable as conversation with him. She thinks about all the times before when she snuck out of the office to eat lunch on her own and regrets it.

When they return to the office Phil is staring at his computer screen. Kate notices that Debbie has gone from his desk.

"Kate, come into my office, I need to talk to you," he says. Phil doesn't have an office, so Kate pulls up a chair next to his desk and the piles of books and files that surround it like a wall. Jay watches from his desk on the other side of the room.

Phil picks up a book and examines its spine.

"I need you to stop writing about the lido," he says, running his hand down the spine of the book, eyes down.

"What do you mean? Who is going to be writing about it instead?"

"No one."

"No one? But it's one of our ongoing stories, we can't just stop it."

"It's not one of our stories anymore."

"But I just wrote a story about the petition for the paper — your paper!"

Phil puts down the book. "That's today's news; it won't be tomorrow's."

"But I don't understand. I thought you loved the story. Where's Debbie?"

Kate looks around the desk, desperately looking for a flash of yellow, only half registering the madness of it as she looks up and down Phil's book piles and around the rest of the office.

"Paradise Living has offered us some extremely lucrative advertising," says Phil quietly. "It's too much to refuse. It would be diplomatic if we stopped the story."

Kate can feel her stomach tensing. She worries that she will cry, and she feels absurd for it.

"Diplomatic? How could you? After all the articles we've written about Paradise Living and how they're messing up the Brixton we know and love. It was you who asked me to write this story in the first place! That's not diplomatic, that's selling out."

She is aware that her voice is coming out of her body louder than she expected. Jay is watching her, half standing in his seat as though he is about to say something.

Phil picks the book up again and then slams it down on the desk.

"Selling out? This is not your newspaper, Kate. Do you think that local papers make any money? No, they don't. You're lucky to have a job. Jay's lucky to have a job." He is waving his arm now, pointing at Kate and Jay and then at himself. "I'm lucky to have a job. I've done my best, but this is just the way the world works. People advertise, and it pays our wages. Stop being so fucking naive."

Kate flinches, tears hot in her eyes.

"And I think you should step back from your involvement in it too," continues Phil. "It doesn't look good to our advertisers if one of my journalists is out there with a placard. I think you've become much too involved personally — this is your *job,* Kate."

She stands up, her body shaking. Jay is standing up too.

"I think that's enough," Jay says firmly.

"I do too," replies Phil, turning in his chair so that his back is facing the room. "Take the afternoon off, Kate. I'll see you tomorrow."

Kate leaves the office crying hot, angry tears, but as she walks farther they become

315

tears of panic. She replays Phil's words over and over in her mind, but it is more than that — it is a feeling of spinning wildly out of control. It hits her outside Sainsbury's and she slumps to the floor.

This is what it looks like to see a person crumple. You think that bones and skin are suitable scaffolding for a person, but when a person is crumpling you realize that we are not built of strong enough stuff. Being a human can be like being a cobweb in a storm.

Kate's are not dainty tears that she can uncry by breathing and sniffing deeply and looking up quickly. They are heaving, wretched sobs that rack her body. They are violent tears that make her shake and gasp for air like a tortured animal. Her brain tells her to stop, please stop, but her heart spills out of her eyes. Her nose streams and sweat drenches her skin. She is drowning in her own terror. She is a soft toy gripped in the teeth of an angry dog and it's shaking her and shaking her.

People walk past her, embarrassed by the sight of her crying on the pavement. The people look to Kate like they are on a television screen. Normal life is suddenly a complex show. People walking and laughing with friends or dashing down the escalator seem like skilled actors, getting through the day and managing to play life with a conviction that Kate suddenly cannot muster.

The attack of the Panic is not a fight she feels she can win. Instead she sits and waits for the pummeling to be over.

Finally a woman with a pram looks down at her and asks if she is okay.

"I'm fine," Kate replies. Because what would anyone do if she said no?

She sits on the floor and cries.

"Kate."

The voice comes to her like a hand, softly prodding her and reminding her where she is. She looks up. Rosemary is standing over her, leaning on her shopping trolley, a look of deep concern on her face. And in that moment there is no one else in the world that Kate would rather see.

"It's okay," says Rosemary, and as Kate pulls herself off the floor the old woman wraps her arms around her and hugs her tightly, fiercely. And she holds her together.

CHAPTER 47

Kate tucks her legs beneath her on the sofa and takes the cup of tea that Rosemary is handing her.

"Thank you," she says quietly, wrapping both hands around the mug for the warmth. She looks out the balcony doors. A butterfly lands on one of the lavender plants and Rosemary's swimsuit drips quietly onto the floor. The sun is high and warm and Kate imagines it sparkling on the surface of the lido. She feels like she has just been shaken awake from a very long sleep full of troubled dreams.

Rosemary sits in the armchair and faces Kate, watching her.

"I guess I should explain what happened," says Kate. She starts to recount the argument with Phil about Paradise Living and the articles, but Rosemary interrupts.

"Right now I don't want to hear what's happening with the lido, I want to hear what's happening with *you.*"

Kate wonders whether there is much difference between the two. She thinks, not for the first time, that it has only been since she discovered the lido — or it discovered her — that she has really started to live. When she floats in the cold water it is as if her sense of self and all the anxieties that are carried with that float away too. She is not Kate in the water, she is just a body, surrounded and protected by water and sky. The water makes her feel like she could do anything.

"I started getting panic attacks when I moved to London," she says, remembering her mother and stepfather driving her from Bristol with all her things, Kate wrapped up in her duvet because it wouldn't fit anywhere else in the car. Her excitement grew as they got closer to the city and her new home. Even being stuck in traffic seemed exciting: the traffic looked different from Bristol traffic with its red buses and beetle black taxis.

"I had always been anxious, but it got so much worse once I was in London," she says. "I loved it here, I still do. But I found myself feeling overwhelmed."

After Kate's parents had left she had gone out for a walk, deciding to leave her unpacking until later. She wanted to smell the new smells and feel the warm pavement under her feet. People walked faster in London and she found herself picking up her pace to match theirs. She loved the music of the people, cars, and buses; she loved the cinema with the film names spelled out in tall letters; she loved the smell of cooking spices and coffee in Brixton Village. She soaked it all in until she felt dripping with it day after day until she just couldn't absorb anything more. And soon she found herself looking at her feet rather than around her; London became a muddle of feet and sidewalks. Every now and then she would look up and find the view terrifying.

"I can't explain it when it happens," she says. "I think of my panic as a creature that follows me and can suddenly kick me in the back of the knees. But it's like it lives inside me, too — sometimes I feel like it wants to rip me apart."

She thinks about the people she lives with whom she doesn't know one bit. She thinks about the people she watches on Facebook, like Joe and her former friends in Bristol, and wonders for the first time whether they really are having the best time or whether, like her, uncertainty sits on their shoulders like a child with its arms gripped tightly around their necks.

Rosemary watches her.

"It has gotten better. I do feel so much better. But it still catches me every now and then. I'm sorry, I feel embarrassed."

"There's no need to feel embarrassed," says Rosemary. "You've seen me when I couldn't look after myself, when I could barely stand. And you looked after me. There is absolutely nothing to be ashamed of."

Kate is crying quietly, the tears dripping down her face without her really even noticing them.

"Have you talked to your family about this?" Rosemary asks.

"I spoke to my sister when she came to visit," Kate replies, remembering her sister's hand reaching out for hers on the side of the lido. "It took me a long time, though, and I still haven't told my mum and stepdad. I don't want to worry them."

She pictures being back in Bristol with Erin when they were young and both still lived together, and the feeling of home fills her up like water rushing into a canal lock. Sometimes she wants to float on this feeling and rush right back into the past. She wonders if Rosemary feels the same way and she reaches for her hand.

Rosemary squeezes it, her skin dry but warm, and doesn't let go. They stay like that for a while, holding hands in the quiet of Rosemary's living room. Both women feel a sense of relief, their hands reminding each of them of something they had nearly forgotten. Rosemary feels Kate's warmth flowing through her fingers and up her veins, feeling like the piece of wool that holds a child's two mittens together, stopping each one from getting lost.

The door buzzes. Rosemary stands up and walks slowly to the phone, listens, and then presses the buzzer. A few minutes later there is a knock on the door of the flat. Rosemary opens it and Jay follows her into the living room.

"I tried your house first," he says. "This was my second choice. I was going to try the lido next."

Kate sits up on the sofa, wiping her face and feeling aware of the mascara rings around her eyes.

"You found me," she says quietly.

"I'll make you a cup of tea, Jay," Rosemary says, disappearing into the kitchen and opening and closing cupboards and drawers, louder than Kate thinks is quite necessary.

"Phil was out of line," says Jay, moving to

the sofa and sitting next to Kate. He looks at her intently as he talks, his eyes bright like a child's.

"He shouldn't be taking the money, and he shouldn't have said any of that to you.

"But fuck him. I have something more important to tell you. I just got a phone call from the *Guardian*. A journalist who works there lives in Brixton and heard about the protest. They want to buy one of my photographs for the paper. They like the story — anti-gentrification, community in the big city, rubber ducks . . ."

He is talking quickly, and Kate can feel his body vibrating slightly next to her.

"The *Guardian*?" she asks, trying to imagine how it would feel to see her name printed in a national paper. She imagines what Erin and her mum would say — how excited they would be. She feels her heart racing.

"But that's not all, they want a comment piece to go with it. An article about the lido and what it means to people and how the community has been fighting to save it. I told them I knew someone but I needed to ask her first. You will do it, won't you, Kate?"

And then he kisses her. He takes her face in his hands. She is so surprised that hers stay by her side. He lets go and steps back, looking dazed.

"I'm sorry," he says. "I don't know why I did that. I'm just excited, and I'm really angry too."

"Do you always kiss people when you're angry?" asks Kate.

"Not always."

They both laugh. Heat flows through her as if she has just taken a deep sip of whiskey. She is not sure how she feels about the kiss, or him, but she doesn't mind — she feels comfortable and safe and the warmth tickles her whole body. Rosemary appears with a tray.

"Let me take that," says Jay, standing up and taking the tray with the teapot and mug from Rosemary.

"You need to help me persuade Kate that she's brilliant: the *Guardian* wants her to write an article for them about the lido."

"Kate, that's wonderful," says Rosemary, looking at her proudly. "A byline in a national paper!"

Kate blushes.

"I'm not sure I can do it," she says quietly. "I just write about missing cats and dogs for a local paper."

She thinks about the first day of her journalism master's program and how confidently the other students had spoken about their achievements — and how many achievements there had been. To them the world was something to conquer and they were determined to get from it what they wanted, what they deserved. They were each confident of their own name and its right to be printed: Kate never felt certain of hers. She remembers the classes where they would critique each other's work. Comments and opinions flowed easily from her classmates but she struggled to take their words as a comment on something she had created outside of herself, rather than a personal attack. It was impossible for her to untangle what she wrote from who she was.

"Oh, no, you write about much more than that, Kate," says Rosemary. She walks slowly to the bookshelf.

"Tell me this is just about cats and dogs," she says, handing Kate a scrapbook. It has a plain red cover and Kate can see the edges of newspaper poking out from inside. She opens it and sees her words staring back at her: all her articles about the lido are carefully stuck on the pages. Her other articles are there, too — all the stories she has written since Phil gave her a chance and she started writing real stories for the paper. She imagines Rosemary cutting out each page from the newspaper; the slightly jagged edges of each page failing to hide the shaking of her hands. Jay's photographs are there too. Kate looks at the pictures of Rosemary and the other swimmers smiling at her or staring defiantly into the camera.

"You can do this, Kate," says Rosemary. "Tell our story."

"Only if you help me," replies Kate.

Jay clears his throat.

"I think I should leave you to it," he says.

He looks at Kate for a moment as though he is going to say something more, but instead he nods at them both, realizing that the most important thing now is for Kate to write her article.

After the front door clicks shut quietly behind him, Rosemary and Kate sit next to each other on the sofa and Kate takes her laptop out of her bag, trying not to think about Jay and the kiss.

"I don't want to just write about why I love the lido," she says. "It should have your story in it, too — yours and George's." Rosemary nods and smiles, taking a quick glance at the photo of her and George on their wedding day, the two faces smiling at them.

As Rosemary talks, Kate writes and feels herself relaxing as she does so, as though she is drinking a hearty soup and getting stronger sip by sip. They drink wine and talk about the lido and George and the people they have met there. When the article is eventually finished Kate saves it as "The Lido" and emails it to Jay before she can change her mind.

CHAPTER 48

After Kate goes home, Rosemary chooses a record and puts it on the player. She rarely listens to music on her own but tonight she lets it fill her apartment. She imagines her neighbors pricking their ears up in surprise. Perhaps they will wonder if their old neighbor has died and a new young couple has moved in — it would seem the only reasonable explanation for the sound of the Beatles coming through their walls.

She places the sleeve of *Please Please Me* on the table, looking at the faces of the four young men staring down from the top of a flight of stairs.

George's love of the Beatles had surprised him. He didn't like the fuss around them — he didn't like fusses in general. But he did like the Beatles. He bought the record on his way home from the fruit and vegetable shop one day, the album and a bag of carrots under his arm. They listened to it and danced together.

As she listens Rosemary remembers Brixton as it was then. She remembers the old red double-decker buses, nothing like the imitation ones on the streets today. She remembers Granville Arcade bursting with color and flavors: it was where she and George discovered sweet potatoes and okra for the first time. George didn't think of the stallholders, like Ellis's father, Ken, as competition — he talked with them like old friends, his kindred spirits who loved the earth and its bounty as much as he did. He was as excited as a puppy as he sniffed the skins of mangoes and examined the tough flesh of wrinkled pumpkins. As he discussed the vegetables she wandered among the other stalls looking at the bright West Indian fabrics that hung like folded sunshine. The newspaper headlines always surprised her at the time: she wondered if the journalists who wrote about "The West Indian Problem" had ever tasted a sweet potato.

It was around that time that George started to teach at the lido. On Sunday mornings he would head to the pool, a towel slung around his shoulders and a tune on his lips. Rosemary came with him and swam in the free lane and then sat on the decking, watching George show the children how to doggy paddle or front crawl or dive depending on their age. The younger ones would beg him to show them a swan dive. He would stand on the side of the pool and suddenly pretend to trip, turning it into an elegant dive as he fell. It made the children scream with laughter.

There was one girl, Molly, who was afraid of the water. Her mother wanted her to learn how to swim, so she sent her along with her older brother every Sunday. Her brother would jump into the pool and immediately start swimming a splashy front crawl, but Molly would stay by the steps, frowning seriously in her flowery swimsuit and gripping onto the ladder.

But one day she did make it into the water. George cheered and held on to her, keeping her afloat. Rosemary asked her after the lesson what had changed.

"I'm still a bit afraid," said Molly, "but the swimmers looked like they were having fun. I didn't want to be left out. So I told my afraid to go away."

Rosemary wonders if Kate's panic will ever stop chasing her, or if she will learn how to tell it to leave her alone. And what is Rosemary afraid of? She thinks of the lido and George breaking the surface with his body as he dove into the water. She is terri-

fied of waking up one day and feeling lost
— the places she and George loved having
all gone for good.

CHAPTER 49

Seeing her own name, "Kate Matthews," printed alongside her article in the *Guardian* feels surreal but thrilling. Kate looks at it again and again, rereading her words about the lido, its potential closure, and Rosemary and George's love affair with it (and each other). Her phone rings twice, both early in the morning. Her mum and Erin have been out to buy copies as soon as their local shops opened.

"I'm still in my pajamas," says Erin on the phone. "I explained to the shop assistant that I was buying five copies of the same paper because my talented sister has an article in it! I even showed her the page."

That morning Rosemary greets Kate at the pool waving a copy. She has already asked Ahmed to pin a cutting to the noticeboard and has attached copies herself to the mirrors in the changing rooms. Rosemary's pride, and the excited morning conversations with her mum and Erin, cheer Kate up, making her forget for a moment the argument with Phil and the fear around the closure of the lido. She can't stop smiling.

Over the course of the week, Kate's article and a heat wave bring more swimmers to the lido. Brixton swelters. On Saturday, several people tell Ahmed that they read about the lido in the paper and have made the trip there specially. He hands out leaflets to everyone who comes in. Geoff is interviewed on the local radio, and then on Radio 5 Live. Soon the "Save Brockwell Lido" Facebook page has hundreds of likes and the petition has been signed by nearly nine thousand people.

A queue tangles into the park.

"We've been waiting for hours," moans a teenager, scuffing her shoes on the pavement and hugging her swimming bag across her chest.

"What would be the point in doing something people didn't want to queue for?" says her father. "A long line shows you something must be good. You just need to be patient. Cheer up."

Telling a teenager to cheer up is like telling a plant to water itself. It would if it could.

The teenager waits in the line, focusing all her energy on hating her father. Later on when she is inside the gates she will have to focus on not having fun. Every now and then she dares a smile and then checks around her guiltily in case anyone spotted her mistake.

For many children, the lido is the only beach they know. They lie on towels stretched out on the concrete and imagine they are dozing on beds of sand. They don't know that salt water doesn't taste the same as chlorine.

"Don't let them catch you," says a little boy. "You'll get eaten."

Adults are sharks and children are fish. It's so obvious that the children wonder why the adults look so confused as the children splash screaming away from them. A little girl squeals. She is littler than the boy and he suddenly remembers his position as Older Brother.

"It's okay," he says. "You're just a fish but I'm a dolphin. Sharks don't bother with dolphins because they don't taste good and besides a dolphin is as big as a shark. If you ride on my back, you'll be safe."

Little Sister grabs tight around Older Brother's neck and is the safest person in the pool.

Their mother watches and wonders at the fragile world her children live in. What does it look like to them? She holds her book open on the pool deck but can't remember any of the story; she is too involved in peering over the top at her children playing in the water. Will they remember playing here when they are older? And will she be able to give them a childhood that they remember as having blue and sunny skies?

A man lies on the edge, his arm trailing into the water. Sunglasses balance on his face and he looks through them at the sepia sky. He drags his arm slowly through the water, feeling the ripples that his fingers create on the surface. He is dreaming of Jamaica. He has never been, but he remembers the stories that his grandfather told him when he was young. When the sky is particularly blue in Brixton he likes to look up and imagine he is looking at the same sky that guarded his grandfather when he was a little boy.

On the decking Rosemary leans back in a metal chair and tilts her head to the sky. The sun is warm on her face and chest and she lets a sigh escape her. Two birds chase each other and a plane waves its jet trail behind it like a streamer. She wonders where it is heading: perhaps it is carrying Frank and Jermaine off to their honeymoon. They have left a member of staff in charge of the bookshop and Sprout, the window filled with love stories this week.

Rosemary tries to imagine what it would be like to travel in an airplane. Would her ears pop as the plane took off, and would she feel terrified to leave the ground beneath her? What would her home look like from the air? Would she even be able to spot Brixton and the blue of the lido? She grips the arms of her chair and taps her bare feet on the decking to reassure herself of where she is. A splashing sound comes from the pool as a group of children jump in at the deep end.

"Will you pass me the sunscreen, please?" Rosemary asks, opening her eyes and turning to Kate, who is sitting in the chair next to her. Kate is wearing a swimsuit and has a towel around her waist, sitting with her legs stretched out and crossed at the ankles. A magazine is balanced on her lap. Her face is a poster of contentment.

For once, as well as swimming, they let themselves just relax by the pool. It is an unusually hot Sunday, and it seems as though all Brixton is here lounging by the water. Kate had suggested it to Rosemary, who remembered all the summers she had spent by the lido throughout her life and agreed. She had also been surprised by Kate's suggestion of doing something so indulgent as lazing in the sun and thought it would be very good for Kate.

Rosemary takes the sunscreen bottle from Kate and rubs the lotion into her face and onto the tops of her shoulders. She loves the smell. In the summer she would rub it into George's back, enjoying the feeling of his firm body under her hands. When she finished she would kiss his shoulder blades, tasting his sweat and the sunscreen and the tang of chlorine.

"Pass me one of those," says Rosemary, pointing at the pile of magazines next to Kate's chair. Kate looks at the pile and back at Rosemary.

"Really? They're rubbish, I'm sorry," she says.

"I need some rubbish," says Rosemary, reaching for the magazine that Kate passes to her. "It's too sunny for Shakespeare."

She takes the magazine and sinks back into her chair, flicking open its glossy cover. The two women sit for a while until Rosemary breaks the silence by snorting loudly. Kate looks up at her.

"What is it?" she asks.

"Nothing, nothing, I'm sorry."

But after a few minutes Rosemary snorts again, and this time her snort turns into laughter that she can't control.

"What's so funny?" asks Kate, rolling up her magazine and lightly batting the side of Rosemary's chair with it.

"Is this what you young people care about now?" asks Rosemary, pointing at the magazine in her hands.

She picks it up and reads out loud: "Are you too self-obsessed? Turn to page thirty-four. Eight flawless foundation tips every woman MUST know. These three stars wore the exact same dress to a party. Stuff you think he wants in bed, but really doesn't. The 'superfood' that is actually making you gain weight. Fear of missing out could be ruining your life. What your social media profile says about your love life . . ."

There is something about Rosemary's serious voice reading out the words that sounds absurd.

"Stop it, stop it," Kate says. "I get it."

"Honestly, though," says Rosemary once Kate has stopped laughing, "I'd give anything to have my good knees back, but I wouldn't want to be your age again now."

"I'm going to swim," says Kate, standing

up and dropping her magazine and towel onto the chair. "Can I get you anything?"

Rosemary shakes her head and waves Kate away. She places the magazine back on the pool decking and watches as Kate turns and slips into the water in the shallow end, ducking underwater before she begins her slow breaststroke.

As Rosemary watches Kate she wonders what keeps her up at night and what she worries about as she falls asleep. And what was she like at Kate's age? She was already married, living in her flat with George. But she remembers the insecurities. It was rare that she got dressed up and went out, but each time a dinner party or the Christmas dinner with the other library staff came round she would stand in front of the mirror asking George to tell her if the dress was too short or too long, whether her makeup was okay, and if her hair looked fussy or too plain. He always smiled and told her she looked beautiful but she didn't believe him. She would believe him now — she was beautiful. She hopes Kate realizes it before she is eighty-seven.

Rosemary closes her eyes, the sun pink behind them. She listens to the familiar sound of splashing and voices and a train on the other side of the park until the noises

339

don't sound like noise anymore.

When she wakes up Kate is climbing out of the pool.

"How was the water?" asks Rosemary, picking up the magazine again and trying to pretend she wasn't sleeping. The magazine is upside down.

"Lovely, of course," says Kate, smiling. They watch the water together for a moment.

"You're burning on your shoulders, Rosemary. Let me help."

Kate squeezes some sunscreen onto her hands before Rosemary can object. She stands behind Rosemary and places her hands on her shoulders, rubbing the cool lotion gently into the bare skin between the straps of her swimsuit where Rosemary cannot reach.

The feeling of Kate's hands on her skin makes the hairs on Rosemary's arms stand up on end. She feels warmth spreading up her neck and down her spine. Kate's fingers rub gently and Rosemary blinks quickly, the feeling of hands on her bare skin making it hard to breathe. She closes her eyes. Droplets of cold water from Kate's hair fall onto Rosemary's shoulders and make her skin tingle. A warm breeze tickles her toes and the sun kisses her face. Her body feels like it is smiling, singing, and weeping all at once.

"I'm just going to put on a little more, I don't want you to burn," says Kate, squeezing more sunscreen onto Rosemary's shoulder blades and continuing her gentle massage.

Rosemary relaxes into her chair. She is finding it hard not to cry at the feeling of being touched on her bare skin.

"There we go," says Kate, gently holding Rosemary's shoulders with both hands for a moment before removing them.

"Thank you," says Rosemary, taking a deep breath.

"I'm just going to change into some dry clothes, I'll be back in a minute," says Kate, picking up her bag and walking toward the changing room. As she walks away Rosemary looks up and notices a burned patch between her shoulder blades.

CHAPTER 50

When Kate wakes up it is already bright
outside. She opens her window while she
gets ready. She can hear two children playing in the next-door garden before school;
she imagines them muddying their school
uniforms while they play, or perhaps they
are still in their pajamas. They giggle and
shriek like drunk monkeys until their
mother calls them in for breakfast. The
sound makes her think of Jay, remembering
his face lighting up when he first spoke to
her about his nieces and nephews. They
haven't spoken about the kiss. Every now
and then since it happened she has caught
him looking at her in a way that makes her
feel self-conscious, but not in a bad way.
Like there is a bright, warm light shining on
her. He hasn't brought it up, so she hasn't
either. Instead they have carried on as
before. She can't decide whether she minds
or not. She has thought about calling Erin

to talk to her about Jay, but her own indecision stops her. She needs to work it out in her own head first.

A car backfires in the road, a garbage can lid clatters, and someone shouts, "Fuck you."

Kate dresses quickly, putting her swimsuit on first. It now feels a normal way to start the day: pulling the tight fabric over her bare skin and scrunching up a pair of pants and a bra into her bag.

She pulls on a dress and a black cardigan, and then changes her mind and swaps it for a yellow one.

As she steps out of the front door she is greeted by a blue sky that promises a good day. The door of the neighboring house opens and two children in too-big school uniforms waddle out like ducklings, followed by their mother who is carrying two sports bags and has a book bag slung over her shoulder. She nods at Kate, who nods back and smiles.

"We like yellow," says the older child, pointing at Kate's cardigan. Kate suddenly realizes that apart from school uniforms and funerals you very rarely see children wearing black, and she wonders why she ever wears it herself. Black clothes never bring compliments from small children. She

343

thinks about the outfits that she used to wear when her mother first started letting her choose her clothes in the morning: tartan leggings and floral T-shirts, bright pink shorts and a lime green jumper, and her frog wellies even in the summer. It took her a long time to realize that her clothes didn't add up to something that made sense, or that it was even possible for clothes to have a right answer like a complicated math formula.

When Erin had started college she no longer had a school uniform and her morning routine suddenly became a lot longer and more complicated. Kate could sense the stress coming under Erin's door like the sliver of light she usually checked for when she went to bed at night.

"Mum, where's that shirt?" Erin would shout down the stairs, wearing her jeans and bra and clutching a towel to her chest.

"It was on your floor so I washed it. It's still drying."

"But I need to wear it!"

"Can't you just wear another one?"

"No, because then I'd have to change my jeans and my shoes."

Sometimes Kate would see Erin sitting at her desk in the morning drying a piece of clothing with a hair dryer.

"Why is your top wet, Erin?" Kate would ask at the breakfast table.

"It's not wet, it's nearly dry. And it's Mum's fault."

"Can't you just wear another one?"

"Oh, don't you start."

The memory makes Kate smile. Erin is still just as concerned with her clothes, but she has relaxed a lot too. Since they spoke at the protest Kate and Erin have been texting each other most days. Kate called Erin the night before to wish her luck at the fertility clinic and Erin asked if there had been any progress with the campaign. It feels good to be speaking more honestly with her — as though Kate has finally found a friend who was always there but whom she just never noticed before.

Kate locks the front door and starts her walk to the lido. A fox crosses the road in front of her and gives her a sheepish glance, making her think of someone heading home after a night out passing people on their way to work. The bins need collecting and the air smells of rubbish. A purple buddleia blooms outside one of the houses on her street, radiating a heavenly smell. As Kate passes she thinks that this is what her city is: the sweet and sour next to each other.

The lido is empty. The morning sun

makes the pool's surface look like a sheet of tinfoil. A fleece is flung over the back of the empty lifeguard's chair.

As Kate approaches the reception desk she wonders if Ahmed passed his exams. He won't know for another few months, and she remembers the painful wait after she did her A-levels. The summer was heavy with anticipation and her friends drifted apart, not wanting to see one another and be reminded of their own worries. When August finally came round she was too nervous to open the brown envelope herself. Erin did it in the end. She ripped the top of the envelope like she was a child tearing the paper off a Christmas present, but she was surprisingly gentle when she told Kate the results (lower than she'd hoped, but good enough to get into university). Kate wonders how Ahmed will approach that brown envelope. Will he open it himself? Will he do it straightaway or nurse the envelope for a while before tentatively peeling at the corner, his bedroom door firmly closed and his family trying to hide the sound of their breathing on the other side?

She wants to tell him that she knows how he feels but he is not at the reception desk. Neither are any of his colleagues. The desk is empty apart from a rubber duck sitting

346

by the till. It's been there since the protest photoshoot but it is the first time that Kate has noticed it. With the absence of people it is as though the rubber duck is the guard of the lido. Kate nearly asks it where everyone is, before remembering that it is made of plastic.

That's when she spots movement in the café and hears voices inside. The last time she was in there was for Frank and Jermaine's wedding. She thinks about the paper flowers and the bow on Sprout's collar as she pushes open the door.

Sprout bounds out of Kate's thoughts and across the room to her, brushing white fur against her legs.

"Hello, lovely," says Kate, taking the dog's silky ears in her hands and stroking them. Sprout's tail thumps heavily against her calves. Kate senses that people are watching her before she sees them. She looks up.

Everyone's clustered around the café tables, some sitting and some standing or leaning against the coffee bar: Frank and Jermaine (just back from their honeymoon), Hope, Ellis, Jake, Ahmed, Geoff, and the rest of the lido and café staff as well as the other faces that frequent the lido like the weather. The teenage boy with his jumper zipped high up to his chin; the new mother with the sleeping baby resting on her chest, its mouth slightly open and a patch of dribble on its mother's shirt. The back-stroker and the yoga swimmer, the woman who wears her nudity like a ball gown in the changing room, the friends who share shower gel and gossip, the man who wears the wetsuit and the snorkel. And in the middle of them all is Rosemary.

"I wondered when you'd get here," she says. Her hands are wrapped around an empty mug of tea. Ellis has his hand on the back of her chair.

"What's happened?" asks Kate, standing up and letting Sprout go. The dog weaves between Frank's legs and lies down on his feet.

"It's over," says Rosemary. "They've won."

"What do you mean?" asks Kate.

"We have four weeks," Rosemary says, too loudly. Her voice is shaking. "Four weeks." She almost shouts her last words and a baby starts crying. The young mother stands up, holding her child closer to her chest and swaying her gently. Kate has never heard Rosemary shout before and is shocked by it.

"I'm sorry," Rosemary says quietly. The mother shakes her head and smiles kindly. She bounces her baby as she walks, making "shh" noises. She reaches the other side of the café and pushes open the door and the sun splashes her in gold as she paces alongside the pool. For a moment Kate imagines that everything is fine. The lido is still there, looking just as beautiful as ever. Perhaps there has been a mistake, and there is still something they can do.

"Who told you?" Kate asks Rosemary, turning back to face her. She meets her eyes and barely recognizes them, they are so full of anger and sadness.

"I got a letter from the council," Rosemary says. "They sent one here, of course, but they sent one to my flat too. I wish they hadn't done that."

Kate meets Rosemary's eyes.

"I know I should have called you," says Rosemary, "but I knew I would see you here for your morning swim. I didn't want to tell you on the phone."

Rosemary looks down at her feet.

"They're fucking bastards," says Ellis, turning away from the group and leaning against the coffee bar.

"What are we going to do?" says Kate.

"Nothing," says Rosemary. "It's over."

"It can't be over," says Kate. She looks around the room at the faces that are written with disappointment. As she watches

349

them the Panic creeps out of its box inside her.

"I read the letter too," says Jermaine. "And I'm afraid I think this time it really is. The council members have decided to accept the offer from Paradise Living. They say they tried to find alternatives, but in the end there were none. The lido has four weeks left and then it will close. And then as soon as the sale is completed, Paradise Living will be the legal owners. From then, they can do what they like with it. Which we all know means closing it to the public, turning it into a private club for their tenants. Filling in the pool and turning it into tennis courts."

Kate's stomach churns. The cloud that she has managed to chase away for so long comes to rest above her head and a numbness flows through her. She hates herself for promising to help, for caring, for failing.

No one knows what to say so they say nothing, looking down or out at the lido. Kate watches Rosemary in the middle of them all, her face pale and her eyes turned to the table. After a while Rosemary starts to speak again, her voice softer now and shaking.

"I just wanted to say . . . ." Her voice wobbles and she coughs quietly and then starts again.

"I just wanted to say thank you."

She looks up at Kate, fixing her with her bright blue eyes, shiny with tears. Looking at her, Kate's eyes fill too. She brings a hand to her face. Then Rosemary turns and looks at the others, too, the sad huddle of misfit friends who came together to try to save their lido.

"Thank you for trying," says Rosemary. "It means a lot to me that you cared that much. And I know it would mean a lot to George too."

Kate notices Rosemary's voice catch as she says his name, and it makes her eyes swim with tears again. Kate pictures the photograph of Rosemary and George on their wedding day that she saw in Rosemary's flat, and George's black recipe book that now stands proudly on her shelf. She remembers the first image she saw of the lido on the front of the flyer Rosemary made: an image of a man diving into the still water.

The lido started as part of Kate's job, but it has become so much more than that. She has learned to swim again, but more than that, she has remembered how to live. Helping Rosemary Peterson save Brockwell Lido was a way of proving something to herself.

But now that is all over. She has failed.

"We did our best," Rosemary continues, "and I really appreciate that. But sometimes our best is just not good enough."

Kate listens to Rosemary and feels something inside her break.

Around her, the others try their best to offer comfort. Hope moves her chair closer to Rosemary and rests her head on her shoulder, but Rosemary doesn't move — it is as though she is frozen in her chair, facing out and watching the water.

Eventually the group reluctantly loosens: the swimmers have to go to work or school or home. They leave the café quietly. Frank says a sad goodbye then links arms with Jermaine, calling Sprout to follow them. Ellis, Jake, and Hope do the same, moving close to Rosemary and trying to find some soothing words, before disappearing quietly. Rosemary ignores them all, unable to meet their eyes. Kate doesn't want to leave Rosemary alone but is late for work.

"Please," says Kate, fighting back tears as she looks at Rosemary, "can I at least walk you home?"

Rosemary shakes her head.

"I just want to be on my own," she says.

So Kate steps out into the park. The day doesn't look so beautiful anymore. She walks with her head down.

Once she is alone Rosemary sits at the table looking out at the lido. She watches the light on the water and the clock that kept on ticking even after time stopped. The lifeguard goes back to his spot and the pool gradually fills with people. In the late morning a school group arrives, the children giggling as they fill the colorful lockers with their schoolbags and scramble into the water, energetic because of the prospect of the school holidays starting next week. A few use the ladder but most jump, sending droplets exploding into the air like fountains. The schoolteachers watch from the side, arms heavy with towels and trouser legs wet from the splashing. For now the lido is just the way it has always been. The way Rosemary thought it would always be.

As she sits, she tries to remember it all. The day it opened, the way it felt to swim there during the war, and then George and everything that happened after they found each other in the park on the edges of a glowing bonfire.

The café gets busy around lunchtime, full of prams and groups of women who ask about the vegan brunch, and elderly couples who sit and read the papers. But the waiters don't ask Rosemary to move, instead they leave her at her table with her empty mug and carry on their work around her, seating groups and asking others to wait on the decking. She barely notices anything around her; she is too lost in the past. As she watches the pool she sees herself scrambling over the lido wall at night with George; remembers him proposing in his swimming trunks; pictures him jumping into the water as he taught swimming classes on Sunday mornings, her watching him proudly from the side.

When the afternoon turns into evening the café staff sweep the floor and bring in the chairs from the deck, stacking them upside down on tables. The barista takes the coffee machine apart and cleans it, carefully wiping the shiny metal pieces. Finally Rosemary stands up slowly, stretching her stiff back and wincing at the pain in her knees, before making the short walk to her flat. It might be where she lives, she thinks as she walks, but her home is behind those brick walls and in that perfect rectangle of blue water.

As Kate returns home from work and lies on her bed, Rosemary arrives back in her flat, turning the key in the lock and quietly shutting the door behind her. She drops her keys on the chair and heads to her bedroom, kicks off her shoes, and climbs into bed. On two sides of Brixton the two women stare at their ceilings and cry.

"I'm sorry, George," says Rosemary as she cries.

"I'm sorry, Rosemary," says Kate.

CHAPTER 51

After hearing the news, Kate imagined she might find it too painful to keep swimming at the lido. But when it comes to it, her morning swims are the only thing that get her out of bed. At the *Brixton Chronicle* she avoids eye contact with Phil, working quietly on her outstanding stories and going back to some pet announcements, too, in order to avoid further conversation with him about her work. She settles back into the routine she knows well, typing at her computer and fixing her eyes on the screen. Occasionally she looks up and catches Jay watching her and she gets the sense that he is looking right inside her and can see exactly how she feels. She wonders if she should talk to him, but thinking he can see her pain is too much to bear.

In the lido's final four weeks, it is a lifeline. And Kate holds on to it. In the water she pretends that nothing has changed. How can things be bad when the water is so blue and the sun is now in the full swing of summer? As she swims her wonky but peaceful breaststroke it is as though she is protected, sheltered from the future. She knows the lido will close. But when she swims there is nothing but the feeling of the cold water around her and the hot sun above.

It is not just Kate who frequents the lido throughout July — its final month. It's as if all of Brixton's swimmers have come to say goodbye.

One morning she spots Frank in the water, and the next day there is Jermaine. They nod at each other as they swim past. Another day Kate bumps into Hope, who has brought her granddaughter, Aiesha. She spots Hope on the side, wearing flip-flops, a swimming cap, and a bright yellow swimsuit that hugs her plump body. She holds the hand of a little girl who Kate guesses is about seven.

"Be careful on the side, poppet; it's slippery," Hope says. "Don't forget to put your goggles on now. Let me help you down the ladder, sweetie. Hold the sides tightly; be careful now, my angel."

Kate watches as grandmother and granddaughter slip into the water. Aiesha immediately swims away and Hope is left on her own, a look of total love on her face. As Aiesha stops and puts her feet down, Hope looks up and spots Kate. They wave at each other.

On a Sunday Ellis comes with Jake, who Kate notices is a much stronger swimmer than his father, but who slows down so his dad doesn't get left behind.

As well as the regulars, there are others too. Kate hears them talking in the changing room, saying that they never even knew the lido was there until they read about it in the paper and heard that it was closing. When they say this Kate feels a tightness in her heart. Just like her, they found the lido when it was too late.

There is only one person missing. Kate swims on her own without her friend to guide her and correct her corkscrew kick.

Once she has dried off and is dressed again, Kate makes the short walk across the road to the building where Rosemary lives. She looks up at her balcony, spotting it by the pots of lavender. The washing line hangs empty like a bare tree.

When Kate reaches the entrance she presses the buzzer to Rosemary's flat. As she waits she remembers the meal she shared with Rosemary here, back when hope still existed. The sun is hot on Kate's shoulders but her damp hair is pleasantly cool around her neck. After a moment she hears the familiar voice on the other end of the intercom.

"Hello?"

"Rosemary, it's me, Kate."

"Oh, hello," replies Rosemary.

The intercom buzzes softly in both of their ears, as though the phone is afraid of silence and hums gently to fill the gaps in the conversation.

"Can I come up?" asks Kate eventually.

The buzzing seems to grow louder.

"Not today, I'm sorry," replies Rosemary.

Kate doesn't know what to say. Before she can say anything Rosemary continues.

"I'm sorry, I'm just busy."

Kate wants to ask her what she is doing, but the hesitance in Rosemary's voice stops her. Instead, she says, "I missed you at the lido today."

Kate thinks of the first time she swam with Rosemary: how the old woman seemed to become young in the water, and how she, Kate, felt the unsteadier one. She had felt then that Rosemary's strength was tucked away beneath her dry-land clothes, a hidden power unleashed not by a cape but by a navy blue swimsuit.

"Yes, well." Rosemary's voice is quiet. The intercom chips in with its gentle buzz. "Will I see you there tomorrow?" says Kate.

"No, I don't think so."

Despite being on the other side of the road, Kate can still hear laughter from over the walls of the pool and the background noise of conversation coming from the queue that lines up outside the entrance. Kate hears Rosemary sigh.

"I just can't," she says.

"Okay, then," Kate says after a while. "But I still hope you change your mind."

After one last look back up at Rosemary's flat, Kate crosses the street toward home. As she walks, her hair dripping down her shoulder blades and the pavement hot beneath the thin soles of her pumps, she hears Rosemary's voice in her head. *I just can't.*

She knows that it must be hard for Rosemary but she worries that despite it all, Rosemary will regret not coming in these final weeks. And Kate misses her. Swimming at the lido in the final weeks has been better than not swimming. Realizing that she will never swim in the lido with Rosemary again makes a suffocating sadness rush through her. Kate walks more quickly down the street before the Panic can catch her, or the knowledge she is all alone again.

CHAPTER 52

The sound of splashing pierces the quiet of
Rosemary's flat. She shuts the balcony
doors and the lido is silenced. The room is
quiet again.

Rosemary pulls the curtains across the
doors and the living room falls into a cool
blue shadow. It is a mess: boxes are scattered on the floor, books are piled underneath the bookshelves, and black garbage
bags bulge in the corner. It is the kind of
mess that typically comes from a thorough
housecleaning.

She had started with the bookshelves,
removing each book and dusting it and wiping the shelf. It took so long though that
she had to stop halfway through. Half the
books sit on the floor waiting to be returned
to their clean shelves. The furniture is in
disarray. She managed to pull the sofa out
so she could vacuum behind it, but then
she couldn't seem to push it back in place

so it juts out into the room.

As she cleans she listens to today's voice-mail messages, the voices of her friends filling the corners of her flat like perfume.

"I took Aiesha to the lido this morning," says Hope as Rosemary reaches for the feather duster. "She is swimming so well now. She doesn't even need to use water wings. I wish you could have seen her."

Hope clears her voice and Rosemary turns from dusting the coffee table to look at the machine, waiting for her friend to continue talking.

"I will pop in and see you again tomorrow. I know you've said you can't, but I hope I can persuade you to come and swim. I know it's hard, but it's not long now. I hate that you are missing it. Anyway, goodbye for now, I'll see you tomorrow."

The machine clicks and Hope's voice changes into a deeper voice, a man's voice. The voice coughs.

"Mrs. P? It's Ellis. Just calling to check on you. There's a bag of tomatoes and this season's strawberries with your name on it when you're ready to come and see me next. Well, that's all really."

He coughs again.

"Goodbye, bye."

"Goodbye," Rosemary replies. Her friends

had all been keeping an eye on her, she knew it. It was as though they were taking turns in either calling or coming to visit. Each time they tried a new tactic, trying to get her to leave the flat and go to the lido. But none of them had managed it.

She puts down the duster and looks around the room. With all the boxes and bags and disturbed furniture it looks as though she is moving out or going on holiday. But where would she go? She sits down on the floor and leans against the sofa, remembering Kate sitting there and typing on her laptop while Rosemary slept through the flu. It is quite comfortable there. Even though her flat is on the third floor, sitting on the carpet makes her feel close to the ground and it slows the spinning inside her head. She wants to lie down so she does, slipping down the side of the sofa and stretching out on the floor. Crossing her hands on her stomach she lies there and stares up at the ceiling.

There is a thin crack branching out from the lamp in the center of the room and a patch of peeling paint in one corner. She wonders if she could paint it but she can't remember where the paintbrushes are. Perhaps she threw them out, along with the stepladder and the electric drill.

She suddenly feels exhausted. *It must be the tidying,* she thinks. She has done too much too quickly. She closes her eyes. Even with her eyes shut she can see the thin crack and the peeling paint; she tries to focus on it instead of the blue sky and rolling clouds that are trying to fill her mind. Perhaps her neighbors have some paint. She will ask them in a minute.

Rosemary is woken by the sound of a knocking on her door. She sits up quickly, feeling dizzy as the blood fills her head. Steadying herself against the side of the sofa, she stands up slowly and shuffles to the door.

"I'm coming, I'm coming."

She opens it and is surprised to see Jay standing in the corridor.

"Rosemary," he says.

"Jay."

He almost fills the doorway, his scruffy hair glowing around his head as though he is standing in front of a bright lamp. He wears a kind smile, but Rosemary frowns at him.

"How did you get up here?" she says, peering around him down the corridor.

"Someone let me in downstairs — can I come in?"

"Well, I suppose you're here now," she

365

says, turning back into the flat. He follows her, closing the door behind him. He looks around the room, taking in the mess, the rearranged furniture and the bags in the corner.

"I'm tidying," says Rosemary, sitting down on the sofa.

"I can see that."

She sits and watches him, not saying anything.

"Shall I make us a cup of tea?" says Jay after a while.

"I've just made one," she says, picking up her cup and taking a sip. It is cold.

"Oh, I must have fallen asleep for longer than I thought," she says, handing him the mug.

"I'm sorry, did I wake you?"

She waves her hand and shakes her head. She wishes she hadn't said anything; she is embarrassed to have fallen asleep in the middle of the day. What time is it? She looks at her watch: one fifteen. Jay carries the mug into the kitchen. He returns a few minutes later with two steaming cups. He hands one to Rosemary and then sits down next to her. They sip their tea.

"How is Kate?" Rosemary asks after a few sips. "She has tried visiting. And phoning."

"She's quiet," Jay replies. "Really quiet.

She keeps her head down at work. I've been trying to cheer her up but it's hard to know what to say. She doesn't want to talk. I think she's just so disappointed. I'm sure you both are."

He turns to look at her. His fingers are wrapped together around his mug and Rosemary thinks he looks like a worried little boy. It makes her sad, but despite her reluctance to let him in, there is also something nice about having him there sitting next to her. Being with him makes her feel as though she is reaching out to Kate and holding her hand, but without having to look at her face and see the sadness there or the reflection of her own sadness in her eyes.

"She really misses you, Rosemary. And I know it's not my place to say it, but I really think you should go and visit the lido. There are only a few days left — you should be there, not stuck up here. I know it's hard but I worry that you will regret it if you don't go. You need to say goodbye."

He lets out a deep breath, as though he'd been practicing the speech in his head on the walk there (he had).

"Are you on your lunch break?" Rosemary asks.

He looks at his watch. "Yes, but I've got a bit more time."

367

"Thank you for coming, I do appreciate you using your lunch break to come and see me. But as you can see, I'm very busy. I should have started my spring cleaning a long time ago. There is really a lot to do. I just don't have time to go swimming."

She stands up but then sits back down again as though someone has pushed her heavily into the sofa. She sighs and looks at him. His green eyes watch her, waiting for the truth.

"I just can't say goodbye," she says eventually, quietly. She looks from Jay down to her hand and twists her wedding ring around her finger. It is looser now than it used to be — her body may have filled out but her hands have become thinner. She twists it around and around.

When George died two years ago she went to the lido after his funeral. The ceremony was in the morning. The mourners were a small group: local people and a few of their childhood friends, the ones who were still alive, and their families.

"Thank you for coming. He would have been so pleased," she kept saying to people. In her head she wondered what she was saying. He'd be pleased that they'd come to his funeral? How could he be pleased when he was dead? But she still kept saying it; she didn't know what else to say.

She wore a black skirt suit that she had borrowed from Hope. It was too big and the material kept giving her static shocks. She didn't care that it wasn't right, though: the only person she wanted to look nice for was in a wooden box.

"Please, take some sandwiches, they are only going to go to waste," she kept saying as people left the wake. She wrapped sandwiches and sausage rolls in tinfoil and handed them to people like children's party bags. The flash of tinfoil parcels could be seen carried awkwardly against black suits as families headed back to their cars or the bus or walked home.

Once everyone had left she sat and ate a few stale egg and cress sandwiches, realizing that she hadn't eaten all day. Then she moved onto the coronation chicken and the sausage rolls. When she had ordered the food from the caterers she had no idea how much to order. She couldn't imagine people really eating at the wake. But she learned that it wasn't true what they told you: death didn't really make you lose your appetite. People ate and they drank — she was glad that she had decided at the last minute to get some wine as well as tea and coffee.

Rosemary sat and worked her way through the stale buffet. One of the catering staff came into the room to collect the trays and caught her with pastry crumbs on her fingers and on the collar of Hope's black suit. She brushed them off, ashamed, and gave him a particularly large tip.

"Can I help you clear up?" she asked, scooping crumbs off the tablecloth and into a paper napkin, which she folded neatly.

"No, we have everything under control. You should go home, Mrs. Peterson."

She brushed a few more crumbs into napkins, slowly collected her handbag, and said goodbye to the staff, accepting their condolences with a nod and a "thank you."

But she didn't go home, at least not for long. Instead she picked up her swimming things and went to the lido. By the time she arrived it was late afternoon and the sky looked like a bruised peach. The pool was busy with children and the sound of the lifeguard's whistle blowing in an endless loop as the children bombed into the water, splashing everyone, were told off, and then bombed in again.

In the changing room she peeled off her clothes, letting them fall into a black puddle at her feet. In her purse she found a fifty-pence coin in the pocket next to George's picture. She folded her funeral suit into the locker, locked it, and pushed open the changing room door.

The noise hit her first, then the cold. Splashing, children laughing, the lifeguard's whistle, the wind. She walked slowly to the ladder.

As the water took her in its arms she realized the strength of the effort and concentration she had been giving to just staying standing all day. She leaned back and let herself be carried. The cold water felt like hands on her body and fingers in her hair.

Water washed into her ears and over her face and for the first time all day she let herself cry. As she floated she watched the sky and a ball being thrown above her as children played around her. She caught sight of the big clock that had watched her for most of her life.

Turning onto her front she kicked off in a slow breaststroke and she thought about George. George as a young man diving from the high diving board, stretching his arms like a bird shaking its wings. George swimming through her legs underwater. George kissing her by the pool in the dark. George lying in the sun like a lizard and her watching him and loving him. She couldn't swim enough lengths to remember him completely, to remember their life completely.

Around her the children continued jumping onto floats and jumping off each other's shoulders, ignoring the old woman who cried as she swam. They didn't even see her: she was invisible. The one person who always saw her was buried in the cold ground.

She stayed until the lido closed. Cleaners mopped the floor around her as she changed. When she walked out through the reception area she watched the lifeguards pulling the cover over the pool. Her fingertips were puckered and her chest hurt from having stayed in the cold water too long. The bruise had spread across the sky and it was now nearly dark. There was nowhere else to go except back to her empty flat.

When she arrived home she didn't turn the lights on. She put her wet swimsuit in the kitchen sink and walked through to the living room, where she sat in his armchair. There was a blanket on one of its arms and she pulled it across herself, tugging it tightly over her lap and up to her neck. She sat in his chair in the dark all night, staring into the empty living room. As the sun rose she fell asleep.

Now Rosemary looks up at Jay, trying to

think of pulling herself up, up and out of the tears that sit at the bottom of her throat. She thinks of a string lifting her from her shoulders and she shuffles and sits up straighter on the sofa.

"I've said goodbye to him once before, I can't do it again."

"Okay," Jay says. They sit together for a little while longer. Before he leaves he helps her put the books back onto the bookshelves and straightens the sofa back into its place. He picks up the bags from the corner and hangs them over his shoulder as he heads out of the door.

"Tell her . . ." says Rosemary, and then stops.

"I'll tell her," says Jay. She closes the door on him, listening to the sound of the garbage bags rustling as he walks down the corridor toward the lift. She hears the ping of the lift and then the clatter as the doors open and close and then she is alone.

CHAPTER 53

Today is the lido's last day. In the evening Geoff will be closing the doors for the last time. In a few days, Paradise Living will exchange contracts.

The *Brixton Chronicle* office is quiet — Kate is the first one here. Phil arrives shortly afterward but heads straight to his desk without saying hello. Ever since the argument he has been avoiding speaking to Kate or looking her directly in the eye. Kate has taken to wearing her headphones all day. Sometimes she listens to music but a lot of the time she doesn't.

Phil has sent her an email with some admin work to do and she starts silently, trying not to think too much as she types. Jay arrives and they look at each other and nod but Kate isn't in the mood to talk. Their kiss seems a long time ago. She focuses on her screen.

As she types, she wonders if Phil will ever

give her serious articles to write again. She should look for freelance work on the side. It will mean some late nights, but now she doesn't have the campaign to occupy her and will be stopping swimming, too, she has more free time.

And that's when she starts to cry. At first the tears come quietly; they drip down her face and onto her keyboard and she doesn't bother to wipe them away. She keeps staring at the screen but all the words swim into one another. She can't keep quiet anymore and a sob rips out of her chest, making her whole body shake.

Jay is out of his seat and standing next to her, his arms on her shoulders.

"Kate, Kate," he says, his voice muffled through her headphones. She doesn't move or take the headphones off so he pulls them gently off her ears and turns her chair around to face him.

Phil sneaks glances over the top of his computer screen as Jay crouches down and takes Kate firmly in his arms. She lets herself be held and he holds her tightly. She leans her head against his chest and listens to the thumping of his heart through the soft cotton of his T-shirt that smells of coffee and newspaper print.

She wants to say something, to explain

what is pouring out of her, but she can't. She feels exhausted, twisted and squeezed like a wet towel wrung out to dry. Eventually her sobs quiet enough for her to speak.

"I feel like such a failure," she says, "and I can't believe I'm crying again. You must think I'm crazy. Maybe I am crazy. But I'm just so tired. I wanted to get this right. I can't believe it's really going to close — that today is really the final day."

Kate thinks about Rosemary, realizing for the first time that her closest friend is an eighty-seven-year-old woman whom she only met because of a story about a lido that needed saving. She thinks about Rosemary's swimsuit and how it used to hang defiantly from her balcony like a flag.

"It will be okay," says Jay, his arms still tightly around her body. She waits for him to say something else but he doesn't, and she realizes he probably doesn't know what to say, just like she doesn't know what to say, doesn't know how to make herself or Rosemary happy, doesn't know how to fix things, doesn't know what she is doing with her life. Maybe the truth is that nobody really knows anything, they just do a good job at pretending. Most of the time.

"It will be okay," says Jay again into her hair.

By now Phil is standing, hovering next to Kate's desk. She looks up at him over Jay's shoulder and is surprised to see that his face is twisted in concern. He reaches down and pats her shoulder. It is an awkward, shaky pat. She flinches at his touch; she is so surprised by it.

Kate imagines herself floating above this scene right now and looking down on herself: crying, tightly embracing her colleague in the middle of the office, her boss's hand on her shoulder. They are alone, surrounded by messy piles of files and papers. There is a photo of Rosemary by the lido pinned to the board behind her computer. How did she end up here? Outside the office the city spins around them. Libraries close and coffee shops open, stones are thrown through the windows of estate agents, people stand on buses to let pregnant women sit, another lorry hits another cyclist, a wedding party piles onto a vintage double-decker bus, and people swim for the final time in a lido under the sky.

Phil clears his throat as if to speak. Nothing comes out. He coughs and tries again.

"It will be okay," he says, echoing Jay.

"But what if it isn't?" says Kate, wiping her eyes and sitting up a little straighter. She looks at them both, and around the newspaper office. Jay and Phil are quiet.

"What if it isn't?" she says again. Something inside her shifts, like a creature stirring. "I know it's just a swimming pool, but it's not just a swimming pool to Rosemary, or Hope, or Ellis, or Ahmed, or Geoff, or Frank, or Jermaine. All these names I didn't even know a few months ago."

She is looking straight at Phil now, her mascara-smudged eyes holding his gaze firmly.

"There are so many things that seem not to matter. We live with them and we walk past them and we think 'it'll be okay' or 'it doesn't matter' or 'that's just that then.' Cities change and property companies buy out communities to build more million-pound flats, and 'it doesn't matter.' But then one day you wake up and realize actually it does matter. There are so many things that really don't matter, like whether I'm going to have macaroni cheese or spaghetti Bolognese for dinner or whether I look fat in a swimsuit or what my hair looks like today or whether my old university lecturer thinks I'm doing well in life. Somehow those are the things I used to spend my time worrying about and not the other things."

Her voice shakes at first, but it gradually gets stronger, firmer. Jay has let her go and is leaning against her desk, watching her.

"The lido isn't just a hole in the ground filled with water that a bunch of people happen to swim in every now and then. It's bigger than that; it's so big that if you can't see it, you're not using your eyes the way you are supposed to. Meeting Rosemary taught me that. And if it's not the lido, it's the library, or the youth center, or that building where that man who has lived there all his life is getting thrown onto the street. All these things that this newspaper writes about every day, or should do. They all matter. And it's not okay. It's not fucking okay."

She stands up. Phil hops back a little, as though she is going to hit him. She picks her jacket off the back of her chair and her rucksack from the floor.

"Excuse me," she says, "but I have to go now." And she walks out of the office and down the steps onto the street, not looking back. The sun greets her with open arms.

CHAPTER 54

Kate phones Geoff on her way and tells him her plan. He listens quietly as she talks.

"Okay," he says eventually. When she arrives at the lido he is waiting for her by the reception, holding the keys. Ahmed isn't working today. The pool behind is empty — it has already received its last swimmers and is awaiting the final removal of equipment.

"I'm not sure why I'm doing this," he says, handing Kate the bunch of keys, "but it's worth a shot."

"Thank you," she says, taking the keys from him and holding them carefully in her hands like something that might easily break.

"Will you tell the others?" she asks.

"I'll see what I can do."

Then he turns and heads out of the front door for the last time. Kate searches the metal fist of keys for the right one. She hears footsteps — someone is jogging toward her.

She looks up and sees Jay, his camera hanging from one shoulder and a duffel bag slung over the other.

"I got your message," he says, stopping in front of her.

His cheeks are pink from the jogging.

"You don't have to," she says. "It's a mad idea, really — we might get fired. Or arrested."

He steps forward, placing one foot over the threshold.

"I want to," he says. He takes another step until he is inside the reception area. She looks at him as though she is deciding something, and then steps back, letting him in. Together they close the door behind them and Kate locks it. She wants to tell him she's sorry — for being so distant and for barely speaking to him since they kissed. But the thought of the lido keeps her focused.

"Let's get something to cover the door," she says and Jay follows her down the empty corridor. Between them they carry a table from the staff room and prop it in front of the reception doors. Then they search the exercise rooms, carrying furniture to the front of the lido. When they are finished a barricade of tables, chairs, and exercise bikes blocks the entrance.

"That should do it," Kate says. There is another entrance through the café so they do the same thing there, locking the door and moving the tables and chairs in front of it. The room looks bare; the baristas and waiters have already cleared away the coffee machine and their aprons are hung over the end of the coffee bar. Kate imagines them lifting them over their necks for the last time.

There are a couple of tables left in the café and Kate sits down at one, taking her laptop out of her rucksack and setting it up. Then she starts to write.

As she writes Jay explores the empty lido, taking photographs as he goes. The water is still and blue, the empty lifeguard's chair watching over the silent pool. He takes a photograph of the clock and the empty snack shack by reception. The shutters are pulled down, making it look like a beach hut in winter. He walks down the corridors, photographing the afternoon sun catching on dust in the empty yoga room.

As he heads out onto the decking to cross back to the café he hears the sound of voices coming over the top of the lido wall.

"Don't pull the plug on our lido," they shout.

Jay steps back into the café and snaps a

photograph of Kate at her laptop, her face full of concentration. The noise makes her look up. He takes another photo.

"Sorry," he says, "I couldn't help myself. They're here."

She stands up, looking expectantly in the direction of the door. As they walk toward the reception area the sound of voices grows louder. She reaches for his arm.

"Don't pull the plug on our lido!"

Kate and Jay peer through the windows at the large crowd gathered outside, holding placards and a large banner in front of the lido doors. The noise is so loud that Kate imagines they must be wrapping partway around the lido as well, forming a wall of bodies and blocking the entrance. She spots Ellis — he turns and waves at them. Jake is there, too, with Hope, Jamila, Aiesha, and Geoff. Next to them are Frank and Jermaine. Sprout has a flag tied to her collar with "Save Brockwell Lido" written in capital letters. Kate spots the teenage boy and the new mother with her baby on her hip and her husband at her side. The yoga instructor is there, too, along with the lifeguard and the rest of the lido and café staff.

"I can't believe they all came," she says to Jay.

"They wouldn't be here if it wasn't for you," he replies, holding her gaze. She smiles nervously and brushes her hair away from her face.

There is a plump figure at the end of the line whose face Kate can't see. He turns around and smiles — it is Phil. He is holding a placard. Kate can feel her heart beating quickly inside her chest.

Phil turns again and looks through the window, nodding at Kate and she nods back.

"What now?" asks Jay.

"We wait."

CHAPTER 55

The protesters stay all afternoon. Ellis and Jake pass around beers; Frank offers biscuits. Locals walk past and take photographs; some join the line and are handed spare placards. As they stand in the sun Kate sits in the café and writes. She sends a new article to a few national newspapers and local blogs and shares the link to the petition everywhere she can. The number of signatures rises steadily throughout the day. Each new signature gives her a jolt of happiness. She thinks about the people in her community who want to help right to the end to keep the lido open, and she feels less despondent. It might be hopeless, but she is not alone. She just wishes Rosemary were there.

"You better come and see this," says Jay in the early evening. The setting sun streams through the café windows and lights up Kate's hair. She looks up from the laptop.

"Is it the police?"

"Not yet, but I think they might be reps from Paradise Living."

They walk to the reception area and peer through the windows. Hope is standing apart from the protesters and talking to a group of men in suits. Kate spots the councillor from the meetings among them; the rest she doesn't recognize. Hope is holding her placard tightly across her chest and waving her arm. Ellis leaves the crowd and joins the conversation.

One of the men points at the lido; another looks at his watch. Kate can't hear the conversation, she just watches through the glass, wondering whether the police are on their way and how long their makeshift barricade will last. Jay stands close to her and she feels the warmth of his shoulder against hers. After a while the group of men take a last look at the lido and then walk quickly away. Hope and Ellis return to the group. The crowd parts and Hope pushes through, coming close up to the glass so Kate can hear her.

"Who were they?" Kate shouts through the window. "And are they sending for the police?"

Hope shakes her head.

"It was a group from Paradise Living. I

386

certainly gave them a piece of my mind!"
she says. "But they're not doing anything
today — I think they want to get home to
their dinners. But they'll be back tomorrow.
They said we have tonight to clear out of
their building and then they will be taking
action. 'Their' building. The cheek of it.
They don't even care about the lido — and
to hear them call it 'their' building . . . But
I suppose it is, or will be when they exchange contracts."

Jay looks at Kate. The crowd of protesters
are looking at her too. Kate thinks about
the prospect of being thrown out by the
police, of handing the keys over to the suits
from Paradise Living. The thought makes
her feel sick and makes her breathing
quicken. She pictures her Panic, creeping
up to ambush her.

"What do you want to do?" Jay asks. Hope
is still there, standing by the glass waiting
for Kate's response. For a moment she
wishes she could ask Rosemary or Erin what
to do. But then she feels strength rising up
inside her.

"I'm not leaving until they drag me out,"
she says.

Hope smiles and shouts her reply back to
the others so they can hear. The group
outside cheers.

"Are you sure?" says Jay.

"Yes, I'm sure."

Suddenly she doesn't feel afraid. She can see her Panic nearly as clearly as she can see Jay in front of her, but this time she refuses to look it in the eye, refuses to acknowledge it is there. She wants to be here until the very end, doing something even if it comes to nothing. Trying. The lido may still close for good but she wants to know she did everything she could.

"I'll stay with you then," says Jay.

"You don't have to."

"I know."

He watches her and thinks how different she looks now from the girl who used to pass him on the stairs in the office or wave at him across the street. She is just as lovely, but it is as though a light has been switched on inside her. She glows and he stands in her warmth.

CHAPTER 56

Rosemary's flat is still in disarray. The more she tidies, the more mess seems to accumulate. At points throughout the day she can hear cries of "Don't pull the plug on our lido" coming from the park. Occasionally she peers out the balcony window at the protesters wrapped around the lido walls, standing back slightly so she can't be seen, before returning to her tidying. It tires her, and she spends a lot of time napping stretched out on the sofa, trying not to dream about the lido.

As she wakes up from a long sleep she realizes slowly that it is evening and the balcony door is still open. The protesters have fallen quiet by now. The curtains are flapping and the room is shrouded in the near darkness of dusk. A chill rushes through her and she stands up and walks slowly to the bedroom to fetch a cardigan. The bedroom is just as untidy as the living room, with boxes spread out across the floor from her cleaning. She weaves her way through them and opens the doors to her wardrobe, searching for something warm. She reaches up to grab one of the sweaters folded neatly on the top shelf of her wardrobe. As she tugs, she drags down not just the cardigan, but the box that was resting next to it. The box tips, the lid opens, and as it falls to the ground piles of black-and-white glossy sheets come spilling out. Dozens and dozens of photographs. It is raining smiles.

Rosemary watches and waits for the rain to stop. George is everywhere, smiling at her. She kneels down, picking photographs up at random.

George grinning from the diving board, his face turned to her just before he dove off the edge, checking that she was watching him. George stretched out on the side of the lido, a book open over his face, his arms behind his head and his feet crossed at the ankles. George teaching a class of children to swim the front crawl: he is standing on the side of the pool stretching his arms in the air in a mock crawl stroke and the children are watching him and laughing.

She picks up another photograph — this

one of her. She is wearing a striped swimsuit and holding two ice cream cones — in the photograph the one-piece is black and white but she remembers the suit was white and red. The ice cream is dripping down her hands and she is stretching the cones out toward the camera, her mouth open wide. George made her hold them while he took the photograph but the ice cream started to melt until it was dripping off her elbows. He just laughed and laughed.

There is one of the two of them, both leaning on the side of the pool and kicking their feet behind them, water spraying into the air and catching the sun. Hope took that one of them, just before they both ducked under the surface and kissed each other underwater before leaping back up for air.

Here is the lido covered in snow and George in a woolly hat, a scarf, and swimming trunks, standing on the side and grinning. Here Rosemary and George both dive in unison from the deep end. They look like each other's shadow they are so perfectly in time.

She gathers the photographs in her lap, stroking George's face on each one. Her life is spread out around her, disordered. Some of the photos are shadowed by a thumb in front of the lens or have caught the glare of the sun to the point that you can't see the faces. But she remembers what the faces look like. And throughout the photos is the lido, the thread that holds them together, the place they keep coming back to. Their home. She has to do something. It can't be the end.

CHAPTER 57

The crowd stays until it is dark. Kate keeps looking along the line for Rosemary but she doesn't come. She checks her phone for messages, but there are none from her. Kate calls Rosemary's flat but it goes straight to voice mail. She doesn't leave a message; she has tried too many times and knows Rosemary won't answer. But the thought of her alone in her flat not able to come and say her last goodbye to her lido makes Kate terribly sad. She hopes that Rosemary won't regret it once it is closed for good. There will be no chances for goodbyes then.

Instead she texts Erin, telling her about the plan, and about Rosemary's absence. Her sister replies immediately.

"You're awesome! I'm thinking of you. And about Rosemary — maybe she'll come round still. It must be hard for her. Sometimes hope can be the most painful thing."

Kate reads the text back and suddenly

thinks she understands why Rosemary hasn't been in touch, hasn't visited the lido, and won't let anyone see her. Better, perhaps, to cut yourself off and not let anything or anyone — the light on the water or the comforting words of a friend — give you hope.

The crowd breaks apart slowly. Frank and Jermaine wave to Kate through the glass and walk away holding hands, their placards over their shoulders and Sprout trotting behind them. Hope leaves with Jamila and Aiesha, and Ellis, Jake, and Geoff follow behind.

"We'll be back in the morning, dear," Hope says through the glass, before turning and walking away. As she turns to leave, Kate spots a figure walking toward the lido entrance. Kate realizes it is Ahmed. In all the excitement of the day, she suddenly realizes that he was the other person missing from the protest line.

"Sorry I'm late," he says through the glass as he reaches the window and pushes his face up close. "Geoff told me about your plan, but I had my final exam today. I meant to come straight after but my dad insisted on taking me out for dinner."

He blushes, and it makes Kate smile.

"Congratulations!" Kate says. "You're a

free man now!"

Ahmed smiles and stretches his arms out wide as though he were a bird and could take off right then and there.

"Well done, mate," says Jay, raising a hand before remembering the glass. Ahmed raises his arm, too, and they do a sort of salute at each other and laugh.

"I wanted to come and wish you luck for the sit-in," says Ahmed. "But I also wanted to tell you an idea I had — a way we might still save the lido."

Kate raises her eyebrows and looks at Ahmed intently, trying desperately to slow the beating of her heart. Hope is the most painful thing.

"Go on," she says.

"It might be nothing," says Ahmed, suddenly growing nervous.

"Please," says Kate. "We need ideas."

So Ahmed tells them.

"Well, I was thinking about the lido after the exam. I was feeling bad for missing the final day, even though I knew the exam was important. And I suddenly remembered a conversation I had with your sister, Erin, Kate. D'you remember, that day at the rubber duck protest?"

Kate nods, remembering Ahmed and her sister talking intently on the side of the pool.

"Well, I remember her talking about a module she did on the rise of branded places and things — you know, like the Barclays and then Santander bicycles in London, the Emirates stadium . . . And I suddenly thought — if it can work for them, perhaps it could work for the lido?"

As he says it the seed of hope shoots roots inside Kate's chest.

"Go on," she says.

"Well, perhaps we could find a company who might be interested in advertising at the lido. With the press that it's been getting — and hopefully will get now that you've locked yourself in here" — he pauses and they all smile — "well, maybe that might be of interest to an advertiser. I've done some research into some companies and have drawn up a list. And maybe if any of them are interested, it could keep the lido open."

He finishes and puts his hands in his pockets, looking at Kate and Jay, waiting. Kate wishes she could leap through the glass and take this wonderful young man into a big hug.

"It's brilliant, Ahmed," she says. "Really brilliant. And surely it's got to be worth a shot?"

At that moment Kate's phone rings. She

396

looks down and, to her surprise, sees Rosemary's name. She turns it around so that Jay and Ahmed can see who's calling. She takes a breath and then answers.

"Rosemary," she says.

"Kate, I'm so sorry. I made a huge mistake."

Her voice is shaking.

"Rosemary, are you okay?"

Rosemary sniffs and her voice brightens slightly.

"Yes, yes, I'm fine. I'm good actually. But I've just realized what a fool I've been. I should have been braver — it was simple cowardice that stopped me from coming to the lido, and from seeing you, from talking to my friends."

"It's okay," says Kate. "I understand how hard it must have been for you. Must be for you. It's so nice to hear your voice again."

"And yours, too, Kate. Listen, I've been thinking" — her voice is even faster now and sounds stronger — "this can't be over yet. There must still be something we can do."

So Kate tells her where she is, and about her plan for the sit-in.

Rosemary laughs, and the sound of her laughter gives Kate all the strength she could ever need.

"I admit I've heard the sound of protesters, but I had no idea you were locked inside! My goodness. George would have loved that: a proper sit-in. You, Kate Matthews, are much braver than you think."

Now it's Kate's turn to blush as Jay and Ahmed watch her, listening to her half of the conversation. She looks up from the phone at them and suddenly remembers Ahmed's idea.

"Rosemary, Ahmed has had this wonderful idea about another way we might be able to save the lido. I think he could do with someone to help him, but obviously I'm locked in here . . ."

She explains the idea to Rosemary, though she is fully on board anyway.

"Is Ahmed there?" Rosemary says. "Tell him he's a very clever man."

Kate repeats the message to Ahmed, who blushes again, and then she turns back to the phone.

"So do you think you could help Ahmed, Rosemary? You two could go to the meetings together and you could make your case for the lido, just like you did at the town hall."

"Yes," Rosemary replies, "whatever it takes."

Once Kate has hung up the phone, she

turns to Ahmed.

"It seems you have a business partner for your plan."

CHAPTER 58

Eventually Kate and Jay are alone. The empty lido is silent. It feels bigger now, a hollow shell or a castle that they are guarding alone for the night. Kate shivers slightly, wondering if she has made a mistake. But she wants to be here to the end. The lido has welcomed her like a new home and she wants to stay inside the safety of its walls until the very last moment — until she is forced to leave. And hearing Rosemary's voice again, and knowing she hasn't completely given up, has given her a renewed sense of purpose.

"I'm starving," Kate says after a moment's quiet.

"Me too," says Jay. "Shall we see what we've got?"

They walk back to the Lido Café and unpack their bags onto one of the empty tables. Kate brings out a packet of Hobnob biscuits and a quiche in a tin. Jay has sandwiches, KitKats, and two cans of gin and tonic. At the bottom of their bags are more supplies to last for a week — just in case.

"What a feast!" says Kate.

"Did you make this?" asks Jay, pointing at the quiche. Its crust is wonky and slightly burnt at one edge, but it looks good, and Jay suddenly notices how hungry he is.

Kate smiles widely.

"I did!"

She sounds incredibly proud of herself, and it makes Jay want to reach across and pull her into his arms.

It suddenly turns dark.

"Shit."

There is a pale light from the moon outside, but the half of the room away from the windows is plunged in darkness. Jay fumbles his way to the light switches and tries them all.

"They've probably shut off the electricity," he says.

Kate disappears behind the coffee bar and kneels down, searching for something.

"I wonder if they're still here," she says as she searches. Eventually she stands up.

"Here we go," she says. "I thought they had some left over from Frank and Jermaine's wedding. I'm surprised they're still here."

She comes back to the table carrying several large candle lanterns and a box of matches. She lights the candles and the room glows in a warm orange light. The candlelight and their faces reflect on the glass windows. Outside the lido is dark and still.

"Perfect," says Jay, pulling out Kate's chair for her to sit down and then sitting down too.

"Thank you. Shall we eat?"

She pulls a knife out of the tea towel she had wrapped it in and cuts them both a piece of quiche. The cans make a satisfying hiss as they open their gin and tonics.

"Cheers."

"This is delicious," says Jay, taking another bite of the quiche.

"Thank you. I'm not much of a cook but I'm learning. George has been teaching me."

Jay looks confused but Kate explains: she has been working her way through George's notebook of recipes.

She stops.

"I'm so happy Rosemary has agreed to help Ahmed. But do you think she will be okay if the plan doesn't work? I don't know how she'll recover from the loss of the lido.

Her whole life revolves around it.'

They both quietly consider Rosemary and her lido.

"It must be so hard for her," he offers eventually. "Yes, this has been her whole life."

They look out at the lido in the darkness, imagining all the things that Rosemary has seen here and all the people she has met. How many times must she have swum here? Too many to count. They eat the rest of their strange dinner quietly in the candle-light. The summer night presses its face against the window, stars shining in the sky and reflecting on the surface of the pool.

"What do you think will happen tomorrow?" Kate asks eventually, sipping her gin and tonic and feeling a warmth rush to her cheeks.

"I don't know," he says. "We'll probably get kicked out in the morning. Get arrested for trespassing perhaps."

Kate sighs.

"Hmm, yes."

She looks out across the dark water and thinks about all the times she has swum here over the past few months. She lives only fifteen or so minutes away but before being assigned to the story she had never been. She wishes she had known about it sooner.

"I suppose I should feel afraid," she says, "but right now I don't."

She sees herself in the window and for once she doesn't shrink away from her reflection. She holds her gaze firmly. *Here I am,* she thinks. *I am here.*

She turns back to Jay.

She thinks about how much of the past few years she has spent feeling afraid. The Panic has ruled her life for so long. Before she found the lido she felt as though she was balanced on the tip of a diving board, terrified by the height below her. But she is finally not afraid anymore. She is ready to jump.

So she stands up, reaches across the table, takes Jay's face firmly between her hands, and kisses him. He blinks in surprise and then kisses her back. They push their chairs back and stand up awkwardly, their lips still pressed together. Then he pulls her closer to him, their hips touching and his arms wrapping around her waist. His mouth is warm, his beard rough beneath her fingers. She pulls him tighter into her until their chests are pressed together, their hearts beating quickly together like clapping hands. This kiss is different from their first, and she realizes why. It's because this time she is ready — she's ready to be loved.

They kiss in the candlelight, learning each other's faces. After a while they pull apart and cover each other's cheeks, ears, chins, necks with small soft kisses. He kisses her eyelids; she kisses his cheeks. But it is not long before their mouths are together again.

After a while she pulls herself away from him slightly and looks at his face. He looks back, putting a hand on her cheek.

"God, I've wanted this for a really long time," he says.

"Me too."

She only realizes it as she says it. She might have been too afraid before, but this is what she wants. He is what she wants. She kisses him again then untangles herself, catching her breath.

"If this is the lido's last night, I think we should swim," she says, pulling her dress over her head as she says it.

"It would be wrong not to," he replies, unbuttoning his shirt. Their clothes make a trail behind them as they head out to the pool. It has taken her a long time to get there, but she is finally not ashamed by her nakedness. Jay yelps as he climbs in and it makes her laugh. The moon watches over them as they swim in the cold water.

"I'm not used to it!" he says. She laughs again and ducks underwater, her hair spreading out around her like seaweed. She stretches her hands in front of her and opens her eyes, looking at her pale skin and the shape of Jay's body swimming in the distance. She's not sure if it's him or the cold water making her heart beat so fast. She bobs back up for air and swims toward him.

At first they laugh and splash water at each other like children. Then they stop playing and start swimming quiet lengths side by side. He floats on his back and she does the same. She tries to count the stars but there are too many to even start.

They swim until their bodies are tired and shivering. Then they heave themselves out of the water, their skin cold but tingling.

"Towels?" says Jay.

They each take a lantern and their pile of clothes and Kate leads him down the corridor to the reception area, both of them dripping onto the floor as they walk. She searches behind the reception desk and pulls out a box filled with white towels, relieved that the staff left everything intact when they shut up the lido for the last time. They wrap them around each other, hugging each other for warmth before letting go.

"It must be late," she says, suddenly aware of the passing of time as though she has come up for air after being underground. The clock above the desk tells them it is half past midnight.

She becomes aware of the energy she has given to the day: to writing the articles, to sending out the petition, and to caring so much. She is exhausted. Even the relief of hearing Rosemary again and knowing her friend was back on their side had taken its emotional toll on her. She carries the box of towels, her pile of clothes, and her large rucksack, and Jay follows her to the yoga studio. Holding the lantern, Kate looks around until she spots the yoga mats in the corner. She puts down the box and starts dragging mats into the middle of the room, unrolling them and stretching them out in a large square. He helps her until a mattress-sized portion of floor is covered in yoga mats and towels that they drape over like fluffy sheets.

"Perfect," he says.

Kate bends down and pulls a sleeping bag out of her rucksack and opens it over the mats and towels. She only has one, but she thinks it won't matter.

The room glows in the candlelight and the two of them are reflected in the mirror that stretches the length of the wall. On the other side is a long window. Outside it is completely dark. Kate's hair drips onto her shoulders and she hugs her towel tighter to her body and shivers.

"Come here," Jay says, wrapping his arms around her and kissing her. They kiss standing up, then kneeling down together, then they both lie down among the pile of mats and towels. She leans across and blows out the candles. In the darkness he lies behind her and pulls her tightly toward him until they are lying as one S-shape made up of two bodies. She can feel his heart beating against her back as they hold each other tightly.

"We might get arrested tomorrow," she says quietly as she drifts toward sleep, "but I'm glad I'm here."

"Me too."

They fall asleep in pale moonlight that peeks in through the window and shines on the mirror as though on a lake.

CHAPTER 59

The next morning at ten o'clock Rosemary is due to meet Ahmed in a café in Brixton Village. She arrives early and finds them a table in the corner facing the market. She watches people passing by the window or pausing to look inside. It feels good to be out of her flat. After a week of inactivity she can feel a new energy flowing through her, making her jittery and almost but not quite distracting her from the pain in her knees. She taps her hand restlessly on her lap as she waits for Ahmed. Her heart matches the beat of her tapping as she thinks about the lido and how badly she wants this plan to work. When she spots Ahmed at the door, an iPad tucked under his arm, she waves. He asks the waiter for the Wi-Fi code and heads over to the table.

"Don't you look like a new man," says Rosemary, pulling him into a hug. At first he seems awkward but then he lets himself sink into the old woman's strong embrace. "I hear you have finished your exams," she says, stepping back and holding his arms, looking at him and smiling. "Well done, you."

She remembers all the times she has seen him studying at the lido reception, Post-it notes dotted around the desk. The memory of the lido and the thought that it soon might just be a memory sends a pain through her chest, but she tries not to let her smile drop.

"I don't know if I've passed them yet," Ahmed says shyly.

"Oh, I just know you have. Don't you worry."

They sit down together and Ahmed talks Rosemary through the different companies he wants to try and what they should say to them. She is impressed with the spreadsheet he has drawn up on his iPad — it is very neat and she tells him so, causing him to blush again.

Rosemary has never imagined herself uttering the words *Hello, may I please speak to your advertising department?*, but over the course of the morning she uses them nearly twenty times. They take turns calling on Ahmed's phone. Rosemary phones a company, then Ahmed types the information on the iPad. Then Ahmed takes his turn to call and Rosemary writes down the notes.

After several hours they have worked their way nearly to the bottom of the list but have no confirmed meetings. Ahmed sinks heavily in his chair, disappointment spread across his face. Rosemary feels on the verge of tears. But she thinks of Ahmed, and she thinks of George. She tries to think what George would do. George would be kind to this young man.

"I think it's time for some more tea," says Rosemary, patting Ahmed gently on the shoulder before shuffling to the counter. As she goes Ahmed picks up his phone again.

There is a small queue, and as Rosemary waits she spots a stack of *Brixton Chronicle*s by the till. She picks one up and immediately recognizes the face on the front.

"Local Journalist Stages Sit-In to Save Brockwell Lido," reads the headline. The photo is of Kate sitting in the empty café, the doors open as she looks out toward the pool. Next to her is a rucksack with a sleeping bag poking out of the top. *Jay must have taken the photo and sent it in to the paper,* she thinks, and the thought of the two of them there barricaded in the lido behind a wall of chairs and exercise equipment makes Rosemary smile and grow a little taller.

As she makes her way back to the table a few minutes later carrying a tray with the tea and trying very hard not to spill it, she spots Ahmed talking animatedly on the phone. He looks up at her and does a thumbs-up. Her hands shake even harder now, sloshing the milk in the small jug onto the tray. A waiter comes out from behind the counter and helps her with the tray, placing it gently on the table and giving her a little nod. She nods back and thanks him.

By the time she has sat down and wiped up the spilled milk, Ahmed is off the phone and beaming.

"We've got a meeting for tomorrow!" says Ahmed. And this time it's him who leans forward to hug Rosemary.

CHAPTER 60

Waking up, it takes Kate a moment to remember where she is. She looks at the ceiling of the yoga room and listens to Jay breathing heavily by her side. She doesn't want to move so lies as still as she can for a moment, listening to the soft noises in the empty lido. Pipes creak and she can hear the birds outside but otherwise it is quiet. Jay is warm next to her and she edges closer to him, enjoying the sensation of his body. It feels strong and soft and makes her feel as though if she fell over she would be okay. She wraps an arm around him, her heart racing at the feel of his skin on hers. It reminds her of her first swim at the lido: how her heart leaped at the shock of the cold and her whole body seemed to wake up and come to life.

She stares at the ceiling and wonders how long it will be until the police arrive. Will they come today? Or tomorrow? Could they

413

arrest her? And what would that be like? She has never had so much as a parking ticket before. And what about Rosemary? What if Ahmed's plan doesn't work? What will she do when the lido is closed for good, turned by Paradise Living into a tennis court for the rich? The day stretches ahead of her like the depths of the sea that plunge down into darkness. She can't see what is down there. She doesn't want to look. So instead she turns and rests her head on Jay's chest and he sleepily tucks her under his arm.

After a few moments he wakes up, too, kissing her on the forehead as he does so.

"So it wasn't some crazy dream?" he says sleepily.

"Nope, you're stuck here with me, I'm afraid."

He yawns and pulls her closer to him.

"We should get up," she says eventually, and after checking to see no one is outside the window, they stretch and rise from their makeshift bed, passing each other the clothes strewn around it and dressing quickly but unselfconsciously.

Then they return to the café, open the doors onto the lido, and sit down to a strange breakfast of leftover quiche and Kit-Kats.

"It seems weird how quiet it is," says Kate once they are finished and are both leaning back in their chairs watching the water. "It's like everything is okay."

"The calm before the storm," says Jay. "Any news from Rosemary or Ahmed?"

Kate checks her phone and shakes her head. She knows they must be busy working on the plan, but right now Kate feels like she and Jay are the only people in the world, trapped as they are together behind the walls of the lido.

The water winks invitingly in the morning sunshine. She has of course seen it many times before, but she still marvels at the shade of blue. As the water shines Kate walks to the edge. It is just too inviting. This time Jay doesn't join her; instead he stays in his chair, watching her and smiling.

"I can't believe I didn't think to bring a swimsuit to a sit-in at a lido," says Kate as she strips off her clothes. "This is my chance to be the only person to have had the lido all to herself."

Naked on the edge she is aware of Jay watching her. She is conscious of the curves of her imperfect body. But she doesn't mind. She climbs down the ladder and slips into the water.

For a moment she sinks under the surface

and opens her eyes. The pool stretches ahead of her, completely empty apart from a few leaves that spin slowly in the water. It looks like a stage before the actors arrive. Then Kate bursts up for air and starts her wonky breaststroke.

What irony, she thinks as she swims alone through the cold, *to have such calm and such beauty when things are so bad.* It could be her last swim at the lido. The thought rips her apart but the feeling of the water, the sun on the surface, and the simple joy of the here and now holds her together again.

Once she is tired she climbs out, dries off on the side, and pulls her clothes back on.

"God, you are so beautiful," says Jay as she sits next to him at the table. And for once, she feels like she just might be.

By midday, they hear noise over the lido wall.

The protesters are there again with their placards, but this time they are joined by a group of police officers who follow them across the grass. Kate's heart sinks and she feels her skin beginning to prickle. This must be it — they are about to get kicked out or arrested. The keys will get handed to the police and, when the sale of the lido is completed, to Paradise Living. And then it will be over.

She reaches for Jay's hand and he squeezes it tightly.

Kate spots Hope talking to one of the police officers and trying to hand him a placard. Eventually the whole group arrives outside of the lido doors.

One of the police officers is a man in his fifties, with sergeant's stripes on his uniform; the other three are much younger — two women and one young man with a beard. Their uniforms look box-fresh and they seem slightly nervous as Hope again tries to hand them a placard. The oldest officer tries to push through the crowd of people to get to the door, but Hope, Frank, Jermaine, Geoff, Ellis, and Jake form a barrier between the officers and the lido entrance.

"Please step aside, we don't want a fuss," Kate hears the officer say.

"We'd rather not," says Frank. Jermaine stands close next to him, their arms linked together. Sprout barks at their feet.

"I hear there are two people inside there — we want to talk to them."

The officer speaks loudly toward Kate and Jay, who are pressed close to the glass.

"Can you hear me?" shouts the sergeant.

Kate and Jay nod as they peer at him over the top of an exercise bike that is currently forming the front line of the barricade. Jay's hand is still entwined in Kate's. She can feel her stomach churning, her heartbeat rocketing.

"Now I suggest you leave the building voluntarily," says the officer, "otherwise steps may be taken to remove you."

"I really hope you don't mean that, Billy Hooper," comes a voice from behind the group of protesters.

The police officers and protesters turn to give way to Rosemary, who is walking up to the lido entrance with Ahmed at her side. She looks at Kate through the windows and nods, giving a smile that slightly steadies Kate's beating heart.

"Mrs. Peterson," says the officer. He looks down at his hands and suddenly looks not like a fiftysomething officer of the law in a smart uniform, but a young boy in scruffy school clothes.

"Those are my friends inside there," says Rosemary, staring Sergeant Hooper in the eye when he eventually looks up. They look at each other for a moment, and then Rosemary continues brightly, "Now, how are your children? And I heard you just became a grandfather! Congratulations."

After a short back-and-forth with Rosemary, Sergeant Hooper turns back to Kate and Jay, and the group of protesters gathered around them.

"Look," he says, "I'll be honest with you. At the moment you're not breaking the law by being in there. The building's owners — at this stage still the council — need to obtain a court order asking you to leave. After that, if you still refuse to move, then we'll be instructed to come and forcibly remove you."

Kate and Jay look at each other.

"The court order can take several days," says the sergeant, seeing their concerned expressions.

"Well, then," he continues, turning this time to Rosemary, "we will leave you to it for today, Mrs. Peterson. But tomorrow we will be back to check that everything is aboveboard and peaceful. If any damage is caused — then they could be in real trouble."

Kate nearly laughs — why would they damage the very place they are trying to protect?

As he is about to go, the younger officers following closely behind, he turns back and speaks to Rosemary and to Kate who is pressed up against the glass.

"Between you and me, we all think it's a shame to see the lido go," he says. "I used to swim here as a kid — we all did. But I'm afraid the law is the law and whether or not any of us like it, Paradise Living is going to get its hands on this building. It's a done deal."

He nods at Rosemary and turns away, he and his colleagues heading across the grass and away into the park. As she watches them leave Kate's breathing finally returns to normal and she lets go of Jay's hand.

"How'd you do that?" asks Kate. "He seemed almost afraid of you, Rosemary." The other protesters huddled around to hear why Sergeant Hooper was so shy around Mrs. Peterson.

Rosemary waves her hand as though it's nothing. "He used to come into George's shop when he was a boy. His dad was out of work quite a lot and Billy had four brothers and sisters, so George would always put some extra things in the bags free of charge. He tried to do it so no one would notice, but Billy was a smart child."

"That was kind of George," says Jermaine.

"Well, he was a kind man," she replies.

The protesters chat for a while, congratulating one another on their small victory.

"So I guess now we just wait for the court

order?" says Kate to Jay. He nods.

"It could be several days — do we have enough food to last several days?" he asks.

"I'm not sure," replies Kate. "We'll work something out. I hope."

With the new news about the court order, the protesters stay for the afternoon but then decide they are safe to leave Kate and Jay, knowing that no one will be able to remove them just yet.

"See you tomorrow," they shout through the glass as they wave goodbye.

Eventually the only ones left are Rosemary and Ahmed, standing close to the window where Kate and Jay peer through on the other side. Rosemary tells them about the meeting they have secured for the next morning.

"Well, it was Ahmed who did it really," she says. Kate notices how much more confident he looks, as though the exams and his idea have turned him from a teenage boy into a young man. She wishes she could go to the meeting with them.

"But who would guard the lido then?" replies Rosemary. "No, you and Jay need to stay right where you are — keeping our lido safe."

"So tomorrow is the deciding day," says Kate, looking nervously at the three of them.

"I suppose it is," says Rosemary. After that they all fall quiet, each imagining what the next day might hold. The evening shines on them and on the lido, although at that moment no one is there to enjoy it apart from the pair of mallards that drift quietly across its surface.

CHAPTER 61

Ahmed meets Rosemary at the bus stop opposite her flat wearing a suit that is too big for him.

"Sorry about this," he says, pointing at the baggy jacket when he spots Rosemary. "It's Dad's. My mum said she'd buy me my own suit when I pass my exams. If I pass my exams."

"Well, I think you look dashing," says Rosemary. "I've never seen you look so smart."

Rosemary is wearing a pale blue skirt suit. When she put it on this morning she thought the color reminded her of the lido, so it felt appropriate. Ahmed smiles and holds his arm out for her.

"Are you ready?" he says.

"I think so."

"I'm a bit nervous."

"Me too."

Their bus pulls up and with arms linked

together they step on and find two seats near the front. As the bus pulls away and continues down the road Rosemary looks out of the window, watching her Brixton rolling past. They skirt around the park and turn right down Brixton Hill, passing the church where the homeless men sit and drink Special Brew hidden in plastic bags, past the cinema and the road that leads to Frank and Jermaine's bookshop, and alongside the underground station with people pouring out onto the street. She looks down Electric Avenue, trying to spot Ellis, but all she can make out are the crowds of people weaving between the stalls with their striped plastic awnings. Then Brixton becomes the rest of the city and she stops recognizing the streets and the shops. The cafés and parks become someone else's home patch.

They pass through Kennington and alongside the Imperial War Museum with its cannons standing guard outside the entrance. They go past Lambeth Palace, the turrets shining golden in the late summer sun. As they cross Lambeth Bridge both Rosemary and Ahmed look up and down the river on both sides, at the London Eye and the Houses of Parliament in one direction and the towering glass buildings in the other that flash brightly with the reflected light. The bus continues on past Westminster Abbey, Big Ben, and Parliament Square, where a group of protesters hold placards and have tied banners to the railings. Rosemary tries to read the signs but can't quite make them out. She wonders how long they have been there and what it is that they are fighting for. She wonders whether they will win their fight. She hopes that they do.

At Trafalgar Square the bus slows with the traffic, and Rosemary and Ahmed watch Nelson on his column and the bronze lions with their mouths slightly open as though they are about to speak. Tourists and pigeons crowd the square and the living statues of Charlie Chaplin and the Tin Man collect coins in hats on the ground.

Eventually the bus pulls up on Regent Street, its final stop.

"Thank you, driver," says Rosemary as Ahmed helps her off.

The bus pulls away and leaves them standing on the pavement. The stop is outside Hamleys toy store and the street is packed with children and their parents heading in and out of the shop. Hamleys staff stand by the door, some wearing red uniforms, others dressed as children's characters. A group of Chinese students have their photo taken next to a giant bear.

"Excuse me, excuse me," says a mother as she pushes past them, holding her daughter's hand and heading into the toy store. For a moment Ahmed and Rosemary are frozen on the sidewalk, watching the people bustling around them and hearing the buses and taxis passing behind them. A cyclist shouts at a bus driver and a car beeps its horn at people dashing across the road. Above them the pale-fronted terraced buildings tower into the blue sky, decorated with uniform columns and black railings on each tall window.

"Come on," says Ahmed eventually.

Rosemary holds on tightly to his arm as he steers them along the street. Shoppers walk past them, knocking them with their bags or nearly bumping into them as they look down at their phones. They turn onto Beak Street; it is quieter here so Ahmed stops to take his phone out and check they are heading the right direction. Rosemary waits as he looks at his phone and then up at the streets around him.

"Hmm," he says, "we might have a problem. My blue dot tells me we're here but that's not the street we're on. So I'm not sure which direction we need to go."

He looks at the blue dot again, looking around him in confusion.

"I'm sorry, I don't want to make us late." Rosemary reaches into her handbag and brings out a battered old *A–Z* guide. "Might this help?"

Ahmed laughs and takes the book. Together they lean over the pages and find their street and where they need to go.

"Okay, got it," says Ahmed.

"Sometimes you can't beat an old faithful," replies Rosemary, putting the *A–Z* back inside her bag.

They arrive outside the building with a few minutes to spare. The front is glass and they can see inside to the reception where a woman wearing red lipstick sits behind the desk talking on the phone. She has gray hair but she looks very young. *Perhaps she moisturizes really well,* thinks Rosemary, watching her.

Lightbulbs hang from the ceiling by red cords and behind the desk is a rough-looking chipboard wall. The ceiling looks like it is made of wooden packing crates. Maybe this office is new and they only just moved in. It certainly looks quite sparse; next to the reception desk is a glass table with a cluster of chairs in varying heights. There is a beanbag, a high stool, a dining table chair, and a leather armchair. Someone sits awkwardly on the beanbag and checks their watch.

A young man with a ponytail passes in front of them and walks up the steps. The receptionist greets him with a wave and he swipes his card at the gates on the left and continues up some stairs.

Rosemary and Ahmed turn to look at each other.

"Ready?" asks Ahmed.

"Ready," nods Rosemary.

Together they climb the steps and open the doors.

"Hello!" the receptionist says brightly once they reach the desk. "How can I help you?"

"We have an appointment," says Ahmed, reaching into his pocket for a scrap of paper where he has written down the details, "with Tori Miller at ten o'clock. The names are Rosemary Peterson and Ahmed Jones."

The young woman checks her computer screen and nods at them.

"Yes! I'll let them know you're here."

"What's that?" Rosemary asks, pointing to a tall glass and metal machine on one end of the reception desk.

The young woman smiles and stands up. Her top stops just above her belly button, as though it has been chopped off with a pair of scissors.

"It's a smoothie maker," says the young woman, beaming. "Would you like a smoothie? Or a coffee? I can ask our barista to make you one if you like?"

"Oh no, no," says Rosemary, shaking her head. She wouldn't have said no to a cup of tea, but she isn't sure she likes coffee and never knows what all the names mean. Cappuccino, macchiato, flat white . . . The words don't make sense to Rosemary.

"Well, why don't you take a seat for now then?" says the young woman. "I'll take you along when they are ready for you."

They head over to the seating area and Ahmed perches awkwardly on the dining chair. Rosemary chooses the armchair and immediately regrets it as she sinks into the deep cushions as though the chair is trying to swallow her.

Rosemary crosses and uncrosses her hands in her lap. She smooths her skirt and checks her watch. She takes deep breaths, trying to stay calm and not to think about the importance of this meeting. But she can't help it. Images of the lido play out in her mind. The order is jumbled, though: one moment she pictures the lido a few months ago when she swam with Kate for the first time, and then she is back swimming there as a teenager during the war. Then she sees

George, swimming with her after the riots when they both needed calm. She sees him smiling at her and jumping into the water. And then she imagines the lido closed and turned into a private club, the pool cemented over and the lifeguard's chair gone.

"They're ready for you now," says the receptionist. Rosemary opens her eyes and looks up, remembering where she is. Ahmed nods at her. He helps her out of the chair, and together they follow the young woman through the security gates and down a long corridor. At first the woman walks quickly, but once she sees that Rosemary and Ahmed aren't keeping up she slows down and walks just in front of them. Eventually they come to a closed door at the end of the corridor.

"Okay, here we are!" says the receptionist, opening the door onto a large meeting room. A group of about ten people are sitting around a long table. Rosemary feels her hands shaking so holds them tightly in front of her.

"Your visitors are here. I'll leave you to it now."

The group around the table nod and the receptionist closes the door. Ahmed and Rosemary stand at the front of the room in silence.

"Hello, I'm Ahmed Jones," says Ahmed

eventually, after a deep breath. "We spoke on the phone."

Then he remembers his father's advice and walks forward to shake hands with everyone around the table. He tries to keep his hand firm and strong.

The people around the table nod at Ahmed.

"Nice to meet you."

"And this is Rosemary Peterson," Ahmed says.

Rosemary is still standing at the front of the room, unable to move. Ahmed moves back to stand at her side.

"We read about you in the paper," says one of the men behind the table. "It was a lovely article."

"That was Kate," says Rosemary. "My friend Kate wrote the article."

The people round the table nod.

"Shall we introduce ourselves?" says a young woman in the middle, Tori, who tells them she is the head of advertising, and the group then go around saying their names and their job titles. Rosemary tries to remember the names but they and the job titles roll into one another until she is convinced that someone is the head brand director advertising executive.

Once they are finished, Ahmed smiles at

Rosemary, and then at the rest of the room.

"As you know, we're here to propose to you the idea of advertising at Brockwell Lido," he says. "In the summer Brockwell Lido welcomes hundreds of visitors every day. We hope advertising could work well for all of us — we get to keep the lido open, and you get a unique advertising opportunity. The bottom of the pool, for example, could be an excellent place to advertise. Over the past few years there have been dozens of aerial photographs of the pool in papers and magazines across the country, talking about the latest heat wave. But to better explain why this is so important to us, my friend Rosemary would like to say a few words."

He steps back again and nods to Rosemary. The group turn to her expectantly.

"Do you have a PowerPoint presentation?" asks a man at the table.

"A what?" says Rosemary.

"Do you need the computer?"

"Oh no."

"Right."

There is silence and Rosemary suddenly feels uncomfortable in her skirt suit surrounded by so many people who are so much younger than herself. In the lido it never matters — they are all the same once they are stripped of their dry-land clothes. But here, the fresh young group with their similar haircuts and outfits intimidates her.

"Why don't you tell us about the lido?" says Tori. She leans forward, resting her arms on the table. The others turn their chairs so they are facing Rosemary. Ahmed turns to her, too, smiling and trying to encourage her. They all look at her, waiting.

The fear of letting their final hope slip away, of making a mistake, freezes her to the spot. This is her last chance, and she knows it. Rosemary can feel herself shaking, so she closes her eyes and pictures a calm expanse of water. The water is striped with ropes, separating the slow, medium, and fast lanes. On one side a clock ticks, watching the swimmers in the cool water. She opens her eyes.

"In Brixton we have a lido," she says. "And I have been swimming there for eighty years. The lido is my home. But it's not just me — it means so much to our whole community."

At first her voice shakes, but it grows stronger as she tells her story. The group watch her and Ahmed stands close by her side.

"I've learned that more than ever over the past few months. It's funny how it takes the threat of closure for people to realize quite how special a place is. It's like nowhere else I know. Things can be busy and stressful outside, but once you are in the lido everything is okay. When people visit it for the first time they can't believe how calm it is compared to the rest of Brixton. That's why it's so special — it's somewhere to escape to without having to leave your own community. Some people call it Brixton Beach — it's the only beach that many of the children there know. In the summer it is heaving with people. Parents stretch out on towels or swim in the water with their children. You get people of all ages — teenagers trying to impress each other by jumping in, little ones learning to swim in the shallow end, businessmen shrugging off their worries. And me."

She pictures the lido as it would look now in the height of summer: the laughter of the children, the splashing of the water, and the sun warm on her face.

"And what about you?" asks someone at the table. "What does the lido mean to you? There are other pools in London — why fight for this one?"

Rosemary closes her eyes. She sees the cool blue water.

"It's true that there may be many more

important things to fight for and more important things going on in the world," she says as she opens her eyes. "I keep saying to myself: Rosemary, it doesn't matter."

Last night she sat on the edge of the bed and repeated it to herself over and over, trying to convince herself that it didn't matter so she wouldn't have to go through with the meeting, wouldn't have to stand up in front of these strangers and risk failing at this final opportunity. Failing herself, failing the lido, failing George.

"But it does matter. It does matter. Just like it mattered when the library closed."

Her voice is getting louder, and she is shaking. She puts one hand on the table to steady herself.

"The library used to get full in the winter. It was somewhere for people to come in from the cold. After the library closed, where did all those people go who had nowhere else to go when it rained? I never knew where they went and I felt like it was my fault for not fighting harder.

"When my husband, George, died I felt like it was raining every day and I had nowhere to go. He was my dry place when everything was terrible outside. He was eighty-five. He had a good run of it. I shouldn't make a fuss and it's not unusual

435

to be in my position. We had a very lucky life."

Her life was punctuated by his smiles caught as he emerged from under the water and the reassuring hum of his snoring. He used to keep her up at night and sometimes it made her angry. She misses being made angry by the sound of him sleeping next to her.

"But you see, well, the truth is I miss him."

Rosemary takes a sharp breath and busies her fingers with the buttons on her jacket, doing them up and undoing them and then doing them up again. One of the buttons is coming loose. It dangles from its thread like a flower with a broken neck hanging from its stalk. She smooths her skirt, wipes her face, and looks up.

"There might be other pools, but they could never be the same. My George isn't at those other pools, he is at our lido."

The group watch her but she barely notices them now.

"When he died I sat in his chair and I tried to feel him around me. It sounds silly I know but I'm not ashamed that I did it. But, well, it didn't really work. I tried to make it work but it didn't. He just wasn't there anymore. But when I'm at the lido, I feel him. I remember him everywhere."

George is in the way the mist sits on the water in the morning, he is in the wet decking and the brightly colored lockers and in the sharp intake of breath when she steps into the water, reminding her that she is still alive. Reminding her to stay alive.

"Maybe it's true that the pool doesn't make much money. Maybe I am a ridiculous old woman. But I can't let the lido go. I can't let my George go."

Ahmed reaches an arm around Rosemary's shoulder and holds her tightly. The strength of her feelings has exhausted her. There is silence for a while, then a man in the group stands up.

"We're going to consider the possibility of advertising at the lido. But we need to think about it first. We will call you later today." The others stand up too.

"But thank you for coming in, Rosemary. You, too, Ahmed."

Rosemary looks properly at the group opposite her for the first time since she started talking. Tori's face is red. Others are blinking vigorously, as though they have something in their eyes.

Ahmed shakes hands with everyone again and says a final goodbye. The receptionist is waiting on the other side of the door and leads them back to the entrance.

"Shall we get a taxi?" says Ahmed. "I think you deserve it."

She nods and he flags one down — Rosemary is too tired to speak. When she gets back to her flat she will go to sleep, she thinks. She knows she should go to the lido and update Kate, but somehow she feels that for now she just needs to go home and be on her own. In the back of the cab Ahmed watches London through the window again as Rosemary leans on his shoulder and closes her eyes. As she drifts into sleep she realizes they have done everything they can. There is nothing left to do.

CHAPTER 62

On the third day of the sit-in Kate and Jay anxiously await the arrival of the court order. They move between the café, the lido edge, and the reception area, peering nervously out through the barricade. Every time Kate hears new voices outside the lido her heart leaps, wondering if it is someone come to deliver the court order. Every now and then she glances to the clock that hangs above the pool, feeling as though the hands are moving slower than they ever have before.

The line of protesters is smaller today: Frank is on his own while Jermaine runs the bookshop; Ellis is here but not Jake, who is manning the stand for his father. They had been apologetic, wanting to be there until the very end, but life had to continue. Hope is perhaps the loudest protester, shouting "Don't pull the plug on our lido" every time a passerby crosses through the park outside the lido. At lunchtime a small crowd gathers — locals on their lunch break who have come to see the sit-in they read about in the paper. For a while it is noisy as these newcomers join the group and Kate watches them from behind the reception doors. Hope hands out placards and Ellis takes photos on his phone. Later, when the new protesters have drifted back to their offices, Ellis posts the photos on the Save Brockwell Lido Facebook page.

The day draws on but there is no sign of either the police, the council, or Paradise Living. As they wait, Kate paces around the lido and up to the reception door nervously. She considers another swim, but the thought of them arriving while she is in the water — naked — puts her off. She showers in the empty changing room and then works on her laptop, checking on the petition. The numbers have increased overnight and continue to climb throughout the day. She checks Twitter, where the hashtag "save our lido" is being used by local residents and swimming enthusiasts. As she works, Jay sits quietly beside her or heads to the reception area door to talk through the glass to Hope and the other protesters. Hope and Jake break the line briefly in the afternoon to stand by the lido wall, Jake shouting at Jay to go and stand on the other side by the pool.

Kate follows him until they are next to each other on the decking looking up at the brick wall. After a moment they see something flying through the air. Jay leans and stretches his arms, catching a soft plastic lunch bag in his hands.

"I hope it survived the journey!" shouts Hope over the wall. Jay hands it to Kate and she unzips the bag. Inside is a tinfoil package — she opens it to reveal a slightly squashed slice of ginger cake.

"I thought you might be getting hungry!" shouts Hope. "It's homemade!"

Looking at the flattened cake, made specially for her and Jay, Kate feels her eyes growing wet. She fights back the tears and shouts "Thank you!" over the wall. Kate thinks about when she first moved to London and how until a few months ago she barely knew anyone here in Brixton, let alone anyone who would make her cake or think to check if she was hungry. She and Jay share the large slice and it tastes just about the sweetest thing she has ever eaten.

"I wonder how Rosemary and Ahmed are getting on," says Kate as they eat. "Their meeting should be over by now."

The thought sends them into silence

again. The happiness Kate felt while eating quickly passes as she remembers that they will soon be thrown out of the lido. And then what? Back to her house and her housemates who know nothing about this campaign — who probably haven't even noticed she has been missing for three days?

As if understanding her thoughts, Jay puts an arm around Kate and pulls her toward him, holding her tightly. Kate's phone buzzes in her pocket and she moves away from Jay to take it out and read.

"Any news? E x."

"None yet," Kate replies to Erin's message. "The police should be here any minute. No word from Rosemary and Ahmed either. I think it might be nearly the end. K x."

"Hang in there," comes her sister's reply. "I'm so proud of what you're doing. E xx."

Erin's words give Kate a little life, but she still feels exhausted and falls back into Jay's arms, letting herself be held.

"It will be okay," says Jay softly, even though they both know it might not.

After a while they break free and head back to the reception area to check what is happening. The group of protesters parts to let Ahmed through. He is still wearing his ill-fitting suit. Kate comes close to the glass

442

and they speak loudly through it to each other. He's alone.

"How did it go? And where's Rosemary?"

"I think it went okay," he replies. "She has gone home to wait for their call — they said they would let us know by the end of the day. I think she was exhausted from it all — she slept the whole way back."

Kate tries to imagine Rosemary standing in a swish office somewhere in front of a group of advertising people, but struggles to picture her anywhere too far from this lido.

She checks her phone every few minutes throughout the rest of the day, but apart from a few more texts from Erin, there is nothing. Ahmed checks his, too, but he has no missed calls and no messages either. At one point his phone rings and he nearly drops it he seems so excited, but it is only his mum asking him if he will be back in time for dinner.

After a while Kate can't stand it anymore and calls Rosemary's flat to ask if she has received any news from the potential advertisers yet.

"Nothing," says Rosemary. "I have been sitting next to the phone since I got back. I'm too scared to move and go to the bathroom in case I miss them."

"I think you can go to the bathroom if

you need to, Rosemary," says Kate.

"Well, you never know — I don't want to miss them . . ."

"Call me when you hear from them okay?"

"Okay."

Still waiting for the sound of the police, or the council and Paradise Living officials, Kate is surprised in the afternoon to hear loud laughter and chatter instead. She follows it from the café, where she had been sitting and checking on the petition and the Facebook page, to the front of the lido. Two lines of girls in brown-and-yellow uniforms, holding hands, are processing through the park, led by two adults. Next to them is Phil. As the group draws closer Kate notices that in their hands the children are all holding pieces of paper that flutter slightly as they walk.

"We're from the local Brownies," says one of the adults as she reaches the group. "We're here for the protest." Ellis and Hope welcome them into the fold. Phil looks a little sheepish, but Ellis reaches out his hand for Phil to shake.

"Most of our girls are from the local school and use the lido for their swimming lessons. They were gutted to hear it is closing. So were we," says one of the leaders.

"And I thought it would be a good story

444

for the paper," adds Phil, eyeing Kate nervously through the glass. They look at each other for a moment and then Phil turns away, his purple cheeks flushing even brighter.

"I have some information for you," he says, avoiding her eyes. "I hear the court order is taking longer than they hoped. But it should be here soon. You've got another day or two at most."

Kate nods, thankful for Phil's comment and wondering where he got his information from. She feels the fear of what will happen over the next few days flooding her body, but tries hard to focus her attention on the children instead, who stand and chatter next to the adults, still holding hands.

"The girls have made their own banners," says one of the Brownie leaders, and the children let go of one another's hands and form a line, turning to face Kate. They hold up their pieces of paper to reveal drawings and paintings of the lido. Each one is slightly different but they all have some things in common: the bright flashes of blue and the smiling faces on the slightly wonky people who splash in the water or stand on the side. Seeing the lido replicated in the unsteady, colorful shapes made by these children makes Kate want to cry again.

The girls turn and show the rest of the group the pictures too.

Jay takes a photo through the glass and Ellis takes one on his phone on the other side.

"Save our lido!" says one of the leaders and the children join in, chanting faster and faster in unison until they are so fast that they break down in giggles and then return to their conversations.

The Brownies stay for a while, and their happy voices remind Kate of the lido on a summer's day. She wonders whether she will ever hear those sounds again.

By six o'clock, the children have left and the lido is quiet once more; Kate tries Rosemary again.

"They said they'd call by the end of the day," Rosemary says as she picks up. "Why haven't they called? It must be a no if they haven't called? They would have called if it was a yes, wouldn't they?"

"I'm sure that's not what it means," replies Kate, but her heart sinks as she realizes that probably is what it means.

"I wish I was there with you," says Rosemary.

"Me too," replies Kate, although she can't help but wish she was in a comfortable bed somewhere curled up in a calm and dreamless sleep.

That night Kate sleeps restlessly, throwing off the sleeping bag in the heat and lying curled up in the towels in the yoga studio. Each time she turns, kicking in agitation, she wakes Jay, who calmly kisses her on the forehead and tells her sleeping body that everything will be okay. He says it for her, but partly for himself, too, as the moon shines in through the studio and on the surface of the sleeping lido.

CHAPTER 63

The sun rises into a pale blue sky. The birds crowd the trees, singing their morning songs in competition like the market traders who shout prices over the top of one another. Bees hover among the wildflowers that scatter the bank around the lido. A man walks his dog and peers in through the lido window, spotting two sleeping bodies huddled under towels in the yoga room. He presses his face to the glass, laughs quietly, and carries on walking, his dog bounding ahead of him through the park. The dog runs up to a bench at the top of the hill where an old woman is sitting watching the view.

"Hello, you," says Rosemary, leaning to stroke the dog's ears. It puts two paws on her knees and wags its tail vigorously.

"Stella, get down!" shouts its owner. The dog jumps off and wanders away to sniff a gnarled tree trunk on the edge of the path.

"Sorry about that," says the owner. Rosemary shakes her head and smiles. The man and his dog walk away over the hill and Rosemary is alone again.

She has been here all morning. When she first arrived the park was thick with mist that clung to her coat as she veered off the path and walked through the grass. It was a slow walk to the top of the hill and she fell heavily onto the bench once she finally reached it.

By now the sun is up and shining on the lido at the bottom of the hill. She watches it turning the brick building golden terra-cotta in the morning light, remembering. If she closes her eyes she can see the still blue water beyond the walls. In her mind she walks through the doors to the lido and sees George standing on the decking. He looks up at her from the pool's edge, waiting for her to reach him so that they can hold hands and jump in together.

She opens her eyes and looks down at the quiet building. The old tree is still there at one corner but it is missing a branch; it never grew back after she and George broke it climbing over the wall. She remembers the splintering of the wood and showering of leaves and how much it made them both laugh. The sound of George's laughter rattles her heart.

From her seat on the bench she can see her whole life in front of her. There is the path that she walked down with her schoolmates, trudging in the rain before jumping into the water in their raincoats. She looks across to the other side of the park where a bonfire burned on VE Day, where the teenagers found their freedom and she found her future in a scruffy face with pink cheeks and a straight nose. Not far from where she sits is the tree where she and George practiced their handstands and felt like the first people to have seen the world from that way round and to have felt the stomach-dropping excitement of falling in love. It is the same tree they stood in front of on their wedding day, his arms tightly around her, her face turned toward his and the bright sun.

Another dog walker passes by and nods his head at her. She hardly notices him as she stares down the hill at the lido. She thinks about the cool water and the pair of mallards sending ripples across its surface. She sees the clock and the snack shop where George bought her tea on their first date. She sees the old diving board, now long since gone, and George diving like a bird. He barely breaks the surface of the water as he disappears underneath. When he bursts back up to the surface he is smiling the way he always smiled at her.

"Rosy," he says. "My Rosy."

Beyond the lido are the rooftops of Brixton and in her mind she walks down the familiar streets. She walks past her flat, looking up at the tall building and the lavender pots on the balcony. She pauses at the market and outside George's old shop, remembering it filled with crates of vegetables and the sound of his voice.

She goes a little farther, and then the city stretches away out of her grasp. The horizon is jagged with buildings and glass tower buildings that reflect the light. They look a million miles away, because this is all that matters — this view from the bench down the park to the lido.

"It's over," she says aloud.

A jogger turns and looks at her. Rosemary looks like she is crying, but perhaps her eyes are just watering from the sunlight. The jogger takes a deep breath and pushes on up the hill and over the other side, leaving Rosemary alone with her view.

CHAPTER 64

When Kate wakes on the fourth day she sits up and reaches for her clothes next to the yoga mats and dresses quietly. The lido is still and the sun streams in through the window. She looks out at the wildflowers on the other side, the red heads of the poppies floating above the cornflowers and tall grass. She looks beyond the flowers into the park, and that is when she sees Rosemary at the top of the hill.

"Jay," she says, gently shaking his sleeping body. He stirs and sits up, rubbing his face and kissing her on the cheek.

"Is it the police? Is the court order here?" he says, looking around him. But the lido is empty and still.

"No, look," says Kate, pointing out of the window and up the hill. He spots Rosemary sitting on the bench.

"What do you think she's doing there?" he asks.

"I don't know, but I don't think it's good. I think it might be over."

Saying the words out loud sends a pain ripping through her chest. Kate knew the end would come but didn't think it would still hurt this much.

Jay wraps an arm around her shoulders.

"Maybe it's time to leave," he says quietly. "Why don't you go and see her?"

She shakes her head.

"Not yet. I can't leave just yet."

"Okay. Shall I go?"

Kate pauses then agrees. He dresses and together they pull aside the tables and chairs until there is a path to the front doors. Kate finds the key and unlocks them.

"I won't be long," he says, kissing her.

"Okay."

Kate opens the door and the sunlight comes streaming in. She watches Jay walk into the park, then closes and locks the door, pulling the tables back in front of them. Back in the studio she sits by the window, watching Jay walking up the hill. When he reaches Rosemary he sits next to her.

They sit for a long time, talking and looking down the park. To calm herself, Kate imagines she is swimming.

The park appears to be empty apart from

Jay and Rosemary and a jogger who is now looping around the far side and heading down toward Herne Hill. Eventually Kate sees Jay stand up and reach for Rosemary's hand. He helps her up and they then walk side by side down through the grass and toward the lido.

Kate stands, too, and runs to the window, watching them. Rosemary and Jay walk slowly toward her, until Rosemary is standing just on the other side of the glass.

Rosemary places her hands up to the glass and Kate puts hers up, too, pressing their palms together through the window.

"It's okay," shouts Rosemary through the glass. "It's over."

Rosemary starts to cry and Kate does, too. Because she knows from Rosemary's voice that "It's over" means it isn't.

Rosemary is holding a copy of the *Evening Standard* in her hand. She unfolds it and presses it up to the glass. Kate looks at her own picture staring back at her. "London Journalist Stages Sit-In to Save Brockwell Lido" reads the headline. The article Kate wrote yesterday is printed underneath.

"Come outside!" shouts Rosemary.

"The police aren't there?"

Rosemary shakes her head.

"It's just me."

Kate runs down the corridor to the reception area and pulls apart the barricade of tables and exercise equipment. Once there is a clear path to the door she unlocks it and steps out into the warm sun.

Kate passes Jay waiting by the door and carries on running toward the old woman standing by the bench, the old woman who has become her friend.

"It's over," Rosemary says as Kate gets closer. "We've won."

Then the two women open their arms and hug each other tightly.

Kate cries, realizing she has done what she didn't truly believe she could do when she first met Rosemary: she has helped. And Rosemary cries, too, thinking about George and all her memories that fill her up like water in the pool. As long as she has her lido, he will always be with her.

"Tell me what they said," says Kate eventually, wiping her eyes and stepping away. They sit next to each other on the bench, arms linked together as Rosemary tells Kate that she received a voice mail from Tori that morning saying they wanted to advertise. They want their brand name written on the bottom of the pool and the price they're paying for it is enough to keep the lido open. They have already spoken to the council who accepted the offer. After receiving the voice mail, Rosemary had immediately called Ahmed, who was on the phone to Tori now, talking through the details.

Then Rosemary plays Tori's voice mail for Kate.

"It seemed a good opportunity. With all the press that the lido's had recently, this would get us the right kind of coverage. So it makes business sense. But most importantly it just makes sense. We were very moved by you, Rosemary. Thank you for sharing your story with us."

"You did it," says Kate, looking at Rosemary proudly. Her eyes are shining.

"Oh, I didn't do it alone. Ahmed was wonderful yesterday. And when they called this morning they said your article in the *Guardian* helped them to make their decision. They want to 'capitalize on the goodwill' I think is how they put it."

"But what about Paradise Living?" asks Kate, a frown starting to appear on her face, as she remembers the catch in Ahmed's plan: the investors who had already put down an offer to buy the lido.

Rosemary shakes her head.

"They were due to exchange contracts today, but when the council members heard about the advertising offer they changed their mind. Apparently there has been some problem with asbestos being found in one of Paradise Living's new block of flats, too — did you not see the story in this morning's *Brixton Chronicle*?"

Kate shakes her head. "Who wrote the article?" she asks.

Rosemary pulls a copy of the local paper from her bag and shows Kate the story. The byline to the article reads "Phil Harris."

"So we did it?" asks Kate, looking back up at Rosemary, meeting her blue eyes that are full of happiness.

"We did it," replies Rosemary. And then she wraps her arms around Kate again.

"Thank you," Rosemary says as she holds her. Kate holds her back and doesn't let go. The two stand in the sunshine and hold each other like they have both just come home. After a while Jay breaks the silence, walking over to them and pointing.

"Look who's coming," he says.

Frank and Jermaine, Hope, and Ellis and Jake. And Ahmed in the back swinging his arms confidently, looking taller. For once he isn't thinking about his exams. The group surrounds Rosemary and Kate, smiling and laughing. Hugs all around. Even Sprout tries to join the embrace. When they let her go Kate spots Geoff and hands him the keys from her pocket.

"I think these are yours," she says.

"Thank you," he says, taking the keys from her. "I'm certainly glad to have these back. Thank you. I mean it, thank you so much."

"I think there is just one last thing to do," says Rosemary once the group has settled.

"Swim!"

"Excellent idea," says Hope, holding up her swimming bag.

Together they troop into the lido, walking past the dismantled barricade of tables and chairs and down the corridor. Kate looks into the yoga room as she passes it, the mats and towels still piled on the floor, reminding her that her nights tucked up against Jay really happened. She reaches for his hand and holds it as they move onto the decking.

CHAPTER 65

As the months pass, the lido remains busy, a queue winding its way out into the park most weekends. Inside, the pool is full of all kinds of swimmers. There is the training swimmer who leaves a bottle of water and a watch on the deck and swims carefully timed laps. There is the backstroker, who only seems to be able to swim backward and who knows exactly the number of strokes until the end of the pool so that she never hits her head on the side. There is the splashy swimmer, who gets a lane to himself (maybe he does it on purpose). There is the underwater swimmer, whom you rarely see as she swims most of her lengths close to the bottom of the pool. And then there is Kate, the corkscrew kicker.

Kate and Rosemary swim their way through the end of the summer and into autumn, pulling their arms through the water where fallen leaves float like boats.

Every day they swim in the cold water and every day they sit for a while on the bench outside the lido, waiting for their hair to dry and talking.

"Same time tomorrow?" says Kate as she stands up to leave.

"Same time tomorrow," says Rosemary.

CHAPTER 66

The fox makes her way through Brixton, her tail whipping behind her as she runs. Even in the daylight she is not afraid: this is her home and she knows she can come and go as she pleases. She runs along the edge of a school: the playground is busy with children who kick through piles of autumn leaves or pick them up and throw them at each other. In the afternoon she returns to the yard once it is deserted, pilfering dropped sandwich crusts and half-eaten biscuits. Once she has eaten she follows the children as they disperse through Brixton and into the park, making the most of autumn's last warm weather. Some head straight for the play park; others swing their swimming bags and run toward the lido.

In the evening she passes by the pubs, music spilling out of them as people open and close doors to step outside and smoke. As they stand around outdoor heaters the fox takes the opportunity to raid the bins at the back until a chef comes out with a new pile of rubbish and chases her away.

At the market the stallholders huddle into their coats in the cold mornings and pull tarpaulin covers over their stalls during the day to hold back the rain. At night the fox runs down the empty street, sniffing for fish heads and bruised fruit in the bins. Around the corner on Station Road the shutters to the archway shops are pulled down — some just closed for the night, others closed for good.

In the early mornings she runs through the mist in the park, passing a few joggers who begin to wrap up in more layers — starting with jackets and moving to scarves and gloves. Their cold breaths cloud the air in front of them as they run and the smell of bonfire smoke clings to clothes like dew to blades of grass.

As the fox makes her daily laps of Brockwell Park the trees glow orange, then red, then brown. Leaves drop like brown puddles around the trunks of trees, leaving the branches bare.

In the lido swimmers tug on their wetsuits to protect them from the cold. The braver ones keep their swimsuits, take deep breaths, and jump.

CHAPTER 67

And then winter comes. The restaurants in Brixton Village hand out blankets to customers who sit in their jackets and warm themselves with cocktails and wine. Farther up the street at the cinema a stand collects coats and food for those who have nowhere to go to escape the cold.

Dog walkers in the park walk faster than they walked in the summer. The tennis courts are empty and the community garden sleeps, waiting for the spring.

A crowd is gathered at the lido, standing in the café and on the decking.

"I hear you have a new job," says Hope to Kate.

Kate smiles. "Yes, I start next week."

"I hear it's at the *Independent*!"

"It's just a junior journalist role," says Kate, blushing. But she smiles.

"That's still brilliant," says Frank, who has come over to Hope and Kate, Jermaine

463

at his side.

"Congratulations, Kate," says Jermaine. "If you ever need any books for research purposes, you know where to come."

"Of course," says Kate, "to my favorite bookshop."

Hope asks them how the shop is doing and they tell her about their plans to hold author talks and feature local authors. As they chat Kate looks across the room. Erin and Mark are here, and her parents, too, and they are currently standing with Jay. The start of a bump is visible beneath Erin's black dress. She called Kate a week ago to tell her the news and they both cried on the phone. Kate can't wait to be an aunt.

She feels herself getting warm as she watches Jay talking with her family. *It's okay though,* she thinks. *He'll be okay.* He spots her watching and turns to smile at her. They hold each other's gaze for a moment and then he turns back to the conversation. She pictures heading home with him this afternoon — back to his flat where her clothes now hang next to his in the wardrobe. She knows it has been fast, but when Jay's flatmate said he was moving out, it seemed like the obvious choice. Closing the door on her old house and shouting a final, unanswered goodbye into the corridor was the best feeling. As she locked the door and posted the keys back through the letterbox for her roommates to collect for the new tenant, she felt as though she was locking her Panic inside too. She walked away and didn't look back.

Ellis, Jake, Ahmed, and Geoff stand together by the coffee bar talking. Ahmed is partway through his first term at university. He is wearing a new suit that fits him perfectly.

She doesn't hear what Hope says the first time; she is lost in watching the people gathered around her.

"I think it's time to go out," says Hope. She places a hand gently on Kate's elbow.

"Yes, yes, of course," says Kate. She looks back across the room.

Hope takes Kate's elbow and guides her out of the doors and into the cold air. Jay and her family are waiting for her there and Hope steps back, letting Kate join them. Jay kisses her cheek. Erin reaches a hand out to her; Kate takes it and squeezes, remembering sitting on the side of the pool with her sister and holding her hand then too.

The crowd gathers on the decking opposite the pool. The water is empty and still, the sky above it gray and full of clouds. The teenage boy is standing with his back to the

465

pool. His shirt is too big for him, the creases still visible across his chest and stomach where it was folded in the packet. His black tie is new too.

He is holding a sheet of paper. He looks down at it and back at the group. His parents stand on one side, watching him. His mother smiles at him and wishes she could step forward and wrap her arms around him, but she knows he has to do this on his own. Once the group are settled in a semicircle around him, facing the pool, he starts to speak.

"I met Mrs. Peterson, Rosemary Peterson, the first time I came to the lido. That was a few years ago now. She complimented me on my swimming — she said I was strong."

His voice has only recently broken and he is still getting used to its sound. Standing on his own and with the pool stretching behind him he looks small, but his voice carries loudly.

"I didn't believe her at first, but she said it every time I saw her. 'You're so strong', she'd say to me. Maybe I wasn't at first, but I kept coming and I kept practicing and she kept saying it to me, and eventually I realized that she was right. I had become strong."

He looks up from the sheet of paper for

the first time. The figures dressed in black and huddled on the lido decking look back at him.

"That's what she did for me — she showed me how to be strong. And I know she did the same for many of you. That's why we are here."

The boy folds his piece of paper and puts it back in his pocket. He walks back over to his parents and his mother steps forward, pulling him into her. He lets himself sink into his mother's arms, resting his head against her body. She holds his head in her hands. After a moment's pause his father steps forward, too, and wraps his arms around both of them.

Hope retells the story of Rosemary jumping in the lido with her school friends in their coats, making the group laugh. She talks about how Rosemary took her under her wing when she first moved to Brixton and started working with her at the library, how kind she was to the schoolchildren who came in to choose their reading books for the school holidays, and how respectful she had always been of everyone's choices, never batting an eyelid at an unlikely romance title or "how to" book.

They nod and smile. Even if they have only known her for a small part of their lives, they think, *Yes, that's my Rosemary.* They feel as though they knew her then too. At the end Hope's voice falters, remembering her oldest friend and wishing she was still here. She wonders who she will share a slice of cake and conversation with each week now and the thought makes her want to climb into bed and not come out. Instead she takes a deep breath and steps back into the group, where Jamila opens her arms and takes her mother into a strong hug.

When it is Kate's turn to speak she looks at Erin, then at Jay. They both nod at her, and it gives her strength. She walks alone to the edge of the lido, her back to the water, facing the group. She looks at the faces assembled on the decking. Her family stand with Jay and smile softly at her, encouraging her.

Across the pool, Frank and Jermaine hold each other, both wiping their eyes with tissues. Ahmed stands with Ellis, Jake, and Geoff. And all around them are the other faces of Brixton who have come to say goodbye. The young mother holds her baby and remembers swimming in the water when she was heavily pregnant and passing Rosemary, who always used to stop to talk to her. The teenage boy stands with his parents and next to the charity shop staff and the owner of Rosemary's and Hope's favorite café. Many of the faces Kate doesn't recognize. Kate looks at them all — Rosemary's friends, her community, her home — and feels a surge of gratitude.

A bird flies above them in the gray sky, stopping to rest in the trees. It makes a loud noise; she looks up and sees a flash of green and yellow in the dark branches. It is a parakeet. She watches it for a moment and then looks back at the group huddled under the café umbrellas. And then she starts to talk.

"When I met Rosemary I felt alone in a world that was much too big for me. I felt afraid all the time — terrified really. I realize now that I was stuck. I needed someone to help me."

She takes a deep breath, remembering crying in her bedroom and feeling like the darkness might overtake her completely and drag her to a place from where she couldn't climb back.

"I first met Rosemary for work, but it never really felt like work. I was there to write her story but she asked me mine. She helped me find my way. Without Rosemary, I may not have discovered this lido. Without Rosemary, I may never have met all of you and found my place in this city. Without her, I would still be lost."

She says the words aloud for the first time, and as she does, it is like a final letting go. "Rosemary saved me. I know she will be remembered for how she fought and won to keep this lido open. But she saved me too. She took the loneliness out of being alone. She was my friend. And I miss her."

A breeze catches her black scarf and makes it dance. She feels the wind on her face. Everyone is silent.

"We all miss her," she says after a while, "which is why I'd like you to join me in remembering her in a special way, our Rosemary."

She turns and walks around the edge of the pool and signals for the others to join her. Kate and Jay look at each other across the water. He smiles. Erin, Mark, and Kate's parents are on the opposite side, too, next to Jay. Brian is folding up his glasses and placing them on the ground behind him. Mark holds Erin's hand. Ahmed stands next to Geoff, who has an arm over his shoulder. Kate looks down the line next to her: Hope and Jamila stand with Ellis and Jake on one side and Frank and Jermaine on the other. The teenage boy stands at the deep end, his parents on either side of him. The three of them are holding hands. Everyone else is there, too, spread around the lido, standing with their feet on the edge.

Kate unbuttons her coat and places it on the decking next to her. She lifts her black dress off over her head until she is standing on the side in her swimsuit.

Then they all start to peel off their dark funeral clothes, too, revealing colorful flashes of swimsuits and trunks, as Kate had requested on her invitation. It was exactly the right thing to do. As they undress and shed their funeral clothes they start to talk and laugh, jumping up and down to keep warm. Kate suddenly remembers Rosemary's story — the one Hope has just repeated — and reaches for her coat on the floor. She picks it up and puts it back on, buttoning it up over her swimming costume. The others see her and laugh, reaching for their coats and jackets, too.

Eventually they are all standing on the edge in their coats and swimsuits.

Kate looks down into the water. She thinks about Rosemary and George, swimming through their lives together here in the lido.

"One, two, three . . ." she says.

And then they jump.

CHAPTER 68

The wildflowers come back to Brockwell Park in the spring. For a while it seems like they will never return; the earth is frozen and cracks and the grass snaps beneath your feet in the frost. But the flowers always come back. When the frost is on the grass and the trees are bare it is easy to forget that they were ever there. But as the new season yawns and stretches to life the green shoots begin to prick through the earth. Tight buds start to unfurl like fists un-clenching. And suddenly the flowers are there. Bright yellow marigolds, creeping buttercups, and daffodils graze the banks. Beyond the park is Brixton and the noise of the city, but here it is peaceful and green.

The park comes to life, filled with families stretched out in the first of the sun. Couples fall asleep on the grass, one resting their head on the other's stomach. Joggers make their way slowly up the hill. A man stops walking down the slope to say, "You can do it," to the woman running up.

At the top of the hill is a bench. It looks down over the park, watching the people enjoying this new sunshine. At the bottom of the hill people walk along the path to the lido, carrying their swimming bags and towels, ready to stretch out and claim their own corner of this beach in the city.

In the fresh wood of the bench is written a message: "For George, who loved this view. And for Rosemary, who saved it."

AUTHOR'S NOTE

This book is a fictional story, inspired in part by my time living in Brixton in South London while I was a student. I was struck by the sense of community in the area, but also noticed the many changes taking place — changes that are mirrored across many neighborhoods in London and other cities across the world.

While this story is made up, Brockwell Lido is a real place. The outdoor pool in South London opened in 1937. The real lido has a long and complex history and really did close for a period in the 1990s. It was partly the campaigning of local swimmers that helped to reopen it. For my story, though, I chose fiction: imagining what would happen if the lido was threatened with closure now.

I have also been creative with the truth about other places in Brixton — I was inspired by the real place but used my imagination to embellish for the purpose of this story.

As a Londoner, I am very fortunate to have several beautiful lidos in my city: Tooting Bec, Parliament Hill, London Fields, and the Serpentine Lido are some of my favorites. But outdoor swimming pools, or lidos, are also spread right across the United Kingdom, and abroad. Many have been shut down over recent years, but some have also been reopened — often due to the determined campaigning of locals. If you have never swum in a lido, I urge you to seek one out and take the plunge. If you do, perhaps keep an eye out for a Kate or a Rosemary in the water with you. I may well be there too. Happy swimming.

ACKNOWLEDGMENTS

This book may have my name on the cover, but there are so many people who have helped to make it possible and who I would like to thank from the bottom to the top of my heart.

Thank you firstly to my family for your lifelong support and encouragement of my writing. From taking me to writing camps and literary festivals, to simply reading everything I presented you. Particularly to my sister Alex for being the first reader of the first draft of this book, but also for teaching me to swim. Your patience and inspiration have changed my life. To Bruno, for the wine, tea, dinners, and generally for loving me the way you do. Also to my dear friends (too many to name individually) for always being on Team Libby — I'm so lucky to have your support.

A big thank-you to my wonderful agent, Robert Caskie, for believing in me and *The*

Lido and for guiding me through this process with such kindness. I couldn't think of anyone better to have on my side. Also to Nathalie Hallam, for all your help taking *The Lido* around the world, as well as Sasha Raskin at United Talent for bringing this book to the United States.

To my brilliant editor Marysue Rucci at Simon & Schuster: I have learnt so much from you, thank you. Also a big thank-you to everyone else at Simon & Schuster, in particular Zack Knoll, Dana Trocker, Amanda Lang, Carly Loman, Jackie Seow, Lauren Tamaki, Martha Schwartz, and Laurie McGee.

Finally, I would like to thank the swimmers past and present who have inspired this book. Over the past few years I have observed and met swimmers from all walks of life who love their lidos as well as their pools, lakes, rivers, and seas. A common trait among them is a zest for life and a great capacity for joy. This book is for you all too, with my admiration.

ABOUT THE AUTHOR

Libby Page graduated from the London College of Fashion with a BA in fashion journalism before going to work as a journalist at the *Guardian*. Besides writing, her second passion is outdoor swimming. Libby lives in London, where she enjoys finding new swimming spots and pockets of community within the city. *The Lido* is her first novel.

Twitter: @libbypagewrites

Instagram @theswimmingsisters

Libby Page graduated from the London College of Fashion with a BA in fashion journalism before going to work as a journalist at the Guardian. Besides writing, her second passion is outdoor swimming. Libby lives in London, where she enjoys finding new swimming spots and pockets of community within the city. The Lido is her first novel.

Twitter @libbypagewrites

Instagram @theswimmingsisters